basanti

basanti

writing the new woman
nine authors, one novel

Annada Shankar Ray, Baishnab Charan Das,
Harihar Mahapatra, Kalindi Charan Panigrahi,
Muralidhar Mahanti, Prativa Devi, Sarala Devi,
Sarat Chandra Mukherjee, and Suprava Devi

Translated from Odia by
Himansu S. Mohapatra and Paul St-Pierre

OXFORD
UNIVERSITY PRESS

OXFORD
UNIVERSITY PRESS

Oxford University Press is a department of the University of Oxford.
It furthers the University's objective of excellence in research, scholarship,
and education by publishing worldwide. Oxford is a registered trademark of
Oxford University Press in the UK and in certain other countries.

Published in India by
Oxford University Press
2/11 Ground Floor, Ansari Road, Daryaganj, New Delhi 110 002, India

ISBN-13 (print): 978-0-19-948986-2
ISBN-10 (print): 0-19-948986-6

ISBN-13 (ebook): 978-0-19-909587-2
ISBN-10 (ebook): 0-19-909587-6

Typeset in Garamond 3 LT Std 12/14.5
by The Graphics Solution, New Delhi 110 092
Printed in India by Replika Press Pvt. Ltd

All attempts were made to contact the legal heirs of the nine authors who jointly
wrote this work. The publishers wish to thank those who have granted the permission
to publish this English translation. In case of any omissions, please contact Oxford
University Press, India, so that necessary acknowledgements and corrections may be
made in the subsequent editions of this book.

Contents

Acknowledgements

The translators gratefully acknowledge the following persons who, as the representative and legal heirs of the authors of the different chapters of the Odia novel *Basanti*, kindly gave permission for these chapters to appear in an English translation by Oxford University Press:

- **Sudha Panigrahi**, for the five chapters of the novel (1, 2, 28, 29, 30) authored by **Kalindi Charan Panigrahi**
- **Asit Mukherjee**, for the four chapters of the novel (3, 4, 23, 26) authored by **Sarat Chandra Mukherjee**
- **Ananta Mahapatra**, for the two chapters of the novel (5, 6) authored by **Harihar Mahapatra**
- **Laxmi Prakash Mohapatra**, for the nine chapters of the novel (8, 9, 17, 18, 19, 20, 21, 22, 27) authored by **Sarala Devi**
- **Dr Sugat Kar**, for the two chapters of the novel (10, 11) authored by **Suprava Devi**, and for the one chapter of the novel (13) authored by **Prativa Devi**
- **Priya Madhab Das**, for the two chapters of the novel (24, 25) authored by **Baishnab Charan Das**
- **Dr Bijoy Anand Mahanti**, for the two chapters of the novel (12, 14) authored by **Muralidhar Mahanti**

Despite our best efforts, the holder of the copyright for the three chapters of the novel (7, 15, 16) authored by **Annada Shankar Ray** has not been traceable. Every step will be taken to obtain permission from the copyright holder should such a person be identified in the future. The translators would appreciate any information leading to unravelling the identity of this person and will gratefully acknowledge the provider of information in the future edition(s) of the novel.

Apart from the above individuals, the translators would like to express their gratitude to the following persons who have been indispensable to the creation of the English avatar of *Basanti* by providing help, by demonstrating interest, and, above all, by instilling hope and inspiration.

Mini Krishnan of Oxford University Press, for seeing promise in the proposal right from the word go and for her sustained friendship and support; Debendra Kumar Das, for making available to us his copy of the revised edition of *Basanti* and for knowledgeably guiding us to and through the materials needed to understand the complex human drama out of which the collective and the first woman-oriented novel *Basanti* arose; J.P. Das, for keeping faith with us and for helping with the placement of an excerpt (Chapter 17) from the evolving translation of *Basanti* in the Odia Literature Special of *Indian Literature* (May/June 2015); Sachidananda Mohanty, for including Chapter 9 of *Basanti* in his book *The Best of Sarala Devi*, published by Oxford University Press in 2016; Ananta Mahapatra, for sharing our passion and helping us in our investigative quest to identify the living representatives of as many as three of the authors involved and to facilitate the obtaining of consent from them; Kamalakanta Mahapatra, for constantly reminding us that there is no worthier enterprise than translating the classics of Odia literature into English; Dr Bijay Kumar Danta, Professor of English, Tezpur University, for his interest in seeing *Basanti* translated and introduced to the wider world and, to that end, helping with his critical insight into the discourse of fiction; and Dr Nandita Mahapatra, Associate Professor of English, Jatiya Kabi Bira Kishore College, Cuttack, for making possible access to her uncle, the son of the author Baishnab Charan Das, and also for leading us to Dr Bijoy Anand Mahanti, the son of the author Muralidhar Mahanti.

We will end with a toast to serendipity for the magical manner in which casements were opened up by a casual tip-off by someone here and a public airing of what we were trying to do there, thus illuminating a terrain that was completely uncharted. An example is the publication on 5 October 2017 in the Bhubaneswar edition of *Times of India* of an article by Himansu S. Mohapatra, 'An Age of Ideas: Feminism and the Sabuja Writers'. The next day people called, wanting to know about *Basanti* and volunteering to give information about many of its authors supposedly sunk into oblivion. For this our grateful thanks to the Bhubaneswar edition of *Times of India*.

Our heartfelt thanks are of course reserved for Oxford University Press for undertaking the publication of the English translation of this vintage Odia novel, known as much for its experimentation with writing as for its envisioning of the new woman.

Basanti

Writing the New Woman—An Introduction[*]

Himansu S. Mohapatra

Imagine the inner world of an Odia novel, published in 1931 and set in the conservative Odia society of that time. The eponymous heroine seems to be a misfit in this society thanks to her unconventional choices. She is friend to a Christian woman. She reads, writes, plays music, sews, and dispenses homeopathic medicine. It also happens that she marries for love. After marriage she comes to her husband's village in Balasore to take up her new role as the daughter-in-law of a zamindar household, managed by her widowed mother-in-law. A life of petty domesticity and social conformity stretches out before her now. She does not, however, give up on her attempts at replenishing her mental and intellectual wardrobe. To that end she leafs through the pages of a Bengali monthly, writes articles for an Odia literary periodical (*Nababani*), and reads Tagore's novel *Gora* multiple times, not

* I thank my wife Swarnarenu for being my support and sustenance, and, above all, my muse during that long stretch of time starting mid-2014 when I was working on *Basanti*. This introduction is warmly and gratefully offered to her.

to mention her locking horns with her husband and his male friends over the issue of emancipation of women. She even runs a school for the little girls in the village.

This aspiration on the part of a young woman for a higher mental plane does not evoke any response from the family. On the contrary, it invites opposition from her mother-in-law and even her husband. The element of surprise is not due to the fact that the novel depicts the agony and the sense of suffocation of a woman seeking emancipation from her narrow domestic confines. Surprise is in the fact that the novel does for the first time posit activism for women in Odia literature, breaking with the earlier tradition of portraying a woman as a glamorous, adorable object. Yes, in Odia fictional literature Basanti is the first ever woman character to have boldly staked a claim to emancipation of women, presented the means of that emancipation and mapped the pathway to it. The blazing presence of *Nababani*, *Gora*, Romain Rolland, and W.B. Yeats in the discourse of the novel is an eloquent testimony to that. Odia prose fiction, admittedly not of long ancestry in the 1920s and 30s, had not imagined such an intellectually vibrant inner world and that too as part of a character's repertoire until the appearance of the novel *Basanti*.

I

Basanti is a landmark attempt at writing a new kind of novel in Odisha in the early decades of the twentieth century. Like all new literary offerings of the time in Odisha, it was published in the journal *Utkala Sahitya* in instalments starting from issue no. 2 of volume 28 for May 1924 to issue no. 8 of volume 30 for November 1926. The work of nine authors, six men and three women, *Basanti* is a fine gift to Odia fiction from the 'Sabuja Age' in literature. This literature was given to exploring new horizons—the Odia word 'sabuja', like the word 'green' in English, is a symbol of youth, novelty, freshness, and so on—during its all too brief life span of 10 to 15 years. The novel was definitely a new undertaking. The newness existed at least at three levels. First, it was a product of a well-thought-out plan for collaborative writing. Second, it was a novel with a focus on women. Last, but not least, it was a novel of ideas. The three levels were, of course, closely intertwined. When a group of writers come together for the express purpose of engaging in an act of writing, one can be sure that a new creative impulse, at once social and literary, is in the air. Was the late 1920s in Odisha, which saw the emergence of *Basanti*, such a time? Did it witness a new creative impulse?

II

Historically, Odisha was a colonial society. But it had begun to experience the convulsions from the changes in the social and economic arrangements introduced by the colonial British administration. Politically, it suffered dismemberment. Its coastal region had been brought under the Bengal Presidency, the southern region came under the administrative control of the Madras Presidency, and its western region had been incorporated into the Central Provinces, Berar. Economically, Odisha suffered by being subjected to the colonial revenue administration's policy of expropriation of surplus from land. Together, these changes in society and economy produced profound changes in culture. It became a battleground for the clashing forces of traditional rites and rituals and modern practices without much anchorage in the Odishan soil. In a word, the modernity Odisha—referred to as 'colonial modernity'—experienced at the time was a product of a 'moral economy' in the process of being displaced by a 'money economy'. Odishan society was forced to accommodate to the latter.

There were, of course, gains to offset the losses. The spread of English literacy, introduced by the colonial administration, gave rise to a deracinated babu class, as portrayed graphically and with a fine touch of sarcasm in Phakirmohan Senapati's turn-of-century classic novel *Chha Mana Atha Guntha* (English translation titled: *Six Acres and a Third*). There was, however, a section within the English educated Odias ready to use the resources gained from an English education, such as a secular outlook and a scientific temper, in order to critically examine the traditional values of caste and social hierarchy, receiving their sanction from the shastras. English literacy also became the main driver of the vernacular print literacy, thanks to the access the educated class got to the technology of print. English education opened the minds of the Odias. They became avid readers of English books and it did wonders for their intellectual expression in Odia. Frieda Hauswirth Das was a Swiss woman who took up residence in Cuttack for a few years during the 1920s thanks to her marrying an Odia agricultural technologist, Sarangadhara Das, whom she had met at the University of California. She writes in her autobiography, *A Marriage to India* (1933), about an avid culture of reading and discussion she had seen at Cuttack. This is what she writes:

> But some students and some young professors from the nearby Ravenshaw College fell into the habit of coming for discussions to my tea-table. Then we would commence reading, plays preferably, and continue till late in the evening.
>
> I had a small well-selected library. My young friends read avidly through my most treasured books, many of which were not kept in the college library. I saw that they got many books on the woman and sex questions into their hands, such standbys of mine as Olive Schreiner, Ellen Key, Havelock Ellis, Forel, besides a whole group of modern plays, some books on sociology and economics, and God knows what. The contagion spread, my books circulated, others were drawn into our discussions.

It was as keen and wide-awake a group of young minds as I had the pleasure of coming into contact with anywhere in the world. (p. 57)

Before proceeding further it may be worthwhile to slip in the remark that the book culture of the 1920s described by Hauswirth Das has left its imprint in the novel *Basanti* in the form of the sheer number of books and authors, Indian and Western, alluded to in its pages. There is of course the great Kalidasa, but more to the point are the references to contemporary works such as W.B. Yeats's 'The Stolen Child', Rabindranath Tagore's *Gora*, and authors such as Romain Rolland, and so on, not to mention political and intellectual movements in England and America in the early twentieth century such as the Suffragette Movement.

III

In the 1920s English education and a wider world mediated by English books had begun to seep into the consciousness of the educated Odias, transforming it from within. The books they read and the ideas they conceived found their way into their Odia writing for which the journals and magazines of the time acted as both receptacles and triggers. *Utkala Dipika*, founded in 1866 by Gouri Shankar Ray, provided an outlet for their restless journalistic minds eager to explore their environs and shine the light into the areas of darkness. From 1897 onwards it was *Utkala Sahitya*, a monthly literary journal published under the editorship of the erudite and cultured Biswanath Kar, which set out to create a national literature for Odisha. It may be no exaggeration to say that the Renaissance of Odia letters was scripted in its pages. It was here that *Chha Mana Atha Guntha* by Senapati was serialized from 1897 to 1899 before being published in book form in 1902. It was here that the serialization of *Basanti* began in May 1924 and ended in November 1926 before being issued as a book in 1931 by a literary organization named Sabuja Sahitya Samiti formed by the 'Sabuja' group of writers. A revised and expanded edition of the novel, used as the source text for this English translation, was published in 1968 by the New Students' Store, Cuttack.

IV

The passage from a single author to multiple authors was a significant aspect of *Basanti*. The novel saw the convergence of two new forces. One was a new writing strategy which the initiators of the novel referred to as a 'collective composition method'. The other was the collective imagining of the new woman. This concerted effort at writing a novel was of course an extension of the other concerted efforts that were being seen in the social and political spheres in Odisha. While Gandhi's call for non-cooperation with the colonial government had galvanized hearts and minds of every Indian, in Odisha it was the regional issue of the reunification of a dismembered Odisha which struck a chord among Odia intellectuals and writers. The important thing was that the Odia nationalism of the 1920s, having co-existed with an internationalist and cosmopolitan outlook, was not insular. The Odia mind was like a sponge, which absorbed new ideas and new trends such as the psychoanalysis of Sigmund Freud, the mysticism of Swedenborg, the modernism of the Yeats–Eliot–Pound–Joyce generation as well as socialist ideas that reached the Odishan shores both directly through people like Frieda Hauswirth Das and via Bengali literature. As one prominent member of the 'Sabuja' group of Odia writers put it in a journal article, published in 1933, their effort was to create a new and fresh—and hence green—literature which, in tune with the international trends, would 'celebrate the romance of a new reality by extending the frontiers of the everyday reality and reaching down to the unconscious' (Baikuntha Nath Patnaik, *Juga-Bina*, 1933, p. 67). Eminent Odia critic Nityananda Satpathy says almost the same thing about 'Sabuja' literature in his acclaimed critical book *From the Sabuja to the Contemporary*: 'The bold and uncompromised images of love, woman and life that the "Sabujas" were the first to draw have become an indispensable part of the mental make-up of the Odia intelligentsia. Besides, the "Sabujas" were the first to create an ambience of internationalism in Odia literary culture' (1979, p. 41).

Again it may be pertinent to observe here that this concern with the deeper recesses of the mind is reflected in *Basanti* in the form of the epistolary and diary-keeping methods employed in many of its chapters for purposes of tunnelling through to the workings of the inner mind. As in the British Romantic period, the attempt of the 'Sabujas' to create a 'language that is green' (the expression is from the working-class British Romantic poet John Clare) was implicated in a desire, though on a smaller scale, to purge society and literature of the dead weights of conventions and outmoded expressions. The 'Sabuja' group, consisting of five writers—Kalindi Charan Panigrahi, Annada Shankar Ray, Harihar Mahapatra, Baikuntha Nath Patnaik, and Sarat Chandra Mukherjee—started, like Wordsworth and Coleridge in their jointly drafted *Lyrical Ballads* (1798), with a volume of poems titled *Sabuja Kabita*. Their second joint venture, however, was in prose, a novel in particular. This led to the birth of *Basanti*. The novel began to roll out in the pages of *Utkala Sahitya*, made especially hospitable to literary innovation and experimentation by the journal's progressive editor Biswanath Kar. Four core members of the 'Sabuja' group, Kalindi Charan Panigrahi, Annada Shankar Ray, Harihar Mahapatra, and Sarat Chandra Mukherjee, were joined by five new members—Muralidhar Mahanti, Baishnab Charan Das, Sarala Devi, Suprava Devi, and Prativa Devi—in bringing the collaborative project to fruition. Baikuntha Nath Patnaik, a core member of the 'Sabuja' group and the one who wrote the journal article defining 'Sabuja', stayed out of the project probably because his forte was poetry.

It is worth pointing out here that the collaborative writing of the kind seen in *Basanti* was first to appear in Bengali literature in the Indian context. In fact in the 'appeal' published in volume 28 of *Sahitya*, Kalindi Charan Panigrahi called for a replication of this Bengali experiment with the 'collective worship of the word', evinced in the case of *Baroyari* (written by twelve authors), *Bhager Puja* (the work of sixteen authors), and *Chatuskona* (the work of four authors) in Odia literature. The Bengali experiment was obviously not the first. *The Spectator*, an influential periodical paper in eighteenth-century England, was the creation of many hands. Sir Roger De Coverley, its central character, though first imagined by Richard Steele, is taken over fondly by Joseph Addison, much in the same way in which the contours of the new woman in the titular *Basanti* are drawn first by the male authors and then taken over and extended by the female authors. The simple point to note here is that the process of adaptation and assimilation or imbibing—be it through translation or transformation or rewriting—is an endless process in literature and is the very condition of literary creativity. *Basanti* is a shining example of this process of adaptation or rather relocation of a new literary trend in the Odishan context.

V

To go from the verse of *Sabuja Kabita* to the novelistic world of *Basanti* is to see a quantum leap in ideas, social portrayal, and analysis. Suddenly the operative concepts of *Sabuja Kabita* such as 'youth', 'fresh', 'green', and 'new' are not fanciful and vacuous any more. They have been infused with a social purpose.

'Sabuja' has gone from connoting romance to signifying social engagement. The 'new' in the 'Sabuja' lexicon turns out to be a concern with writing the new woman in Odisha. It is a significant act of social commitment in an age when the social life in Odisha revolved exclusively around men, especially high-caste men. The woman was not only 'the second sex'; she was 'A-Suryam Pashya', one who cannot throw a glance at the mighty Surya, the Sun, a non-entity, silenced and rendered invisible. Reading and writing were not for her. She married either at puberty or before reaching puberty and invariably the husband she married was much older than her. And she remained confined within the four walls of the home. In her book, Hauswirth Das recollects her frustratingly futile search for some female company in Cuttack. To start with, no woman in Cuttack ventured out by herself. Secondly, they knew no English. Even if they did, they would not seek the company of a white Christian woman.

Under the placid and stagnant surface of the 1920s Odisha, however, something was stirring and simmering. There were definitely some women who were questioning their socially ordained role within a stratified, caste society, were seeing love as the only allowable basis of marriage, and were looking upon education as a means of emancipation. The three women— Sarala, Suprava, and Prativa—who contributed to *Basanti* were surely among these progressives. And Sarala, who wrote as many as nine chapters in *Basanti*, was assuredly the most advanced in her thinking. In fact, it was her that Das met in Cuttack. Das was surprised and shocked by Sarala. The former left a moving account of her encounter with Sarala whom she presented as Vimla for reasons of confidentiality.

A slight figure with bent head slipped into the room. The instant she realized no one else was present, there was a change, and I at once saw that this was not the ordinary, timid, mute,

adolescent girl of India. She threw back her veil with slim hand
and quick gesture. I looked into a pair of very beautiful glowing
eyes. Vimla was an amazingly attractive girl, her greatest charm
lying in the intense mobility of expression. She broke out at
once into a stream of vernacular. (p. 61)

It is not too fanciful to presume that to the people around her,
Basanti, the heroine of the eponymous novel, may have looked
a bit like Vimla/Sarala. It is also no wonder that the character
of Basanti flows largely from the pen of Sarala. It was inevitable
given the fact that Sarala was the living example of the new
woman that the 'Sabuja' literature was trying to imagine. To
read the content of Vimla/Sarala's 'stream of vernacular' is to be
amply aware of her radical feminist thinking. Hauswirth Das
continues her reporting thus:

With amazement I learned that this girl had even had the
audacity to attempt writing. From behind the veil of her
seclusion she had followed the trend of events and had
actually sent an article to Gandhi's paper which he had at once
published. The kernel of the article was this: 'You Nationalists
are clamouring for freedom from the British. Then why do you
not give us, the women of India, within our own social life the
freedom for which you clamour from the British.' (p. 62)

It may be pertinent to observe here that Hauswirth Das also
wrote a novel titled *Into the Sun* (1933), in which she movingly
rendered the journey of Odia women from darkness, signified
by purdah, to light. Many of the women she drew here had
real-life counterparts. Sarala was portrayed in the character
of Rukmini. No wonder Sarala would go on to become what
Hauswirth Das predicted she would, namely a woman political activist and a nationalist. She would also go on to do her
Mary Wollstonecraft act by drafting her famous essay 'Narira
Dabi' ('The Rights of Women', 1934) for which the chapters in

Basanti were a preparation. She added layers to the characteriza-
tion of Basanti, layers such as reading, writing, argumentation,
and speaking out for the education of women in Odisha. It is
these layers that helped in breaking the mould in which the
woman had so far been cast in the Odia novel. The traditional
romance and marriage plot, seen in the early Odia novels such
as Umesh Chandra Sarcar's *Padmamali* (1889) and Ram Sankar
Ray's *Bibasini* (1891), was rewritten in terms of gender.

The mould was, of course, broken more decisively by the
collaborative composition strategy adopted in the novel. The
second number of volume 28 of *Utkala Sahitya* for the year
1925 featured an unprecedented appeal ('Nibedana') for a novel
in Odia to be written by many hands on the topical and highly
controversial theme of women's education. Admittedly the
inspiration for this came from neighbouring Bengal, which saw
the rise of literary clubs and jointly authored novels at the dawn
of the twentieth century. Three such examples in Bangla literature lay behind the appeal: *Baroyari*, written by twelve writers,
Bhager Puja, written jointly by sixteen writers, eight men and
eight women, and *Chatuskona*, written by four writers.[1] There
had, of course, been half a century of novel writing in Bangla
by then. The Odia novel was, however, still in its cradle at this
time and this is what makes this project a milestone in Odia
literature.

To have given a plot outline and then have multiple authors
extend it, expand on it, and flesh it out with characters and

---

[1]   Exact dates of publication of these works are not ascertainable.
They were all serialized in Bangla journals. *Baroyari* was serialized in
Bharati, and *Bhager Puja* in *Jamuna*. *Chatuskona* was written by four
writers who had formed a society named 'Abhyudayika'. My reading
has not enabled me to discover the venue of the publication or its
date. But it is clear from the context that these collective novels were
all published between 1922 and 1924.

incidents without deviating from the socially relevant theme of
rethinking gender roles in Odia society requires a tremendous
amount of skill as well as a belief in a purposive, reform-oriented
literature. It is just not that the main characters of Basanti and
Debabrata are developed by the brush strokes of all the nine
authors involved; even secondary and minor characters are elab-
orated in a similar fashion with one author initiating a character
sketch and other authors ramifying it. This does not mean that
individual styles of authors are erased or dissolved in some kind
of an undifferentiated and uniformized stylistic limbo. Kalindi
Charan Panigrahi's ornate style can be easily marked off from the
restless and tortuous style of Annada Shankar Ray. Sarala Devi
writes in a range of styles: her penetrating probes of the mind,
her polemics—in this she is joined by Muralidhar Mahanti—
and sometimes her florid prose. Suprava Devi and Prativa Devi
pitch in with their realistic etching of the village life, the view
of the zenana, and the domestic space. Sarat Chandra Mukherjee
and Harihar Mahapatra regale with their lightness of touch as
they fill out the details of time, place, and atmosphere, thereby
giving concreteness to the Cuttack setting of the novel. And
then Baishnab Charan Das excels with his fine eye for mind
mapping and melodrama in the two most painful bereavement
chapters, one written from the point of view of Debabrata and
the other from the point of view of Basanti.

VI

The medley of styles in *Basanti* did not escape the notice of the
early readers of the novel. In fact, it was hailed as a singular
virtue of the collective composition method. The best aspects
of the writers' styles came to the fore while their relatively
inferior aspects receded from view. Here is how an early review
by Harischandra Badal comments on the stylistic plurality of
the novel:

For example, we see the coming together of the idealism of Kalindi's *Matira Manisha* (English translation: *A House Undivided*) and the sharp strokes of Sarat Chandra's realistic and reform-oriented pen, just as we see the brilliant blend of Sarala's fine-grained analysis of complex psychological issues in a lucid language with Annada Shankar's impetuous and energetic rendering of the play of apprehension and anticipation in the consciousness. (*Sahakara*, 1933: p. 779)

This observation confirms the theory of the exponents of the collective novel that 'khichdi', if prepared with the right mix of ingredients in their right proportions, will turn out to be a more wholesome meal than plain rice.

VII

Time now for a brief airing of what it is that the nine authors were striving to present in fictional form: Debabrata, a young man and the son of a zamindar, studying in Cuttack College, and Basanti, a young woman also from Cuttack, get to know each other through Basanti's father who has died by the time the novel opens. They get close through their common love of reading and common hatred towards superstitions and injustice. The death of Basanti's mother precipitates a crisis in her life. Debabrata decides to marry Basanti against the opposition of his mother. After the marriage they move to Debabrata's village Similipur, in the northern Odishan town of Balasore, which was, after Cuttack, the second nerve centre of colonial Odisha, and had seen the establishment of Odisha's second printing press by Senapati.

For a time, things go well but their relationship is under a lot of strain because of the strong dislike of Debabrata's mother for a modern, educated woman who reads, writes, sews, and dispenses homeopathic medicine. Debabrata is not strong-willed enough to stand up to his mother and the village ethos. He also does not have it in him to share Basanti's concern for the independence of women. Devotion to the husband appears to him to be the prime duty of a woman. He starts to resent Basanti writing a magazine article on the rights of women and her running a school for the girls in the village. Frustrated by Basanti's questioning of the unequal gender relationship, he begins to assert his traditional male rights over her.

As if this were not enough, he suspects Basanti of infidelity by imagining from a torn piece of a letter he chances upon that she had been in secret communion with a lover. He turns her out of the house in a huff, drives her to the railway station at night, and leaves her there. This is the climactic scene, narrated in Chapter 22. The remaining eight chapters are taken up with Debabrata's realization of his mistake, his deep repentance on learning that the letter he thought was written to his friend Ramesh was in fact written to her distant relative Binod Bihari, a doctor in Burdwan, and finally, his reunion with Basanti and their son born during this period of exile.

VIII

The ending of the novel seems to be somewhat of a let down, a concession to the demands of the previously discarded marriage and romance plot. It is perhaps not entirely surprising in a novel which is an early step in the presentation of the emancipated woman and is, therefore, bound to be in some sense incomplete and contradictory. But this weakness has to be weighed against the major strengths of the novel. These consist not only in imagining the new woman but also in seeing through the facade of masculinity. The novel is as much a compelling portrait of a feisty woman, Basanti, as it is a searing portrayal of a contradictory man, Debabrata, whose bookish idealism is seen to founder on the rock of wealth, social standing, and masculine privileges, which are among his inheritance. The

review by Badal referred to earlier, captures this aspect of the
novel's criticism of Debabrata—which has echoes of Thomas
Hardy's jibe at the pseudo-liberalism of Angel Clare in *Tess
of the D'Urbervilles* (1897)—beautifully: 'The novel *Basanti* is
structured mainly around the conflict between false and illusory
notions about life, born of inexperience, and the knowledge of
the self gained through a collision against reality' (p. 785). This
seems like a general observation that applies to both Basanti
and Debabrata, but read in the context of the happenings in the
novel the collision described above throws the double standards
of Debabrata into sharp relief.

The catalyst of this collision is, of course, Basanti. As we look
back from our twenty-first century vantage point, where wom-
en's emancipation in the Indian society is still not a fact of life,
where the girl child is still not wanted in many quarters, where
a woman is an object of sensual gratification, where a woman
may be free in the superficial sense of being a breadwinner but
not really in control of her life and sexuality, we cannot fail to
be struck by this early articulation of a feisty feminist spirit in
Basanti. The two impressions that abide even after a lapse of
more than 80 years since the publication of the novel are: (i)
it is a novel of ideas about the new woman, one whose charm
even at this distance of time resides in its several debate-centred
chapters, arguing for the emancipated woman, and, (ii) it is a
work of collaboration and sharing. While of the former there are
many later examples in Odia fiction, the latter has as yet seen no
second coming.

Excerpt from the Call for the New Novel in *Utkala Sahitya*

Appeal

Some young writers of Utkala have decided to write a novel collectively. Like the Bangla novel *Baroyari*, which has been authored by twelve writers, this novel too will be written and published by a mixed group of senior and younger writers of Utkala. Every writer will contribute a chapter or two, so the pleasure in the work will be greater, in comparison to the labour involved.

At the moment four writers are ready to undertake the task. Seven or eight, or at least four or five more writers are needed. It is presumed that there will be no dearth of persons in Orissa to act as priests in this yagna. Esteemed Sri Nanda Kishore Bal was working on a novel named *Kanaka Lata* at one time. Scholars believe that this novel, if it had been completed, would have ranked among the greatest novels of Orissa. Sri Bankanidhi Patnaik and Sri Dibyasingh Panigrahi are able to write short stories; indeed, they have a certain reputation for that. Smt. Kuntala Kumari Sabat's 'Bhranti' is a fine story. Smt. Suprava Kar too has crafted an excellent story. Some beautiful stories by Smt. Kokila Dei were published in *Utkala Sahitya*. Smt. Sarala

Dei wields an effective pen, although she has not yet written stories. Sri Dayanidhi Mishra was writing historical stories at one time. Sri Upendra Prasad Mohanty's portraits of society are considered apt and appealing. There are also other silent devotees of literature in Utkal. They could enrich the world of short fiction if they so wanted.

The organizers will be very grateful if they come to know of persons who are willing to contribute to the collective project. They have given the onus of starting the novel to Kalindi Charan Panigrahi, and two others will follow him. The road after that is uncharted. Those who are persuaded by this appeal to contribute are requested to send in their name. The work will be apportioned based on their preferences; that is to say, each writer's portion will be defined.

The contributors will have to abide by certain norms. 1. Each writer will write two chapters, basing themselves on the plot outline given here. 2. Writers will take care to maintain links with the previous episodes. 3. The development of the principal characters will be inversely proportional to that of the minor characters, meaning that the latter should be developed to the right degree so as to rule out anything absurd or disjointed. 4. Characters other than those who are critical to the plot may be created, but they have to be kept secondary, keeping in view their role as enablers of the main characters. 5. The parts are to be completed within the specified time and sent to the address given below. Sri Annada Shankar Ray has been given the responsibility of determining whether or not the submissions are on track and to the point. He can, if the need arises, make changes in the texts in consultation with the writers. 6. The writers will be notified about the parts or chapters they will write after they send us their names. Prior intimation is desirable if any contributor is unable to write his portion due to some mischance. Someone else will be appointed to write their part.

The tone and tenor of the writing in such a work will naturally vary and so will the language used. So some people may laugh it off as a khichdi. Everyone knows, however, that created with the proper ingredients mixed in the right proportions khichdi is superior to rice. If the khichdi comes out delicious, then no one will go on a fast and subject our khichdi novel to derision. The assembly of writers will in fact make it appear attractive and beautiful, like a group photograph.

It is noteworthy that the well known and much acclaimed editor of *Utkala Sahitya*, Sri Biswanath Kar, has pledged to lend his enthusiasm and support to this endeavour.

Kalindi Charan Panigrahi

A. Ray
C/o – Utkala Sahitya
Chandni Chowk, Cuttack

(The 'Appeal' was published in *Utkala Sahitya*, vol 28, 1924, p. 61.)

One*

A morning in autumn.

She is as bright as this autumn morning, her blossoming youth vibrant like the sky, radiant like night-flowering jasmine! In her youthful liveliness she floats over the beautiful, lush green earth like a cool breeze.

Basanti—her name a reflection of her beauty—is the very picture of spring. The intoxicating scent of jasmine seems to have infused her inner being. Her voice seems to echo the mellifluous call of the cuckoo. She is the angelic harbinger of a luxuriant spring, her looks rendered even more exquisite by the bright beauty of autumn.

On this auspicious morning, however, her autumn-fresh face is clouded by sorrow and her tear-soaked eyes resemble an aparajita touched by frost.

Why? What pain can have caused this fresh flower to wilt? Even pain itself should hesitate to torment such a delicate creature. Alas, if only the unseen powers were imbued with a taste for poetry, a sense of beauty!

What could have caused Basanti's sorrow, her feelings of anxiety? She is still single. Not poorly off certainly, for her

* By Kalindi Charan Panigrahi.

circumstances suggest a life of some ease. What can it be if not that her mother—her sheltering tree in this desert of a world due to whom she was able to survive the loss of her father—has taken to her sickbed so soon after her father's death.

Balaram Babu, Basanti's father, was a deputy magistrate in Cuttack. His wife and Basanti, their daughter, made up his family. After his untimely death, mother and daughter had to shoulder all the burdens of life. To live, they used the money that had come to Balaram Babu when he retired. Her mother was careful not to let on to Basanti, even in the slightest way, how precarious their position was. After losing her father, she began to lean on her mother. Nurtured with great care and affection from infancy, she had been like a precious gem to her parents, spared the sting of want and woe. From the day death led her father behind its dark curtain, bringing her face to face with the stark realities of life, she had held fast to her mother, ready to spare no effort to keep her from death's clutches. But alas, the fatal messenger now had her in its grip, brushing aside Basanti's soft hand.

Sitting on the bed, Basanti was busy nursing her mother. To have to live without her mother was a torment impossible for her to imagine. Brought up with the most delicate of care, she had no sense of the thorny ways of the world. She had already lived through 14 autumns, including this one, and during that time the thought for her future had not crossed her mind for a moment. Nor had she ever looked back to the past. At her father's initiative she had studied at Cuttack Girls' School for a few years. This, together with reading newspapers, had created in her the desire to do what she could to improve the lot of women. Otherwise she was like a dry leaf in the wind, unmindful of where she had come from and of where she would wash ashore.

Seated at her mother's side, Basanti nursed her day and night. Her mother had been in the grip of a fever for the past three days with no remission in sight. Basanti knew how to use a thermometer and the basics of how to treat diseases. She had been taking care of her mother using her chest of homeopathic medicines. Though not strong when faced with misfortune affecting her near and dear, she was more advanced than many women of her generation in terms of education and independent thinking. Today she was feeling threatened by some imminent danger, although when it came to helping a person in distress her strength and courage were beyond compare. Using her homeopathic doses she had cured Ram Tiadi, her elderly neighbour, of a chronic illness. She had been criticised by neighbours for this, but because of Balaram Babu and his wife no one had dared speak ill of her. Basanti was unaware of these reactions. Her parents had kept a sharp eye on her character and education and given her a corresponding amount of freedom.

She could have had a doctor come and see her mother, but even the mention of that made her mother wince. 'Why worry so much? You know more than the doctor and you'll cure me sooner. Be happy; go out and play. Why think about a doctor?', she would say. Basanti never went against her mother's wishes. She knew it would worry her mother if she discovered her daughter was concerned about her. She was especially careful not to cause her mother any hurt. Her mother told her to play with her classmates instead of sitting at her bedside all the time, but she found it difficult to leave. When she felt the need for some diversion she would call her classmates there. But even this she did to satisfy her mother; her heart was not in it.

Basanti convinced her friend Suniti, a Christian, to try and persuade her mother to see a doctor. But she repeated her objections. 'No, my dear. Why are you all worrying so much? There's no need. If I need a doctor, I shall let you know.' Suniti pressed on. 'Mausi, the doctor will tell us why the fever's not going down.' Basanti's mother did not relent. 'Let it be, my dear. Do you think I'm such a fool as to make others worry by not being careful? Don't I know how Basanti would suffer if I were to go? Would I willingly put her through that?' Would any mother knowingly inflict pain on her child? Many times in the past Basanti's mother had come down with a fever. Basanti's mother's greatest concern was to protect her daughter from danger, which is why Basanti had not realised earlier how ill her mother really was. It was only when her mother had been laid low with fever that Basanti had fully understood her condition.

For Basanti, only one person could make her mother agree to a visit from a doctor. Deba bhai! But he had not been heard from for days. Not even a letter! Could he really be so hard hearted? Was the old saying true then, that in times of need nobody is a friend? How could someone like Deba bhai be so rude? Deeply hurt—no one knew because of whom—the proud eyes of the Basanti began to well up.

Just then a bicycle bell was heard outside the front door, and it was not long before Debabrata stepped into the house.

Two *

Ravenshaw College in Cuttack had not yet moved to its new complex in Chauliaganj, but the older buildings had already been touched by the enlightened message of the modern era. Within the confines of its small enclosure a fertile ground had been cultivated, and service to the society, nation, and arts had blossomed. There is no record of what those youths achieved after leaving college, but it is not difficult to find evidence of the enthusiasm and strength of purpose of the young students of that time and of the hope they inspired in their countrymen.

There was a student named Debabrata in the third year of college. This young man deserves special mention. He was the son of a zamindar from Balasore, with only his elderly mother at home. A distant relative of his father looked after their zamindari. Debabrata would never have been thought of as studious or scholarly; he paid more attention to a lecturer's clothes, mannerisms, and the way he expressed himself than to what he was teaching. Very quickly in class Debabrata's eyes would lose their ability to concentrate and begin to wander. Almost 40 minutes of each hour in class was spent gazing out of the window

* By Kalindi Charan Panigrahi.

at passing cars and horses, or at passers-by. At home, games, discussions on music, and debates took the place of studies.

Seen from a different point of view, however, Debabrata would have to be considered a leader. He was invited to meetings and functions to speak and to sing. He was skilled at football, tennis, cricket, hockey, as well as other games. If a student was taken ill, the news would reach Debabrata before it did the doctor or the hostel superintendent, and he would instantly arrive at the bedside. If friends were worried about some danger, it was Debabrata who would go out and investigate. On the days of Ganesh and Saraswati puja he had not a moment to spare. If he took it into his head that untouchability was unacceptable, he would sit and eat with someone from the lowest caste in full view of his friends. He was not casual about anything; he did everything in earnest. His strength was boundless, and energy constantly surged through his veins. No matter how hard he worked he never needed to rest. For all these reasons, he had earned his classmates' love and his teachers' attention.

Debabrata's studies began at Victoria School in Cuttack under the supervision of a tutor. However, most of the money he received from home was spent on the theatre, circus, and on musical instruments. His tutor, Harigopal Babu, never got in the way, preferring to remain silent in matters where it would have been futile to attempt to have a say. Moreover, no one had ever heard of Debabrata failing an examination despite the time he spent enjoying himself. If anyone raised the subject, he would say, 'Is it really necessary to study hard to pass examinations? The only reason people spend a lot of time studying is to draw attention to themselves at the university.' His teachers often expressed regret that such a good student seemed to be bent on ruination, but Debabrata was not foolish to let himself be influenced by them. He would answer them directly, 'Your so-called good students are the real fools.'

At this point it is necessary to provide a brief account of how Basanti came to be acquainted with Debabrata. When Debabrata was being tutored by Harigopal Babu, the house they were living in was next door to Balaram Babu's. Balaram Babu was very perceptive and had seen fit to allow Basanti the freedom to come and go. He had also taken the measure of Debabrata. He had been able to gauge the stamina and strength of the young man as well as his character. As a result, Debabrata was given free access to his house. Balaram Babu and his wife considered Debabrata like a son, and Debabrata held them in high regard. It was then that Basanti had taken to calling him 'Deba bhai'. Though Balaram Babu had hopes that Debabrata would become his son-in-law, he never said anything. Nor did he mention it to his wife, only cautioning her to keep a close eye on their daughter and Debabrata.

When Debabrata entered college after matriculation, Balaram Babu invited him to stay with his family. Debabrata declined, opting for the college hostel instead, but he agreed to have breakfast with them every day. He found it difficult to keep his promise, however, as on most days he was busy with social service activities and attending meetings of different clubs.

Despite all the precautions taken by Basanti's parents, she and Debabrata unconsciously began to feel attracted to each other. Every expression of Basanti, whether she smiled or sulked, would deeply affect Debabrata, his imagination feeding off these pictures of her stored in his mind. For her part, Basanti learned to regard Debabrata with a mixture of affection and respect because of his generosity, courage, and restraint. Everyone who witnessed his patience and fortitude in helping the family at the time of Balaram Babu's death had great praise for him. Day by day Basanti and Debabrata's nascent love grew stronger. If Debabrata was taken up with meetings and committee work for a day or two, he felt restless and wanted to rush to Basanti to catch a glimpse of her. Basanti would write to him if she did not see him for a few days. The growing ties between the two youngsters in love took place out of the public eye; only Basanti's mother was aware of them.

But their relation did not remain hidden for long. As already noted, Debabrata's influence in the student community was strong. If he so much as uttered the word 'strike', the order would spread among the students like lightning and instantly be translated into action. If students had grievances to address to teachers, it was Debabrata who stepped forward. Under such circumstances what normally happens came to pass. The students who were jealous of Debabrata started to search out his flaws. It did not take long to discover where Debabrata went and when, to whom he wrote and who wrote to him. A group of students joined together to malign Debabrata's character and began to attack him in public, unfairly, and through insinuation. Debabrata had known for a long time how nasty and ill-mannered some members of the student community could be, realising that education had little effect on such mean-spirited people. He had no other option but to avoid them, apprehensive about what they might do. But their hawk-like eyes were ever watching him, always on the look-out for a chance to take their revenge.

It was Saturday, and the fourth meeting of the Social Service Guild was being held. The subject under discussion was 'The Duty of the Student Community with Regards to the Autonomy of Women'. Debabrata was in the chair. For his adversaries this was a golden opportunity; people who never set foot in a meeting hall were in attendance. Debabrata had no premonition of any danger. He started to conduct the proceedings with his usual openness. After the paper was presented, someone stood up and said, 'Before giving my views on the autonomy of women, I wish to say something about those present, and in particular about those who have become our self-proclaimed champions. I want to know how suitable they are for this task and if they have the moral right to undertake it. Will the members present here raise their hands—no, no, will they place their hands on their hearts—and tell us how many consider themselves suited to be our representatives? I can affirm that there is not even one person. I know every student present in this meeting hall and can tell you what he does and where he lives.'

Another person rose to speak: 'Esteemed President Sir, it is no use trying to hide. This entire discussion is about you. Your deception stands exposed. No one will put up with a leader who lies.' Debabrata's face flushed. Before the president could react, another person began to speak: 'The secret of your clandestine exchange of love letters is out. Here is one of the letters, proving your access to that lover of yours.' The hall broke into a tumult with sounds of derisive laughter and cries of 'shame, shame'. A few members who rose to speak in Debabrata's favour were shouted down. The president instantly exited the hall, and the meeting came to an abrupt end.

This was deeply hurtful for Debabrata, a strike at his exalted sense of self. He had the unbridled enthusiasm and endless courage to rise in protest against thousands and provide a solid and irrefutable defence of his point of view, but he was the last person to suffer an assault on the goddess he worshipped in the deepest recesses of his heart. Sensing that if the discussion continued it would entail further blasphemy against the goddess he revered, he left the hall without a word.

Exiting the meeting brought him no relief. Although in the past he had questioned the propriety of maintaining a relation with Basanti, the sarcasm of his fellow students again made him wonder if he had done something wrong. He wanted to think things through and considered it proper to stay away from Basanti for as long as that would take. Of course doing this would cause him great distress, but that he could well withstand. From that very day he stopped visiting Basanti's house and did not reply to any of her letters.

Basanti grew tired of writing. Two weeks passed. During this period, Debabrata came to the conclusion that the students' aspersions were unjust, prompted only by jealousy, and that his relationship with Basanti was absolutely pure. So the moment he heard Basanti's mother was ailing, he set out on his bicycle.

Basanti's hurt pride had made her promise not to speak to Deba bhai if they were to meet, but the moment he entered the house she forgot her promise and blurted out, 'Mother, Deba bhai is here.' Nirmala Devi motioned to Debabrata to come closer and sit by the bed. Basanti looked at him sadly and said, her voice on the verge of choking, 'Deba bhai, it was our turn to be remembered at last! Mother has been running a fever for the last three days.' 'Forgive me Basanti, I was busy with an examination.' Basanti, of course, knew full well that Debabrata was not the kind of person to let an examination take over his life, but she felt comforted by his thoughtful atten-tion. Forgetting her mother's illness for a moment, she joked, 'Since when have you become such a diligent student, Deba bhai? Mother, did you hear that? Deba bhai has been busy with his studies.' Nirmala Devi answered, a cheerful expression on her face, 'Yes, an examination can surely keep one busy.' For Basanti, Debabrata's presence provided a big boost in morale. With him here, what need was there for her to worry about mother's illness? She smiled. 'Deba bhai, this time you have changed beyond recognition.' Debabrata pretended to take the comment seriously. 'Do things always stay the same, Basanti? These days, if one doesn't study hard how can one get a job?' Basanti responded in the same vein. 'Yes, Deba bhai, how else would you be able to feed yourself unless you get a job? And especially with your mother minding the estate.' 'No, Basanti, I'm not joking. I'm not so light-headed these days.' Basanti was not one to let up. 'How could it be, when, on top of your dhoti and kurta, you have allowed this hat to stick to your head like a leech?' Debabrata smiled faintly. 'Let's stop all this talk. How long has mother been ill? Who's the doctor?' At the mention of her mother's illness Basanti's mind returned to its earlier worries. 'The fever has lasted for the past three days, and she won't let me have a doctor come.' Without another word Debabrata made a move to leave to call a doctor. Her mother signalled to Basanti to get some food ready, but Debabrata said, 'let me go first', and rode off on his bicycle.

Debabrata and Basanti had become attracted to each other, but without being fully aware of what was happening. Neither had any hint from the way the other person acted or spoke that love was blossoming between them. Like the thousand silent notes of a melody trapped in the strings of a lyre, they were in wait for that day when the music would be set free and resound in all directions. They had set sail on the surging current of youth and flowed on. Their minds were weighed down by the longing of love, but they had remained patient in the hope of one day reaping the fruit of love.

Their life of happiness and sorrow turned over a new leaf when the doctor came and diagnosed Nirmala Devi with double pneumonia. She had come down with fever many times in the past, but had kept it a secret and continued her work so as not to frighten Basanti. Oh, the consequences of filial love! If she had known that neglecting her health would render inescapable the command from death's messenger, would she, in the hope of sparing Basanti trivial pain, have pushed her into such deep grief? But who can know or understand this? All man's knowledge comes to naught when faced with the lessons of life; his head, held high and proud with knowledge, bows before these simple facts.

Neither Basanti nor Debabrata could save Nirmala Devi despite attending to her day and night. Before dying she placed Basanti's hand on top of Debabrata's and said, 'Your father dearly wished to see you two as a couple, but that was not to be. Today I am being called by the same messenger. But standing on the threshold of the kingdom of death and acting as the priest to your union gives me untold happiness. I hope the two hands I have joined together today will remain joined forever.' Nirmala Devi had to obey death's inexorable command. Basanti could not, however, be critical of her mother for this death bed confession; she had carried out her husband's wish.

Three*

'Basa, why live here all by yourself? Come and stay with us, my dear.' As she was saying this, Kalyani wiped the tears from Basanti's eyes. But Basanti's grief at the loss of her mother was stronger than this momentary reprieve, and a tear reappeared in the corner of her eye.

Her voice choking, Basanti answered, 'Auntie, please forgive me. I can't leave this house.'

'My dear child, you shouldn't stay here alone right now. Come.'

'Why alone, auntie? Dhania's with me.' Dhania was Basanti's servant, aged 12. 'He's only a boy, what can he do? Come or I'll feel hurt, please come.' Kalyani took hold of Basanti's hands and started to pull her gently. Suddenly Basanti bent down, grasped Kalyani's feet, and cried. 'Please don't feel hurt, auntie. It would make me suffer too much not to be able to obey you. I'm falling at your feet, please don't feel hurt.'

Kalyani freed her feet and pulled Basanti up into her arms. 'Auntie, please don't make me feel even more guilty. It would be very bad not to do as you ask, auntie. Ma is gone ....' Basanti

* By Sarat Chandra Mukherjee.

could not continue. She found shelter in the affectionate embrace of the motherly Kalyani and began to sob.

'Don't, please don't give into tears, dear. It's all right, you don't need to come to our house. Stay here, and Suna can keep you company. Don't cry.' As Kalyani said this, her own eyes teared up. Both of them began to shed tears in silence. Large drops rolled down from the watery eyes of Suniti, who was standing a little distance away. She covered her face with the end of her sari and began to hurl curses at the mysterious deity of death.

Who is this Kalyani, the very epitome of motherliness as she cries holding the grief-stricken girl to her bosom? She is Suniti's mother and Nirmala Devi's beloved friend. Kalyani is truly the bringer of good; all her actions make manifest the inherent sweetness of her name. Twenty years ago, when Balaram Babu built a big house in Petin Sahi in Cuttack shortly after becoming Deputy Magistrate, and brought his newlywed wife, Nirmala Devi, from her village to Cuttack, there was barely a hint of women's education in the urban environs of Cuttack, let alone in the villages. The efforts of a small number of Christian missionaries from Europe kept the light of women's education burning faintly. Kalyani was one among the few Oriya Christian women who had been able to glimpse in the faint light of that lamp a beacon of their glorious potential as women, hidden by years of ignorance.

It is true that Balaram Babu had brought Nirmala from the village without paying any heed to the resentment and criticism of the village elders, but within a short time Nirmala began to feel restless like a caged bird. She had known a life of confinement in the village, but the small liberties of that world—going with friends to bathe in the river or for a darshan of the deity—provided sweet freedom within village life, if only for a moment. The restrictions of the town exceeded those of the village. Going for a river bath in Cuttack was well nigh impossible for a woman married into a respectable family like hers; venturing out into the street alone would have been very difficult. Although these restrictions were not imposed on her by Balaram Babu, Nirmala made an effort to get used to the limited freedom in her life. But that did not last for long. A friend materialized and freed Nirmala from the shackles of restriction, much like a bird who, though trapped in a net itself, first frees its mate by skillfully ripping the net open. This friend was Kalyani.

Nirmala's first meeting with Kalyani was quite the stuff that stories are made of. Balaram Babu's house was next door to where Kalyani lived. Kalyani's husband, Saroj Babu, was a man of refined taste—gardening was his favourite hobby. With his wife he had planted many kinds of flowering shrubs in the small plot in front of his house. Two or three strong and sturdy rose bushes kept the garden lively and bright with their rich yield of fresh blooms. Once, while she was taking a stroll with her husband in that small garden, Kalyani had noticed a beautiful face framed in a window of Balaram Babu's house, her eyes wistfully focused on a rose bush covered in flowers. Kalyani knew that Balaram Babu's wife was about to arrive and quickly understood that the beautiful face she had seen was hers. She wanted to go and speak to her, but Saroj Babu was experienced in the ways of the world. 'Look, don't go now,' he said. 'A married lady in a staunch Hindu family may not take it well. Let me first have a word with Balaram Babu.' Before Saroj Babu could speak to Balaram Babu, however, Kalyani was introduced to Nirmala by accident.

One hot afternoon Kalyani was standing on the veranda, tracing her fingers gently over the madhabilata plant that had wilted in the heat, when she heard a woman speaking in Balaram Babu's house. 'Go Champa, go. Get some flowers from the Babu's house. He won't say no if you ask. Especially since they're for the evening Satyanarayan puja. We're not seeking them for ourselves; it's for God that we're asking. Go right away. If you don't, it will be time for the babus to return home from the office and you won't be able to go.' The speaker's voice was so melodious that Kalyani let go of the creeper and started to listen. But the next moment a voice rang out. 'Which Babu's house, madam? Shall I fetch flowers from a Christian house? I'd rather die. What does it matter if we don't have flowers? Shall I get flowers from a Christian house for Satyanarayan puja?' Kalyani understood that Balaram Babu's wife was asking Champa to fetch flowers from her house, and she was curious how Balaram Babu's wife would reply to Champa's disparaging words. She pricked up her ears and heard Nirmala say, 'Shame on you, you're still caught up in such talk! You're supposed to get flowers from a garden. What does it matter if they are from a Christian or a Muslim house? Do flowers ever get polluted? Does God give consideration to caste? Is God only our father and mother, and nothing for them? All right, don't get flowers if you don't want to, but don't talk against Christians. What would they think if they heard you?'

Kalyani was overwhelmed by what she heard. Her own people had told her that Hindu women from the rural areas were steeped in prejudice, that they shut their ears at the mention of 'Christians'. Not only were these women devoid of education, but the way they dressed and talked was also utterly in bad taste. But what she had just heard was a revelation. That kind of talk and attitude could not belong to any of these uncivilised and prejudiced village women. 'Does God give consideration to caste? Is God only our father and mother, and nothing for them?' It did not take Kalyani more than a moment to understand the generous nature of a woman who could talk like this despite having been brought up in the narrow and prejudice-ridden confines of a village. She was not unaware what villages in Utkala were like. She knew very well that the generosity that could lead someone to say that flowers meant for worship never got polluted was not to be found in even one of the learned elders of such societies. There indeed is bliss in a simple appreciation of another person's good qualities.

At Nirmala's words Kalyani felt a pleasure she never before experienced, and she instantly went over to speak to Nirmala, bringing with her a small basket of beautiful roses she herself had picked.

This conversation 20 years ago had gradually grown into an intimate friendship. Before her marriage Nirmala had carefully studied the kabyas 'Labanyabati', 'Baidehisa Bilasa', and 'Bidagdha Chintamani' under the tutelage of her maternal grandfather.[1] She had thoroughly assimilated these poetic masterpieces, and Kalyani became an ardent follower of Nirmala and started to learn them during her leisure hours. For Nirmala's part, she accepted Kalyani as a teacher when she learned how qualified and generous she was. Under Kalyani's guidance Nirmala became a dedicated student of Utkala and Bangla literature and also began to learn how to sew, draw, and practice other arts. A deep bond developed between them because of their mutual regard for each other, their openness of mind, and not least because they were of the same age. In reality, Nirmala's knowledge of the world and her efficiency were in many ways the result of her friendship with Kalyani.

After that first conversation many things came to pass. Both took up the responsibilities of managing a house, saying farewell to the many amusements and pleasures of youth. Basanti and Suniti were born on the same day, and they too became friends with the passage of time. Like two malati creepers hit by a bolt of lightning, both Nirmala and Kalyani suffered the

---

[1] 'Labanyabati' and 'Baidehisa Bilasa' are the poetical works of the great eighteenth century Odia poet Upendra Bhanja. 'Bidagdha Chintamani' is by Abhimanyu Samanta Singhar.

calamity of widowhood at the same time. Their ties of friendship never slackened in and through these events and disasters.

When Nirmala took to her sickbed suddenly, Kalyani was in
Tangi, where she had 30 to 40 acres of farmland. She had been
there for a week to collect from the farmers the paddy they had
harvested. On her return by a daytime bus, she learned that her
dearly beloved friend had bidden farewell to the world after an
illness of only two or three days. The grief over the death of her
friend pierced her heart like a sharp arrow, but she did not give
into tears. She reasoned that if she broke down and cried, then
the sorrow of the now motherless Basanti would be increased
many times over. Basanti was a child after all, and it would
be impossible to comfort her if the person offering consolation
herself broke down. She steeled her heart and went to Basanti.
She felt her first duty was to comfort Basanti and to convince
her that she was not really without a mother, although she had
lost the person who had given birth to her.

There was another reason why Kalyani wanted to see Basanti
so quickly. Although a Christian, she believed in ghosts. She
had never seen one with her own eyes, but had heard many
times that spirits were up to all kinds of mischief on the day a
person died and on those that followed. Her belief was confirmed
when, on the night of her husband's death, she heard all kinds
of unusual noises coming from behind the house. Kalyani was
afraid to leave the orphaned Basanti alone in her own house at
a time like this. Dhania was only a boy after all; his being there
made no difference. Kalyani felt it would be good if she could
somehow talk Basanti into coming to stay with her. However,
not all plans come to fruition. Basanti was not willing to move
out of her own house, no matter how hard Kalyani tried to talk
her into it.

Kalyani had made up her mind not to cry in front of Basanti
when she went to see her, but faced with a house now devoid of
her friend and with a grieving Basanti, she was not able to keep

her promise. Hearing Basanti's sorrowful plea against leaving her house, Kalyani drew her to her bosom and began to shed silent tears.

Basanti knew that she had no one and that it would be very difficult for her to live alone in such a large house with only the young Dhania for company. Why then did she not agree to Kalyani's request? Basanti had a keen intelligence, far beyond her years, due to the education she had received. She understood instantly what grim foreboding made the loving Kalyani want to take her home. Kalyani was particularly worried that if Basanti stayed in her own house she would feel very sad at the sight of the household objects her mother had used. Basanti knew Kalyani was right, but could she be so self-centred as to abandon the dear old house her mother had lived in since her youth merely to escape her own grief and the toll it would take on her health? After her father had died many had advised her mother to go and live in her village, but Nirmala had not visited her village even once. She had stayed here, enduring all the hardships of living alone in the town. She had always said, 'No, no, I don't want to go anywhere else. Where he spent his last days is the place of my pilgrimage, my sacred land, my everything.' Hadn't Basanti seen how her mother had acted in those circumstances? Mother's suitcase sitting in a corner of the house, her mirror gleaming there still, and her pet parrot eyeing her sympathetically—had all these become meaningless with her mother's absence? The signs of her mother's skilful hands were present in every corner of the house. Her mother had done all the household chores with her own hands, as she had not been able to afford a maid after the death of her husband. Who can say whether such hard work did not contribute to her premature death? With the signs of her mother's sacrifice evident, how could Basanti even think of going somewhere else? No, no, that was impossible.

When Kalyani told her not to stay in the house alone, Basanti could easily guess that Kalyani was afraid there would be visitations from the spirit world. But she thought about it this way: her mother, who had thrown around her a protective cordon of love and saved her from many disasters, risking her very life; would that same mother, now in the world of spirits, think of causing her harm? Even as a ghost she was still her mother after all! If she appeared in the form of an apparition, Basanti would consider herself blessed and warmly embrace her. She wanted to be held in her mother's bosom, even if she was now in the world of the dead.

Basanti was certain her generous, well-meaning, and helpful mother had left for her heavenly abode and was today among the immortals of the three worlds. Were she to learn that her beloved daughter was anxious to abandon her own home, afraid of being harmed by her because she had left this world, how troubled she would be! No, by no means could Basanti allow herself to do that. She could not cause pain to her loving and caring mother, now in heaven. Kalyani quickly understood and said to Suniti, 'Suna, if you won't mind staying at home at night all by yourself, I'll be able to stay here.' To console Basanti Kalyani had told her, 'Suna can stay with you.' But that had not set her mind at ease; she wanted to keep Basanti company herself. Suniti, however, would not let only her mother stay with her grieving friend. 'No, no,' she said. 'I'll be with Boula.' 'Fine then, go and lock up our house. We'll both stay with your Boula.'

Basanti had been Suniti's Boula—her closest and dearest friend—since childhood days.

Four *

At that time there was only one hostel at Ravenshaw College, a long single-storey structure like an army barrack. It was seven o'clock on a Sunday morning. The students in the hostel were engaged in the important daily task of having their tea; other morning chores—such as brushing their teeth—were done with. The hostel was brimming with gossip and laughter, but one room was still closed; possibly its occupant was asleep. A 10- or 12-year-old boy was vigorously tugging at the iron ring on the door, calling out, 'Deba Babu, Deba Babu! Oh, Deba Babu.'

Readers have already met this boy: Dhania—Basanti's servant. Nobody knows his caste, where he is from, or who his parents are. Seven or eight years ago there was a severe drought in the district of Cuttack. On a stroll to the river Mahanadi at that time, Nirmala and Kalyani noticed a naked child under a tree in the huge expanse of the Killa Ground. He was crying piteously, 'Ma, dearest Ma. Where have you gone?' Hearing the miserable cry of the poor child they were overcome with pity. They went over and asked him many questions. But the child was very little; unable to answer, he kept on crying. Thinking the boy's mother had gone off somewhere and would soon

* By Sarat Chandra Mukherjee.

return to press this gem of her heart to her bosom, they waited for some time. Soon evening fell, and the lights installed by the municipality lit up the ground. But there was no sign of anyone. The child continued to cry, 'Ma, dearest Ma. Where have you gone?'

Seeing how emaciated and feeble the boy was, they understood he was the child of some woman afflicted by famine. The unfortunate woman must have abandoned him under a tree in the care of some unknown God and run away. Nirmala lifted the child to her lap and said, 'Kalyani, from today this boy is mine.' To which Kalyani answered, 'No, no, not yours alone, he belongs to both of us.' In the end, the boy stayed with Nirmala. She brought him up as if he was her own son. No one ever made a problem of his unknown background. Only once or twice did Champa, taking exception to Nirmala Devi's excessive affection for the boy, remark, 'Dear me, he's just an abandoned boy raised in a government shelter; no one knows where he's from or who his parents are. So much affection for such a boy! What would it be like if he were one of your own? As the saying goes, "all style and no substance: the footwork is elegant, but the feet unadorned." Nirmala Devi's sharp rejoinder had made short work of Champa's cutting criticism. And, in fact, Champa too had begun to like the boy for his peaceable nature. That boy of yore is Dhania today. As a result of droughts, there is no dearth of such Dhanias in Orissa.

Dhania addressed Nirmala Devi as 'Ma'. With her death not only did Basanti lose a mother, Dhania too lost his. He cried piteously on the day of Nirmala Devi's death, but soon comforted himself and started to take care of Basanti. Although only a young boy, he stayed close to her and tried to help her by doing small chores like fetching water and mopping the floor, which he knew would please her.

Three days have passed after Nirmala Devi's death. When Dhania got up in the morning he saw that Basanti was crying, her head in Suniti's lap. Despite being comforted by Suniti she was grief-stricken. Dhania decided to run and fetch Debabrata. Perhaps Basanti would become calm if he consoled her. Dhania had seen how happy Basanti was in Debabrata's presence and how attentive she was to everything he said.

Dhania had come to the college hostel many times when Nirmala Devi was alive and was no stranger to Debabrata's room. He headed out to the hostel without wasting any time. Readers have already heard him call out, 'Deba Babu, Deba Babu.' Debabrata was not plunged into deep slumber. Hard work and his many misgivings had taken their toll on him, and he lay in bed half asleep. It was in this state that Dhania's call reached his ears, but it seemed to him to be in a dream, not in reality.

Suddenly Debabrata heard someone shout at the top of his voice, 'Hey Deba Babu.' This interrupted Debabrata's sleep, and he got out of bed at once. The same voice again. 'Hey Deba Babu, the messenger from your in-laws' house is at your door, calling out your name, while you're still sleeping soundly and snoring.' Debabrata understood the taunt in the voice. Enraged he ran to the door, but from the sound of footsteps retreating quickly on the veranda before he could open the door he knew the speaker had fled.

Seeing a startled Dhania in front of him, Debabrata said, 'You go, I'll follow.' Dhania was not one to give up. He knew Debabrata had often responded like this in the past, but had not come.

'No, please come with me.'

'Okay, off you go. I'm coming.'

'Do you swear you'll come?'

'I promise I will, now go.' Dhania was walking away, satisfied. Debabrata called to him from behind. 'Hey, Dhania, was someone else calling me?'

'Yes sir. Another sir like you was saying something about your father-in-law's house, trying to disguise his voice by pressing his fingertips against his throat. The moment you opened your door, he ran away.' Debabrata knew it was one of his cowardly classmates playing a prank.

For the past few days the students had been referring to Balaram Babu's house as Debabrata's father-in-law's house, just to irritate him. Debabrata resented such misbehaviour, and yet another case of this by one of them today made his face flush with disapproval and anger. He was already very tense because of something that had occurred two days earlier, which was why he had not slept the previous night. Resigning his sleep-dazed body to the bed, he began to go over events from the recent past.

The incident had happened only two days earlier. When Basanti's mother left the world for good after placing Basanti's hand in Debabrata's, the sound of the conch and the bell of the evening puja came floating in from all sides. To Debabrata it seemed that, like the setting of the sun, the sunset of Basanti's mother's life had also been beautiful. Just as the lovely earth was swathed in the robes of twilight at sundown, his life too had been encircled in a protective veil of love, keeping him from harm. For a while, he was thrilled at the prospect of winning a girl as beautiful, as virtuous, and as qualified as Basanti. But her piteous lamentation shattered his happiness. He immediately understood that he was embarked on an endless journey on the surface of this earth—he, an inexperienced youth without much wit or worldly sense, and his partner, a hapless woman devastated by the loss of her mother.

Moments after Nirmala Devi had breathed her last, Suniti had embraced Basanti and said, 'Deba Babu, what's the point of standing here in silence? Night is advancing. Go and set about making the arrangements.' Debabrata set off in search of people who would carry the body to the burning ghat after asking Suniti to look after Basanti and bidding Dhania to stay close to Basanti at all times.

The night was dark. Debabrata walked back to the hostel and requested the Karana students to help him out. He had no objection to having students of other castes carry the body, but for Basanti's sake he made the request only of Karanas. But only one of them agreed to suffer the biting drops of dew at the burning ghat on the banks of the Kathajodi on that dark night.

Close by the hostel was the residence of a middle-aged Karana professor. Debabrata went to him. Hearing the story, he said, 'All right, let's go. Since you say the girl's alone and in trouble, what person with a heart could say no? Yes, it will be difficult, but to endure suffering for the sake of social service is the true sign of humanity.' Debabrata felt relieved. Someone was listening to their conversation from behind the door. The moment the professor went inside the house, Debabrata could hear an old woman speaking in hushed tones but not make anything out. After a while the lecturer returned and told Debabrata in English, 'Please excuse me. My mother has told me to stay away from a corpse for a few days for family reasons.'

Debabrata was annoyed beyond measure and quickly walked away without uttering a word. Just then one of the professor's neighbours called out to him from behind: 'I'm also a Karana. I consider it my duty to go with you under these circumstances. May I come?' The gentleman worked as a clerk in the court. Standing on his doorstep he had overheard the conversation between the two and seen what had come of it. Debabrata took his hand out of sheer gratitude.

Carrying a dead body from Petin Sahi to Khannagar was not a job to be accomplished by only three people. This worried Debabrata somewhat. The clerk said, 'Why are you fretting? Let's go and look somewhere else. There are many Karanas in Cuttack and not everyone's likely to act the way your professor did.' They started to walk towards Telenga Bazaar. While on their way, the clerk suddenly asked him, 'You're thinking about that professor, aren't you?' A hint of a smile crossed Debabrata's face. 'It's pointless to think about him,' the clerk continued. 'Didn't you see how he couldn't go against even the slightest injunction from his mother? You must wonder why his mother stopped him. It's because his wife's pregnant.' Debabrata could not stifle a laugh, even under the grim circumstances. He could not help unfavourably comparing the 'generous-hearted' professor, who did not lend him a hand out of superstition, to the ordinary clerk.

There were Karana families in the Telenga Bazaar area: lawyers' mohurrars, writers of documents, procurers of clients for lawyers, and brokers. Two men agreed to come, yielding to requests and appeals by both Debabrata and the clerk. The body was taken to the burning ghat towards the end of the night, once the items for the funeral rites had been arranged. But this did not put an end to Debabrata's suffering. With dawn came a severe storm and rain. He and his companions could only sit and wait after placing the body in the waiting room at the burning ghat. But the rain did not stop until well into the afternoon. The two Karanas from Telenga Bazaar started to vent their irritation on Debabrata for no reason and pestered him repeatedly for snacks and tobacco. A helpless Debabrata had to go and buy these in the market, getting thoroughly soaked in the process.

The rain abated around three in the afternoon, and it was almost nine o'clock at night by the time the group was able to return after completing their work. Exhaustion had left Debabrata completely drained. The two Karanas from Telenga Bazaar were not ones to give up. 'Hey man,' they said. 'We've heard that the dead person had only one daughter and no other heir. Is there going to be a feast to mark the obsequies?' Debabrata was astounded at how inconsiderate these two people were being. Seeing him keep mum, the clerk asked, 'Is it absolutely necessary for you people to eat on the shraddha day?'

'Bah, what makes you think it's not? How will we be free of the dead person's spirit if we don't partake of a ritual feast during shraddha?'

Debabrata was rendered speechless with surprise and contempt at their words. The clerk told the two men not to worry; he would arrange a feast to rid them of the spirit.

Debabrata was not someone to tire easily, but where in the world is there a person who would not have been exhausted by the relentless work and pelting rain of the past two days? His sorely tired feet could barely move. He walked slowly to the hostel and opened the door to his room. After washing his hands and feet he went to the kitchen. It was the Saturday feasting night at their mess. The kitchen and the canteen were upbeat with the sounds of cheerful students. One fun-loving young man was singing a line of verse within earshot of another young man, accompanied by matching facial expressions, 'Radha dear, because of you Shyama will not continue to live, princess of mine.' Debabrata was not in a frame of mind to take part in the festivities. Since his first day at the hostel he had spent most of his time in banter and discussions of music with his friends. But what a change had come over him in the last two days! His mind had turned entirely against such frivolity.

Sitting in one corner of the hall, he started to eat. From another corner a student from the opponent group was heard telling another, 'Hey Madhu, have you heard the news?'

'What is it, brother?'

'Oh, no, don't tell me you've not heard. Well, the road is now entirely clear.'

A third student asked, 'Arey, what road?'

'My, my, my, even you haven't heard? Arey, the road to the Basanti pandal!'

All the students burst out laughing. Debabrata knew this low jibe was aimed at him. His ears turned red from shame, and he retreated to his room after eating only a little. He wanted to keep away from these cruel-hearted classmates of his.

All this was the reason for Debabrata's annoyance; but then, why was he having misgivings? He was a college-educated young man, who had never returned from the university examination hall disappointed. On top of that, he owned a considerable amount of property. True, his mother was still alive, but she no longer looked after property matters. Although the agent who looked after the zamindari was a distant relation, he in fact was simply a paid employee. So in reality, the property was his alone. What reason did he have to worry?

At the moment Basanti was at the heart of all his worries and anxiety. Nirmala Devi had left Basanti in his hands and he felt blessed to have her at his side, as blessed as someone who catches the moon by simply stretching out his hand. But the thought of how he would take care of her had left him sleepless the previous night. This is what he thought: the sooner his marriage with Basanti was solemnised, the better. But there were obstacles on the path to this marriage. How would he surmount these?

The first hurdle: his mother Subhadra Devi.

The negotiations for Basanti's marriage with Debabrata had been initiated while Nirmala Devi was still alive. At Debabrata's request, his mother had come to Cuttack from her village to have a look at the bride-to-be. She had stayed for a few days in Nirmala Devi's house and observed Basanti's behaviour and actions. This only confirmed her opinion that Basanti was not the right choice as a daughter-in-law in her house. She did not find fault with Basanti's looks; the main reason for her negative opinion was that she was not keen to have a well-educated girl as her daughter-in-law. She believed that such a daughter-in-law would always dominate her son and that he would slip out of her control after marriage. This would mean a loss of prestige for her and her family. Yes, it was good that daughters-in-law be well-read. They ought to be able to sing the *Bhagabata* and read out *Kesaba Koili* and *Jema Dei Kanda* for their mothers-in-law. But then, heavens, what was all this! Learning English, learning Bengali, reading newspapers, singing—what on earth was all this! The thing she most disliked about Basanti was that such a grown up girl, far from speaking softly in hushed tones from beneath a foot-long veil, wore nothing on her head and her words rang out loud and clear. Again, one day she saw Basanti go out for her morning stroll with Suniti, both of them wearing shoes. What was this if not an invitation to disaster! That her daughter-in-law should wear shoes? No, no, she did not need a daughter-in-law like that.

On her way back to her village she told Debabrata she had selected a girl from Dhardharapur for him. The girl could recite the *Bhagabata*, knew how to make patterns on the floor and the walls with rice paste, and could wear her sari expertly, patterning it like the flowers in a bouquet. So he had no reason for worry. She had left with the promise she would make arrangements for the wedding immediately on her return to the village. During the entire length of her journey from the house to the railway station she repeatedly cautioned Debabrata to stay away from Nirmala Devi's house. Subhadra Devi was a woman after all and knew that if iron came under the spell of a magnet it would become extremely difficult to separate the two. All of this had taken place a short time ago. It was to no avail that Debabrata tried to budge her from her position; Subhadra Devi was stubborn in sticking to her decision that she would by no means make a 'Christianised' girl like Basanti her family's daughter-in-law. Marrying Basanti without his mother's consent would amount to taking a stance against her. Like Basanti, Debabrata too had lost his father at a young age and had become excessively attached to his mother. He lacked the courage to oppose her.

The second obstacle on the path of his marriage: society.

There are many evil people in the world. The number of those who derive satisfaction from slandering and defaming others is not small. No mean and ignoble act, of whatever kind, is beyond such people. Nirmala Devi's character was spotless, but after her husband's death she too was badly maligned by some vile slanderers, who passed for being gentlemen. Nirmala Devi heard all this, but she was a widow—helpless and alone. What could she do? The respectable people of Oriya society also accepted this scandal-mongering as truth, without the slightest scrutiny. For this reason, Balaram Babu's family was regarded as outcaste even while Nirmala Devi was alive.

They never received invitations to social functions. Once, of her own accord, Nirmala Devi attended the wedding of the daughter of a highly educated person, but the cold shoulder she was subjected to by the girl's father and the innuendoes by the girl's mother made her promise never to attend any social function without being invited. No invitation came her way, of course. So from that day forward Nirmala Devi was beyond the pale of society. In the peculiar social set-up that exists in Orissa the misdeeds of parents, proven or not, are always visited upon their children. Consequently, Basanti now became the focus of society's hostile gaze. This was the main reason why the college-educated sons of the Karana leaders of Cuttack did not agree to carry Nirmala Devi's body. Debabrata too would have to suffer the wrath of society if he married Basanti. He was not afraid of society's caprices, but then his mother was also against him. If he decided to risk his mother's opposition and marry Basanti, he would still need the support of some well-meaning people.

Debabrata's greatest worry was this: where would Basanti stay now? It was not safe for her to live on her own. She could of course move to Kalyani Devi's house, but that would only serve to increase society's hostility towards her.

All of these problems greatly disturbed Debabrata, and he was unable to arrive at a solution for any of them. The cool breeze of the last quarter of the night helped his sleep-hungry eyes to close. He fell asleep while brooding over what had happened. This was why he was so late in waking up today and this accounted for Dhania's having to holler for him.

After Dhania left, Debabrata once again lay down on the bed and fell asleep. A little while later the soft touch of somebody's hand woke him up and he saw his close friend and co-worker Ramesh Mohapatra standing by his side, gently patting him. The moment Debabrata opened his eyes Ramesh asked, 'Debabrata, have you heard the news?'

The manner in which Ramesh asked the question took Debabrata by surprise. What could this new addition to his existing worries be? He sat up in bed suddenly and asked, 'What has happened?'

'The potters' colony of Bidanasi has burnt to ashes.'

'When?'

'Last night.'

Debabrata sat there, at a loss. Why was God so cruel? Would all of creation come to an end if the creator prevented the shacks of the poor and the famished from being razed to the ground?

'What's to be gained by sitting and thinking?'asked Ramesh. 'People have lost everything. If we don't do something, their misery will be endless.'

Had it been another day, Debabrata would have been the first to act, but today he asked, bewildered, 'What's to be done?'

'Let's first go and see what's happened. We'll think of what to do after that.'

This satisfied Debabrata. He finished his morning chores quickly and set out with Ramesh on his bicycle. Just before heading out he remembered what Dhania had said. Wasn't he supposed to go and console a grief-stricken Basanti? Debabrata felt uneasy. He thought to himself, he was going on his bicycle and would be able to return soon. He would go to Basanti once back from Bidanasi. What difference would a short delay make?

Before locking the door Debabrata paid respect with folded hands to an image hanging on the wall. Then he set out for Bidanasi with Ramesh. The flowers draped over the image started to shake gently in the cool breeze that came floating in from the Kathajodi river.

This image was that of Debabrata's exemplary father Nimai Babu, who had sacrificed his own life to save an outcaste girl from drowning in the fierce currents of the Budhabalang.

Five[*]

'Perhaps we're late. Looks like there's not room enough in the hall for even a sesame seed. Has the meeting begun?'

'What could I do? It's my fault we're late, but I had to go by Petin Sahi. Didn't get there at all yesterday.'

As they talked, Debabrata and Ramesh got off their bicycles in front of the town hall, locked them, and tiptoed in through the back door. The room was bursting at the seams. No chance of finding an empty chair; in places three people were sitting on two chairs pulled together. The benches were full. Forty to 50 school students were standing on the veranda outside. Ramesh realised that getting a seat inside the hall would be impossible, at which point one of his classmates beckoned to him and pulled Debabrata along by the hand. They barely managed to squeeze onto a bench. By that time the president was already afloat on his waves of oratory, his subject being literature and its relationship to national life. From early childhood Debabrata had been inclined towards literature, and his strongest wish was to serve the literature of Utkala. He gave the lecture his full attention.

* By Harihar Mahapatra.

This was the annual meeting of the Utkala Sahitya Samaj, presided over by Sri Biswanath Das, a gifted writer and scholar of note. His name was well known in the educated circles of Orissa, and his writings appealed to the young, especially to those who were thoughtful and sensitive. The essays flowing from his pen were highly original and would have been a matter of glory for any literature. Das was probably not far along in years, but no attempt to guess his age would have met with success. He looked to be between 30 and 40, but we have it on the authority of his relative Gobinda that Das had just completed his 50th year. There was no grey in his hair, and his voice had not been affected by a loss of teeth. He was capable of fiery eloquence.

The president returned to his chair to sustained applause at the end of his long and well-thought-out speech, which lasted almost two hours. The clock in the hall showed 4.30 p.m. Meetings and functions usually began at 6.00 or 6.30 p.m., but for the past few days it had been raining in Cuttack every evening. The Sahitya Samaj had decided to hold its meeting at 2 p.m. on Sunday and issued a notice to that effect.

After the president's speech it was time to give out awards. Every year, the Sahitya Samaj announced a list of topics for essays, which it published in the newspapers along with the cash prize attached to each. This year was no different, and the editor had received numerous contributions from many quarters. Our Debabrata had chosen 'Love and Literature' from among the topics. That was three or four months ago. Nirmala Devi was still alive, and Debabrata was always welcome in her house. After college he would toss his books in his room and dash off to Petin Sahi on his bicycle. He would return to the hostel after tiffin in Nirmala Devi's house and an exchange of pleasantries with Basanti, a little exercise at the stadium, and a stroll along the riverbank. Debabrata had one overriding passion: reading poetry in the evenings—all else took a back seat.

Shelley, Keats, and Byron were dear to his heart; Browning, Wordsworth, and Kalidasa were among the poets he revered. As he became more and more drawn towards Basanti, his addiction to poetry increased. Debabrata's ties to literature on the one hand, and to Basanti on the other, grew stronger by the day. It was at this time that the topics for the essay competition and the cash prizes were announced in *Utkala Dipika* two days in a row in bold letters. Inspired by both love and literature, Debabrata selected his topic. Without telling anyone, he wrote an essay and sent it in. His motivation was neither the money nor the award; he did this entirely spontaneously and out of pure pleasure. Man's mind is of course highly changeable, his gaze being drawn, even if ever so slightly, to the fruits of his effort and action. But Debabrata had almost forgotten he had sent in his essay. Readers are aware of the stress and anxiety he had been feeling after Nirmala Devi's death. His usual cheerfulness had faded away. The stream of his love had dried up under the piti-less rays of his anxiety, much like the way the fiercely flowing Kathajodi is reduced to a thin trickle in summer. But then this was merely a prelude to its being in spate as a result of heavy downpours from dark clouds at summer's end. The accidental fire that engulfed Bidanasi three days after Nirmala Devi's death added to Debabrata's worries. It was as if he had lost his home along with his mother. When, despite all this, Ramesh broached the topic of the annual meeting of the Sahitya Samaj while returning from Bidanasi, Debabrata answered, 'Not a bad idea to go, yet no celebration retains its charm when there's danger lurking everywhere. You go, I won't.' But Ramesh was able to convince him to attend by astutely reminding him of president Bisawanath Babu's exemplary scholarship and of one's obligation towards literature. They took two different routes from Choudhury Bazaar square. Ramesh was back at the hostel by one o'clock after having had his bath and his food at home. Debabrata's room was still shut. Ramesh was waiting in another room talking with some students from the group at loggerheads with Debabrata. He was trying to convince them of Debabrata's generosity. The sound of Debabrata's door opening made him suddenly take leave of them. By then it was two o'clock.

Debabrata had left Ramesh to go and see Basanti, keeping his word to Dhania and also for his own peace of mind. He was now back home two or three hours later. Readers can well understand that Debabrata had neither bathed nor eaten. After putting his bicycle away he poured two buckets of water over himself and walked briskly into the kitchen. He gulped down his food in two minutes. Ramesh and he then set out for the town hall. Ramesh had no idea that Debabrata had submitted an essay to the Sahitya Samaj. When, after his address, the president suddenly announced the name 'Debabrata Mohanty' among the prizewinners, Ramesh was completely taken aback. Nudging Debabrata with his elbow, Ramesh blurted out the words, 'God, that's you!' Debabrata too was astounded. In answer to Ramesh he only smiled with pleasure and walked slowly to the dais. After Das handed him a white silk pouch containing fifty rupees, Debabrata was about to return to his seat, when the president signalled for him to stand there a little while longer.

The president announced, 'Debabrata Babu has written an enlightened essay on the subject of "Love and Literature". The essay has great originality. A member of the Sahitya Samaj who was immensely pleased with the essay has requested me to give him this pouch of sixty rupees as additional prize money. Debabrata Babu, it is my great pleasure to present this to you.' Saying this, the president handed Debabrata a red pouch.

Debabrata returned to his seat to applause filling the hall. The words that escaped his lips—'I never expected this'—were drowned out in the din, unheard even by Ramesh.

The meeting ended at about 5.30 p.m., after remarks by a couple of members and the vote of thanks for the president. The moment the crowd filed out on to the veranda Debabrata's classmates and acquaintances surrounded him. Some demanded he provide a feast to celebrate, others shook his hand, and still others patted him on the back. Amid such a display of bonho-mie Debabrata parted from Ramesh and made his way slowly towards Petin Sahi. Before leaving he handed over the two pouches with the prize money to Ramesh and asked him to use the money to help the people of Bidanasi. It was a fortuitous gift from God that had come their way.

Debabrata was under the sway of all sorts of emotions. Whoever earns unexpected prestige or prizes is bound to feel pleasure mixed with pride, but we cannot say for certain what Debabrata was going through at that moment. A psycholo-gist, if one had been at hand, would probably have been able to figure things out. These days he was often absent-minded, preoccupied with some weighty thought. What was his duty towards Basanti? He was not able to decide what he should do in relation to her, she whom he had already made his own outside the public eye. Nevertheless, leaving all unwelcome thoughts behind him he went to Nirmala Devi's house almost two or three times a day to find out from Basanti—but also from Dhania and Suniti—if she needed anything, if anything was lacking in the house. But he had precious little to do in that regard because of Kalyani Devi's sincere and loving care and effort. He often met with Kalyani Devi. They would exchange meaningful glances, as well as a few words, and then part. Kalyani Devi too was worried about what would happen to Basanti. Because of the incidents in the past, Basanti had become something of an outcaste. But for Kalyani Devi one possibility still remained: if no other option existed, at least Christian or Brahmo society was open to all. The pretty and virtuous Basanti would be a Lakshmi for any home, a source of joy and prosperity. If her own community rejected her, there was no fear of her being cast adrift. This was why Kalyani Devi was confident and why she waited patiently.

Debabrata was a riddle for Kalyani Devi; she was unable to understand him. Many times she had tried to read his mind and failed. She felt that if he was drawn towards Basanti, then he would at least give some sign of this if not openly state his intentions. How was Kalyani Devi to know the tumult that had been going on in Debabrata's mind over the past few days? In the meantime, Debabrata had concluded there could be no middle path for him; he must either make Basanti his own or distance himself from her. There were many barriers to her being accepted; it was inevitable society would make her life difficult. But to abandon her would be cowardly. His main worry now was what steps needed to be taken in relation to Basanti. Where could she stay? Her own house was not safe; Kalyani Devi's was not an ideal choice. While such thoughts kept playing through his mind, his bicycle found itself halted before a certain gate in Petin Sahi. Debabrata went into the courtyard and saw Champa standing there, leaning against the wall.

'When did you get here?'

'As soon as I got the news about the poor child. Learned about it yesterday afternoon. Alas! Such a fate for Basa apa! How cruel is destiny!'

'Let me ask you something. Where are you living these days? In Manmath Babu's house? They must have other servants and maids. You can see what things are like here: there's no one else to help. You know this house. Your Basa apa would certainly be better off if you could stay here. What do you say?'

'What is there to say? When Ma Saantani was alive...' Champa started to cry.

'Don't think about that now. Whatever had to happen has happened. We're talking about the present. Stay here.'

'I'll come and stay beginning tomorrow. How could I do anything else? I've brought Basa apa up, right from when she was a little girl.' Champa began to cry again. Nirmala Devi's soft and tender heart had held everyone in her thrall. She had won them all over—friends and relatives, servants and cooks—with her affection and kindness. Champa could vividly remember the days past. She could see Ma Saantani's likeness reflected in Basanti's. Is there no value to affection? Are the ties of love so slack? It was because of Nirmala Devi's financial situation that Champa had moved to Manmath Babu's house. Sometimes, after finishing her chores there, she would come to Nirmala Devi's house in the afternoon. The familiar house and door, the plants and creepers were always welcoming. Champa might be the daughter of a milkman, but she was a woman, and thus valued kindness. She had been widowed in her early youth, with nothing and no one—neither home nor children—to call her own. Her only concern was to fill her small belly. Could she not do without the glamour of the sub-judge's house? And why would he object to her spending time in her Basa apa's house? The pull of Nirmala Devi's ties of love was stronger.

Reassured by Champa, Debabrata went inside. Basanti was standing there with folded hands after lighting a clay lamp beside the photograph of Nirmala Devi. The pallu of her sari was soaked from streams of tears. After a while she heaved a sigh. It resonated deep within Debabrata, who was standing on the threshold, before dissolving in the outer air.

At this moment Suniti stepped swiftly into the house, asking, 'How long have you been here, Champa my girl, and where's my dear friend?' She halted at the doorway, managing only to blurt out, 'Deba Babu, why don't you sit down.' The commotion was enough to break Basanti's concentration. Intoning words of love and gratitude for her mother, she came out on to the veranda as she wiped away her tears. While Suniti went inside to get a lantern from Dhania, Debabrata and Basanti went into the courtyard and sat on the stone slab next to the cluster of jasmines. The sky was clear: the battalion of dark clouds had beaten a retreat, defeated by the autumnal moon's cool breeze; the dusky paleness of earth had been removed by the calming bright light. But all this attraction was without effect on the two fresh hearts. It was as if the clouds had sought shelter in Debabrata and Basanti's faces out of fear, and the moon, powerless to blow them away, had admitted defeat. They sat in silence, lost in thought. Basanti's mind was elsewhere, even if her eyes were directed towards Debabrata, who, in turn, was looking in the direction of the roof in an effort to find a solution to his problem. Basanti felt absolutely overcome by grief. She could not focus on only one thing, and was unable to know where she was in the ebb and flow of events. Debabrata too was caught up in the same whirlwind. Having understood how things stood, he was busy searching for some way out for Basanti. Alas! If only the wishes of humans could be instantly converted into action!

Suniti's presence roused them from their thoughtful state. Soon, Kalyani Devi arrived carrying a plate of snacks for Basanti, which the other two also shared. Often circumstances oblige one to do things even if one has no taste for them. Thus they fell to discussing matters relating to the Literary Society, the famine in the district of Puri due to crop failure, and the fire in Bidanasi. Hiding their grief in the recesses of their hearts, everyone engaged in banter for Basanti's sake. Under Debabrata's magical spell Basanti would be transported beyond the harsh realities of the world, but there were also times when the coursing undercurrent of sorrow beneath his tender words of comfort and his affectionate talk would tug at her heartstrings. She gained some slight relief from her unbridled sorrow by shedding tears.

Debabrata did not want to dispel the pathos in the air by talking needlessly about the award he had won. He took leave of everyone after a while and returned to the hostel.

Six *

After classes the next day, Debabrata paid a visit to Nabaghana Das, the court clerk, to consult with him about arrangements for the 10th day funeral rites. They quickly drew up a list of items for a simple ceremony. When Balaram Babu had been a deputy magistrate, Das was his clerk. The babu's considerate nature had won Das over, and Das had taken pride in working efficiently. Balaram Babu had been very pleased with his court aide. Many a time Das had eaten in the deputy magistrate's house, and so he was no stranger to Balaram Babu's family. Every year he gave Basanti some pretty pieces of earthenware on the festivals of Muharram and Baliyatra. After the deputy babu's death Das called on Nirmala Devi frequently, enquiring as to how she was getting along. Balaram Babu had done him a favour by raising his salary, and so Das was completely loyal and always trying to find an occasion to help her in any way he could. He did not forget his duty towards Basanti on her day of sorrow.

He and Debabrata got down to making the list. He decided to ask for leave from work on Saturday and Monday; the leave was granted. From Saturday onwards Das spent most of his time at Basanti's house. Working with Kalyani Devi, he did all

* By Harihar Mahapatra.

he could to make things easier for Basanti. On Sunday, to the surprise of both Kalyani Devi and Das, Debabrata arrived at the house with a cartload of articles from the bazaar. Basanti stood there, dumbstruck, staring at her Deba bhai. Dhania helped unload the items and Champa busied herself putting them away. How had Debabrata come by the money, Kalyani Devi wondered. As a zamindar's son he might have got it from home, but his mother was not favourably disposed towards Basanti's family. Perhaps Basanti had given him the money, but then why would she have been surprised? Such questions were nagging at Kalyani Devi. Seeing Nabaghana Babu standing near her, she asked, 'Did you give Debabrata any money?' 'No, he didn't say anything to me about that.' Their curiosity was piqued, but Basanti had become so close to Deba bhai that their relations were not governed by social conventions or distinctions between what is yours and what is mine. Debabrata never hesitated to offer Basanti a lozenge, nor did he have any qualms about gulping down a ripe guava she handed him. Today, when Basanti saw Debabrata arriving with so many things, the question of where the money came from did not even cross her mind.

The cremation rites were completed smoothly. Gentlemen and ladies of different castes and religious backgrounds attended the ceremony. The clerk, remembering his promise to the two Karana gentlemen from Telenga Bazaar, did not forget to arrange a sumptuous feast for them.

The commotion and disturbance had now died down. Fifteen or sixteen days had gone by since her mother's passing, and Basanti had a clear sense of her situation. Suniti was always with her bosom friend; Kalyani Devi called on her frequently; Debabrata came by at least once a day, as if on a schedule. Despite all this Basanti could feel that time was passing and nothing was changing. There always seemed to be something lacking. Her mind was uneasy, prone to misgivings if anything seemed amiss. She wanted to draw Deba bhai out on several subjects but could not. She hesitated to seek his advice on what she should do. Debabrata knew all this and had made up his mind that Basanti's situation needed to change. She was not a child anymore; her mind had developed through education and thought. Floating on the wings of youth, Basanti harboured another desire in her heart, even as she was deeply pained by the loss of her mother. She knew what Debabrata's mother thought and was aware that other barriers stood in her way. Still, she was not entirely without hope. Although the loss of her mother pained her and left her frightened, she was gradually trying to adapt to her new circumstances. From early childhood she had nurtured a modern outlook and had willingly worked for the cause of women. This was why she took care in reading her books, under the guidance of her mother and Kalyani Devi. Through his conversations and letters Debabrata had also been helping her advance towards her goal. He could often be seen cycling along the road with books he had just bought strapped to his carrier. One might have guessed these were textbooks belonging to him, but curiously enough modern books of literature, of a colour and type similar to these, were to be found in Basanti's almirah. They, it was discovered, had been been a gift from her Deba bhai.

This afternoon Basanti was lying on her bed leafing through the pages of one such book. The sound of a bicycle bell entered her ears and she got up to find Debabrata at the door. They sat together and started talking about this and that. In the course of their conversation Debabrata said, 'That would be fine. Who's saying not to? It would be much better to go to school than to stay put at home. Would you like to?'

'School? That would be very good. But Deba bhai, don't you see the problems it will bring?'

Once a fish has taken the bait, a fisherman twists and turns as he tries to reel in his catch, no matter how big. Often he succeeds. Seeing an opening, Debabrata continued, trying to convince Basanti. Always ready to learn something new, she finally agreed to return to the school she had already attended. Debabrata had been successful; it was natural for his face to glow with happiness. Kalyani Devi too was pleased, and she decided that Basanti would go to school with Suniti.

Suniti attended the girls' school on a regular basis, but Basanti had stopped going almost two years earlier. It is not difficult to guess why. Balaram Babu had strongly believed that people should live according to their principles. Nirmala Devi was devoted to her husband and had adopted his views. But it is not easy to ignore society entirely. In particular, they had to think of getting Basanti married. A Karana girl has to marry into a Karana family after all. At the time, the education of women had only just begun, and there were many who still opposed it. Taking all this into consideration, Balaram Babu had begun to have Basanti educated at home and she had not returned to the school. Debabrata had a great deal of moral courage, and he considered it his duty to always travel along the path of virtue. It was not in his nature to let fear of scandal or calumny deter him from any noble endeavour. So he was ready today, and Basanti's wavering mind conceded defeat when faced with his resolute will.

The decision had been taken that Basanti would go to school, but for Debabrata that was not enough. After much thought he had come to the conclusion that it would be best if arrangements could be made for Basanti to board there. Of course, that might shock conservative Hindu elders, but under the circumstances it was futile to hope to satisfy everyone. The school hostel would be safe and convenient. That would put Debabrata's mind somewhat at ease, and so he decided this should be the arrangement for now. Today he raised the topic with Basanti. Readers know what ensued. In the course of their conversation Debabrata realised that while Basanti was not averse to the idea, Kalyani Devi was not favourably disposed towards it. Although

Debabrata had been partially successful in his mission, he felt dejected as he returned that evening from Petin Sahi.

On his way back he made up his mind to reduce his monthly expenses of fifty rupees by at least twenty and provide that amount for Basanti's studies. Every month he deposited a little money into his account at the post office towards fees for various organisations and subscriptions to monthly magazines. He could dip into these resources if after giving Basanti twenty rupees he felt financially strapped. But he wanted to hide this from her, which is why, much against his will, he openly lied to her when the question arose of impediments to her renewing her studies. Basanti believed him when he said that for her future Nirmala Devi had saved one thousand rupees from Balaram Babu's pension and deposited it in Debabrata's account. Why would she not have believed him? It would not have been surprising for her mother to keep the money in Deba bhai's name. She had been particularly frugal in managing the household expenses because the income from their property was so little. When even this was not enough, she sent away her maid and began doing the chores herself. Basanti broke into a flood of tears when she learned about the money set aside in the face of such hardship. Who would remain unmoved after losing such a giving and caring mother! Basanti was only a child!

Upon reaching the hostel Debabrata met Ramesh, and the two friends fell to talking about the fire in Bidanasi. Debabrata's forte was that he never felt tired and that his will was as strong as his body.

Cuttack was all astir over the fire. Appeals and requests for assistance came out in the newspapers. Those who were trying to determine how it had started claimed that Dama's kiln had set fire to a string hanging from the thatch, causing the conflagration. Nearly 50 huts were reduced to ashes. When the fire broke out around midnight, people had rushed outside for fear of their lives. There was no time to bring anything with them.

In only a few minutes the entire potters' colony was completely in flames. The fire engulfed two women and some 20 cows, the ritual sacrifice of this 'yajna'. Three hundred souls sought shelter under trees, with no rice to eat and no clothes to wear. Hunger had reduced some children to misery, and spells of rain only added to their distress.

It was impossible for the soft-hearted Debabrata to sit idly by. Despite his worries about Basanti he was aware of his duty towards those who had been left homeless by the fire.

Ramesh, his friend, was a first year B.A. student. His purpose in life was to serve society, and he would not back down no matter what opposition he faced. He worked to improve the lot of the disadvantaged and did his best to give them a modern education. When he first joined college he had stayed in the hostel, but he incurred the wrath of the authorities because he was frequently absent doing relief work. A patient in hospital in critical condition, an outbreak of cholera in Pana Sahi or of smallpox in Hadi Sahi, and Ramesh had to be there. How could the hostel authorities accept that? There were endless attempts to intimidate him. Greatly annoyed by all this, he left the hostel and moved to a house in Nimchoudi with a few other students from the Gadjats. As for Debabrata, his talents were multi-faceted and wide-ranging: from devotion to literature to dedication to animals. He recognised true goodness when he saw it, and Ramesh's nobility of spirit did not remain hidden from him for long. They were travellers along the same path; how long could they remain unaware of each other? After his intermediate examination Ramesh had gone to Puri to help provide relief to the people suffering from famine. Debabrata was also bound in the same direction, after a month in Darjeeling for his health. He stayed with Ramesh near Konark, and since that time they had been friends and consulted each other about their future projects. When necessary, the two friends set to work, and working together their enthusiasm doubled. How many times during that stormy night of heavy rain, during the ritual cremation of Nirmala Devi's mortal remains, oh, how many times had Debabrata wished for Ramesh's presence and company! Ramesh at that time was helping pilgrims performing ablutions in the river Baitarani. Though born in a Brahmin family, he was not bound by restrictions of caste. For him, everyone—whether Brahmin or Chandala—was the same. He respected Debabrata and cared for him deeply. Readers already know that he called upon Debabrata and took him along when he received the news about the fire in Bidanasi. Today the two friends were in deep discussion about how to reduce the hardship of the hundreds of people left homeless. They decided to form a committee under the chairmanship of an enthusiastic professor in order to raise funds. Debabrata asked Ramesh to act as secretary, as he himself was busy with other matters.

After their discussion was finished, Ramesh took his leave. Debabrata sat at his table, intending to write a letter. The look on his face was one of deep concern. He stared outside, his head in his hands, and then returned to his task, heaving a long sigh. There is no way of knowing what he was writing or to whom. The windows were shut. The light shone directly on Debabrata, who was seated at the table. His fountain pen slowly made furrows across the paper. When he opened his door after some time he found that most of the students had already eaten and were enjoying a pleasant stroll in the autumn evening. After returning from the dining hall Debabrata sought the favour of the goddess of sleep, but she was not to be so easily appeased. The grace of the goddess is obtained only by chanting mantras, meditating, and making votive offerings. It was foolish of Debabrata to expect to gain such a rarefied object with ease. To be worthy of that grace it is necessary to banish all bothersome thoughts. As long as that had not been done he had to pass the night sleeplessly, in a state of drowsy stupor. The day was not far off when Debabrata's dissatisfied soul would find rest in the tender embrace of the peace-giving arms of the goddess, but the desire of the aspirant has to be granted before that happens— Basanti needed to be steered clear of danger and difficulties.

The letter was sent secretly and delivered confidentially into Kalyani Devi's hands. Tearing open the envelope, she found a letter from Debabrata. Naturally, she was surprised. Debabrata had been there in the morning as well as in the evening, so what need could there be for a letter? There must be some special reason. Might he have written something about Basanti? Something about marriage...? Or the opposite? Hope and fear are two sisters, bonded to one another by a love without limits, admitting neither separation nor bereavement. And so Kalyani Devi's mind was shaken by one as well as the other.

She started to read the letter. Here is what Debabrata had written:

I am writing this in all humility.

This is my first letter to you. I regard you as my mother, reserving for you the same respect and love. This gives me the courage to write. I will put down a few things in simple language. I have often gone to you, hoping to say these things to you in person, but have hesitated to do so, committing these thoughts to my mind instead. Please don't become annoyed reading this. I hope you will take what I have to say in the right spirit.

On the eve of her death Smt. Nirmala Devi left Basanti in my care. I am obliged by dharma to obey that order. The loss of her mother at such a tender age has plunged Basanti into deep grief. She certainly feels comforted by the care shown by a loving, caring motherly heart such as yours, but my fear is that you have been blinded by your fondness for her. You have not had occasion to reflect on the reality of the situation, which is only natural. There's not an atom of doubt about the nobility of your purpose, but, given the state of decadence into which society has fallen, there is no dearth of people who will misunderstand you. In the absence of Smt. Nirmala Devi you are Basanti's mother. How can society, cruel as it is, tolerate this?

You have decided that Basanti will return to school tomorrow. This is welcome news, but where do you think she will stay? It is not safe for her to remain at home. Who would not feel miserable at the loss of a mother, especially a mother like Smt. Nirmala Devi, who showed so much affection towards her child? Basanti is a mere child. Until now she has found shelter from the hard realities of life in her loving mother's embrace. She has not had time to think of her past and her future, her days have been free from worry. She should not be staying in the house by herself now. There may not be any danger since you are around, but every part of the house is associated with the memory of Smt. Nirmala Devi. Wherever she goes, Basanti will always have before her the image of her mother. You must have noticed how every article her mother once used brings her to the verge of tears. That is very natural. It is intolerable for a delicate and tender-hearted girl to have to go through this. You were there the other day when Basanti said, 'It's my mother I see when I look in her mirror.' I feel that for these reasons she needs to move from there. It is difficult, however, to get her to agree. It might be good for her to stay in your house, but she is not willing. Even if she agreed, there would be the worry that she might come to some harm, although there may not be any apparent reason for such a fear. If she were to stay in your house, Basanti would never be far from her own, filled with the memories of Smt. Nirmala Devi. She loved her mother dearly. She is letting herself be overcome by grief. If she stays nearby, she will be inconsolable; if she stays away, then the sorrow that burns in her heart will hopefully be lessened under the influence of a small circle of friends. Maybe the hostel of the Girls' School would be a better option. There would be a lot to distract her there. Also, she would perhaps not greatly object to the idea. If you try to persuade her, she will agree. I feel it would be safer for her to stay at the hostel. Dhania and Champa can keep watch

over her house. Please rest assured there is enough money for
Basanti's boarding expenses.

I await your considered opinion.

Affectionately,
Debabrata

After reading the letter twice over, Kalyani Devi thought,
'Debabrata is so worried about Basanti, but why hasn't he
touched upon what I have been thinking about. Caring for
another's child with such generosity is very rare.' Alas, Kalyani
Devi, how obsessed you are with making distinctions—you have
yet to understand that Basanti is not a 'stranger' for Debabrata;
rather, she is as dear to him as his own self. Their pure feelings
for each other transcend social distinctions. Debabrata's restless
soul will not find peace until Basanti is secure. Hence this
communication to you.

After looking at the situation from all angles, Debabrata had
decided it would be best for Basanti to stay at the hostel. Initially
Kalyani Devi had not been in favour of this, but everything
became clear to her after reading Debabrata's letter. She had no
further objection. Two thin streams of tears silently found their
way down her cheeks. She had to stay away from Basanti. What
would Nirmala think if she knew this? If only Kalyani were a
Hindu, not a Christian, but there was no way out. Unfeeling
society! How much longer can you survive the fierce curses of
hundreds of innocent souls? Many a tender soul has been ruined
by your harsh fetters. The outcome of this oppression will be
dire. Your destruction is inevitable. It is still not too late. Open
your eyes and look around if you wish to survive. Abolish all
prejudice. Connect tradition with modernity.

The idea of Basanti staying at the hostel appealed to Kalyani
Devi, as she took stock of the present situation. Basanti yielded to
persuasion and chose not to protest any longer. When Debabrata
visited in the evening, he heard that Basanti would be admitted
to the school the following day and move to the hostel.

Seven*

Two years later—two long years later—Basanti was alone in her room at one end of the girls' hostel, looking out the window at the evening sky. She was as bright as the evening star, and her delicate body seemed infused with the essence of night jasmine in full bloom.

As Basanti thought back over the past two years it seemed to her that the world had changed little. Some had felt pain, others pleasure, but for Basanti these years had passed in a dream. Like a lifeboat tossed about on the sea after a shipwreck she had had to weather many storms, but today all these seemed to her somewhat unreal. She had room in her heart only for her Deba bhai's infinite love and genuine kindness—this too was a dream come true. Many friends had gratified her with their love; many teachers had given her affection. Kalyani Devi had helped her temper her grief at the loss of her mother. It seemed to Basanti that her small world had been spared the cruel touch of reality and that she had been left free to explore her dream world.

Suddenly her eyes were covered by someone who had crept up from behind, and she felt a delicate hand, as soft as a leaf, on her shoulder, and long flowing hair falling on her chest. 'Sushama.'

* By Annada Shankar Ray.

Basanti made a guess. The unseen young woman laughed and answered 'No,' slightly altering her voice.

'Asita!'

'No.'

'Chhaya!'

'No.'

Basanti became slightly impatient. 'Shame on you. Let me be. Okay, Lila?'

The woman's hearty laughter only grew louder. Basanti stopped trying to guess and said, a little impatiently, 'Well, I give up.'

The unknown trickster removed her hands. Pressing Basanti's cheeks with her fingertips, she whispered in her ear. 'My dearly beloved, what thoughts were you lost in, looking at the evening sky? Were they about Deba bhai?'

Basanti drew Suniti close. 'All right my friend,' she said demurely. 'Who knew you would arrive at this hour?'

Suniti placed a chair near the window and sat silently for two minutes, looking out. She grew serious. 'Did Deba bhai visit you today?', she asked.

Her face was solemn, unlike her usually jubilant and joyful self. Panicking somewhat, Basanti said, 'Go on'.

'His mother has written that she will refuse to meet him if he does not marry into the Choudhury family of Dhardharapur this coming summer.'

'What has Deba bhai decided to do?'

'That's what he came to talk to me about. He says a mother always has her son's best interest at heart and wonders what option he has if his mother is bent on not accepting me. "What right do I have to go against her will?"he asked.'

'And then!'

Suniti related Deba bhai's words. '"I'm willing to suffer to satisfy my mother, but my conscience won't let me sacrifice the happiness of two people for that of one person alone. My life can be ruined, that's not important. But the thought that another life would be too troubles me greatly." After keeping quiet for a moment, he continued. "There's something else, too. I gave my word of honour to Nirmala Devi. Had I not, she could not have died in peace. How can I betray her departed soul?"'

Basanti was shocked to hear about the marriage proposal but impressed by her Deba bhai's lofty thoughts. The tears she shed at this rendered her fair cheeks as delicate as a flower soaked with dew. 'Don't keep me in suspense, dear; tell me what's going to happen. What has been decided?'

'Nothing. Deba bhai is worried. The smile that's always on his face seems to have deserted him. His examinations are only one month away, but he's in a quandary and is neglecting his studies.'

Basanti thought for a long time, her head enfolded in her hands. At last, she looked up at Suniti, her eyes filled with tears: 'My dear, tell him to carry out his mother's wishes without delay.'

Suniti realised how much pain and suffering lay hidden in these few words.

Anguish was welling up from deep within Basanti's heart. How like an innocent flower she was and how closely enveloped by sweet dreams for the future, like a flower by the gossamer rays of the rising sun! The more she tried to console herself by imagining a noble act of self-sacrifice, the more her tears flowed without restraint; the intensity of an unfamiliar pain churned the recesses of her heart. Breaking into laughter suddenly, she said, 'Do you know what I was thinking about just now, my dear? That my life has been one long dream without pain or suffering, only a feeling unlike any other.'

Anguish rent her soft beautiful eyes. 'After all, no one can snatch him away from me in my land of dreams. Why then should I be sad?'

Suniti heaved a sigh. 'Your heart isn't that of a woman, my dear. It's a flower's, filled with the sweet scent of dreams. If you had descended from heaven to earth, equipped like me with a woman's heart, would you be so willing to make such a great sacrifice, sister?'

The examination results for both Debabrata and Basanti came out three months later. They had both passed with distinction—Debabrata his B.A., and Basanti her matriculation. Debabrata had hoped to go to England and return qualified for the Indian Civil Service, or at least to study for his M.A., but he had no idea how Basanti would manage in his absence. With each passing day it was becoming increasingly difficult not to do as his mother wished. Letter after letter arrived. Her requests and appeals were now turning into threats of suicide.

After giving the matter careful thought Debabrata decided that he would not allow himself to be trapped in Dhardharapur; he would marry Basanti even if that meant causing his mother pain. Forget about his studies and his high ambitions, he could not leave Basanti in mid-sea only to satisfy his mother's wishes. Debabrata had Bhisma's resolute will; he did not put off acting on his decision. He had spent the past two years suffering great mental turmoil, pressured from all sides: anxiety over Basanti, the jealousy of his classmates and their taunts and pettiness, repeated demands from home. All of this had left him uncertain, and so Debabrata decided he would act, once and for all.

Strange as it may seem, he did not consult Basanti. He simply assumed she would not say no to this marriage, that her mind had not changed. Of course, Basanti was, indeed, still the same, her heart full of love for Deba bhai, a state that should culminate in marriage. Still, she had her own views. Was it proper for Debabrata to pay no attention to them? Like most men, Debabrata was patriotic, with high ideals, but his high-mindedness was without the redeeming touch of imagination. It never occurred to him to look at something from a woman's point of view. This was a crucial flaw in his personality, and because of it he might in the future be deprived of the bliss of married love.

One day Debabrata suddenly appeared at Kalyani Devi's house and announced, 'Auntie, my marriage is taking place on the 25th of this month. I have come to invite you all.'

Kalyani Devi was taken aback. 'What are you saying, Deba? So the Dharadharapur proposal has worked out?'

'No, auntie, you won't have to travel that far. You will feast on kheer and cakes, sitting here in Petin Sahi.'

When the words sank in Kalyani Devi was surprised. Lavishing praise on Debabrata silently, she asked, 'So, who will be coming to the marriage?'

'Mother won't, that's certain. Let me think now who else. You and Suniti from Basanti's side; from my side, Ramesh and Sarbeswar Babu.'

'Who is Sarbeswar Babu?'

'A wonderful person. He works in Mayurbhanj. He's an uncle of mine, my father's younger brother. He's the only member of our family who has come out in support of our marriage, and he has the courage to translate his words into action.'

'But it pains me greatly, Deba, that your mother won't be there. How will Basanti set up a home in her house if there's tension from the start?'

Debabrata turned away and tried to hide his emotion. In a tearful voice he said, 'Please don't raise that subject, auntie. What's meant to happen will happen. It depends on our destiny and on mother's wish.'

Debabrata took his leave with these words: 'Everything is now up to you, auntie. Mother has deserted me; please don't you do the same. This is my prayer.' 'What are you talking about, Deba?' Kalyani Devi asked, patting his head. 'Am I not your own?'

She had made this fine looking Hindu young man of good character her own by bestowing on him abundant love from her generous heart.

The marriage day drew nearer. Basanti's mind was in turmoil. A sea change would take place in her life within a few days. The person she had had access to only in her dreams would now be with her in reality—but how stark that reality could be! This union would spark off a fire of discontent in one family, and in that conflagration the budding hopes of Basanti and the noble aspirations of Debabrata would be reduced to ashes. She questioned her God desperately: when two hearts come close and seek to consummate their love, why does the world inflict terrible pain on them by placing obstacles in their way?

As the day of marriage approached, Basanti's mind became more and more excited at the pleasurable prospect of their union while all the while being dogged by self-doubt.

Sarbeswar Babu attended the marriage as the main representative from the groom's side and Ramesh Chandra Mohapatra acted as the priest. Readers have already met Ramesh. He is after all Debabrata's secretary, friend, and disciple in the practice of various arts, all rolled into one. Ramesh knew very well that in this wretched society of ours no professional priest would agree to officiate at the marriage and that, if one did, it would only be for filthy lucre. It would be insulting for any educated person to have to seek the mediation of such an undesirable person in a sacred institution like marriage. Which is why he offered to take the troubles of his dear friend onto himself.

Sarbeswar Babu was an impulsive person; never hesitating to do what he thought was right. He acted spontaneously, but never in a way meant to lead to anything untoward. His latest whim was that Debabrata's wedding should be celebrated in a new and different manner. On the morning of the wedding Sarbeswar Babu said, 'My dear Deba, listen to what I have to say. We old fogeys spent our wedding days riding in palanquins, complete with liveried bearers. You, my son, should arrive at your wedding in a motorcar.'

He burst into a roar of laughter after saying this. Maybe he was pleased with what he had just said. A moment later he resumed. 'Another thing, dear Deba. Why do we need lights at your wedding? What need is there for drums and cymbals? The headlights of the motorcar will be our fire crackers, the tooting of the horn our trumpets. Ha, ha, ha....'

The man was whimsical, but quite simple. He laughed loudly and uncontrollably, steadying himself only with much effort.

In the end, that was how the wedding took place. The bride went to the groom's house, riding in the car of Debabrata's literary friend Biswanath Babu. Sri Biswanath Das himself was the main person from the bride's side. He was not simply a lover of literature; he was a social reformer too and happened to have been Balaram Babu's great friend and a leader of the Karana community. Those readers who are expectantly waiting to hear a dramatic account of the marriage will be sad to learn that the members of the bridal group were unable to do justice to the kheer and cakes, or the luchi and pantua. This was because Ramesh Chandra was prone to indigestion, and also because Sarbeswar Babu was in charge. Dhania, the servant boy, devoured the entire feast by himself and found himself running to the hospital for the next few days.

The wedding took place somehow or other. Kalyani Devi and Suniti broke down and cried when the time came for Basanti to take leave, and she too started to shed tears, covering her face with the pallu of Kalyani Devi's sari. She was indecent enough to go against the national character of Oriyas by not lamenting and wailing loudly! Unable to tolerate this, Champa, the maid, remained transfixed for one full hour, and for the next three days she vented her vehement protests against the ways of today's young females, vigorously shaking her flower-shaped nosestud.

After the wedding Debabrata thought he would return home once to see if there had been any change in his mother's feelings. If there was such a thing as a mother's love, then she would not repudiate her only son. If she did, then he would be disabused of all the grand notions he entertained about motherly love; he would understand that his relationship with his mother was based on pure give and take: she would provide love and affection only in return for devotion and obedience. His mind rose in revolt, thinking about this. One day at last he sent a wire to his mother: 'I'm coming home with Basanti tomorrow.'

Eight[*]

The train arrived on time, and Debabrata and Basanti got down at Balasore station. The greeting party from the village included the manager of the zamindari, maid Saniama, the driver of the bullock cart, and the palanquin bearers. Similipur was two and a half miles away, and there was a metalled road running the entire length from the station to the village. Leaving Dhania with the manager, Debabrata decided to cycle to the village after Basanti had been put in the palanquin and the luggage loaded onto the cart.

Saniama had accompanied the palanquin bearers so she could chaperone the new bride. Seeing Debabrata, she remarked, 'Babu, you had your wedding in Cuttack and denied us the pleasure of feasting. Anyway, what's done is done, but do not disappoint us now.'

Debabrata smiled. 'Just hold off your hunger a little while longer. How can it be satisfied the very moment you express it?'

'I'll go by bicycle after leaving our luggage with the manager,' Debabrata told Basanti. 'Dhania will come with the things on the bullock cart.' Basanti agreed.

[*] By Sarala Devi.

Saniama yelled out with authority, and the bearers set off at a trot carrying the palanquin, while Saniama walked quickly alongside.

Saniama thought the flesh-and-blood daughter-in-law perfectly matched the picture the Saantani had painted of her. This new daughter-in-law's ways did not seem at all appropriate. She walked out of the station unescorted after getting off the train. And, as if that was not enough, she kept talking to Deba Babu in the presence of everybody. Deba Babu was a man, and there was no need for him to be discreet; rather, discretion is an attribute required of women. And there was no trace of that in this daughter-in-law. On top of all that, she wore no ornaments to speak of, no nose ring or peacock-shaped stud, no ornament on her brow, no anklets or jingling bells on her feet. There was not even a shawl covering her shoulders, to mark her arrival as auspicious. The only jewellery she wore were a pair of anklets, a pearl ring, an ordinary stud in her nose, and a long necklace that hung like a garland. Just like Bengali Lalit Babu's wife! Her hair was not parted either, and strands fell over her brow instead, resembling a wild bush, again much like the Bengali wife. An ordinary looking chain studded with butterfly-shaped flowers was fastened in her hair. Her pearl earrings dangled but there was no crescent-shaped chain around her waist. There was a thin gold chain the width of a finger instead; no bangles or bracelets adorned her arms. She was not wearing 10 rings, as would have been expected, but only two. My, my! Deba Babu had gone to such lengths to woo and marry a woman like this! How could that be! I've seen so many Mohanty daughters-in-law, but never one as brazen as this. She just strode out of the station and got into the palanquin as if that was routine for her. The mother had had a son after so much effort and hoped to forge ties with a proper family; she had set her heart on receiving and giving and hoped for riches to come pouring in. Good looks are not enough. If only the son had a good job! If only he cared about ensuring the reputation of his father and mother! Debabrata's house came into view as Saniama was on her way, mulling over these things.

Some women came running out to the palanquin. Saniama's friends surrounded her, unable to hold back their curiosity. 'How's everything, dear friend? What have you seen? Why aren't you saying something? Do you have a frog in your throat?' Saniama pretended to be annoyed by the questions. 'Why are these people pecking at my head like crows? You'll all see her in a moment. Don't ask me now why a lens would be needed to see the bangles on her hand. She's like everyone else—nothing exceptional. I shouldn't go on so much, my dears.' Saying this, Saniama pushed her way through the throng and went off.

Saniama had shut the door of the palanquin. As the curious women were trying to pry it open and peek in, the palanquin came to a halt at the front door of the house.

Debabrata had already arrived on the cycle. He had started to go in to see his mother, but had stopped short. When, feeling like a condemned man, he finally forced his unwilling feet to move and went to his mother, she had just risen and come out to sit on the veranda. Debabrata bowed and touched her feet; his mother did not say a word. Like the dark clouds of the Asadha sky, threatening to break open and release torrents of rain, her face suddenly became overcast and her eyes turned watery. Debabrata felt deeply disturbed. A hard jolt from an unknown power forced his muted mouth open. 'Mother, I understand you feel I'm guilty. But how could I not do what I felt was my duty? Mother, what will happen to this helpless girl if you don't accept her?'

'When my son has brought her home as a daughter-in-law, how can I shut my doors to her? Who am I after all?' Saying this, Subhadra Devi burst into tears. Debabrata soothed his mother with great difficulty. Her crying eased. 'Deba, go and have your bath and eat something.' 'Yes mother I'm going.'

Debabrata was now seated in the front room, looking and feeling morose. Two streams of thought were perpetually at war within him: the first, his educated and reformed conscience; the second, the ingrained social beliefs of his society. The first claimed: I have only done what is right. The other answered: What do you mean you have done what is right? Have you done right by hurting your mother, by making her cry and by exposing her to the ridicule of the world, the same person who wishes the best for you with all her heart, whose tender and caring hands have formed every drop of your blood? Don't you see how many people you have hurt by 'doing right'? The first retorted: I don't agree. I do what I feel to be my duty, without hesitating to suffer loss or pain.

Debabrata sat there in a vacant state, torn between these two points of view, his face extremely glum. His moroseness seemed completely out of place, clouding his usually playful and expressive face. His head seemed to droop in shame on its own, and he was unable to look at women and men in his habitual innocent way. He felt as if he was the object of everyone's ridicule, as if he was a criminal, hanging his head because he could not stand the withering frowns. His body was contracting into a shell from a sense of shame, although he was trying to pass himself off as easy-going, amiable, and cheerful. People seemed to be able to see through his façade into the unrest in his mind and were directing towards him their hateful and mocking gaze. That is why he was concerned with hiding his emotions and feelings from public view.

The palanquin came to a halt. Basanti shivered. She was intelligent and could imagine better than anyone what her place in a Karana community in a village would be. After having been slighted by Debabrata's mother once in the past she clearly saw where she stood in society by virtue of her birth. That brief encounter with Subhadra Devi had taught her what it would take to win her mother-in-law's approval. A sense of utter hesitation turned her feet to stone. It was then that her mother-in-law's younger sister opened the door of the palanquin. She held out her hand and slowly led Basanti, saying, 'Come, dear child.' Basanti overcame her sense of inhibition, and walked in softly, covering her face with her silk-embroidered veil.

Basanti went inside the room that had been made ready for her and stood behind the door, left slightly ajar. Determining that she should show the most respect to her mother-in-law and her mother-in-law's younger sister, she bowed at their feet and then sat down, holding herself a little aloof.

The aunt-in-law was a distant relation of Basanti's and was Sarbeswar Babu's wife. Subhadra Devi spoke to her niece Nisamani. 'Nisa, show the face of the new daughter-in-law to everyone, will you dear?'

As directed, Nisa lifted Basanti's veil and showed her face to everyone present. Her exceptional beauty and charm amazed everyone; everyone wondered if they had ever before seen such a pretty face. What surprise was there in Debabrata's marrying someone so beautiful? This thought streaked like lightning through the minds of all who were present.

When she saw the astonishment in everyone's eyes and heard their muffled words of praise, Subhadra Devi, already not favourably disposed towards Basanti, became even more hostile. Saniama had told her all the damning things about Basanti, such as how she had walked out of the station to the palanquin, carried on a conversation with Debabrata in front of her in-law's subordinates, and above all, about what little jewellery she wore. She had become incensed with her when she saw the daughter-in-law walk nonchalantly into the house, before being invited in. But she was aware that she would herself be blamed if she found fault with her daughter-in-law in front of all the neighbours. So she was on her guard. But the admiring glances and words of praise showered on Basanti's beauty goaded Subhadra

Devi into saying, 'My dears! What does it matter if you have good looks; good qualities are what count. Beauty lasts until the burning ghat; it is qualities that survive the world. If you are good, you will hear nice things; if you are evil, you will hear bad things. As the adage has it: "Worship what is good; stay away from what is not."' One of Subhadra Devi's sisters-in-law added, 'Yes, Deba's mother. Very well said. If she does good, she will bring distinction to the families of both her mother-in-law and her father. As the saying goes, "a daughter is a double-edged sword: both helpful and harmful to the two family lines."' Now Nisa's mother spoke. 'Sister, will you go on talking or take a break and see to your new daughter-in-law's needs?' Looking at the women assembled there, she continued. 'You've finished looking now; the daughter-in-law has entered the house. Both her life as well as yours will be spent in this place. It's getting late. Why don't you go home? Let the poor soul take her bath, eat something, and regain her strength. You can all come back later. No one's about to leave.'

They all left one after another.

'Sister!' said Nisa's mother. 'I'm taking leave too. I'll be back later.'

'No, younger sister, how will I manage if you leave? Mustn't you first feed her and see she is comfortable?'

'Let Nisa stay then. If I didn't have chores at home, I surely would too. You don't need to tell me; the daughter-in-law is mine as well. I'll come by later.'

'Nisa, my dear,' said Subhadra Devi, 'stay close to your new sister-in-law. Who will attend to her needs if you aren't around? After all, she's like a wildcat that will take a while to tame. Stay here for 10 or 15 days and visit your mother every day.'

'For such a long time? No, no.'

"That's only a few days, my girl. Why are you so worried? Are you afraid someone will spirit you away? How will you bear to live in your mother-in-law's house?'

Nisa blushed and made her way to Basanti, her head bowed. From there, she shouted out, 'All right, elder mother, I'll stay.' 'Good.'

'She can't stay away for a moment if she doesn't see me when she returns from her rounds of the neighbourhood. I'm surprised she has agreed,' said Nisa's mother. To which Subhadra Devi answered, 'She's a child after all; daughters and daughters-in-law always stick together. She agreed for the sake of company.'

Nisa's mother left.

'Nisa, Saniama has readied some water. Take your sister-in-law so she can bathe.'

Nisa led Basanti by the hand to the room to wash. Basanti's mother-in-law had asked Saniama to smear her skin with ground turmeric paste before giving her a bath. 'Bohu Saantani, your mother-in-law, has asked me to rub turmeric paste on your body. Your skin looks pale and dry. Oil and turmeric will make it shine and glow.'

This was something new for Basanti. In Cuttack she had coated her body with turmeric paste on the Raja, Kumar Purnima, and Khudurukuni fasts at her mother's insistence, but only after much sulking and whining. Otherwise, she had no memory of ever having used it. From early childhood she had been brought up in the town, and had only heard about the way a daughter-in-law was forced to act in villages. She had never seen it herself. That was why she almost turned into a log when she heard the comments, snide remarks, and innuendos after arriving at the house. Seeing the turmeric paste and hearing what Saniama had to say, she realised that she would not easily take to such a life. Saniama was bound to find her behaviour as a daughter-in-law wanting. Since there was no way to cover up these flaws, she decided to say 'yes' to everything for now and to accept it all without a murmur of protest. Only she, who was used to soap and not oil, and no one but she, would know how much sadness and annoyance was veiled beneath her simple 'yes'. If there was one other person in the world who could claim to know this, it was her husband. But from her own plight she could well imagine her husband's state of mind was no better; he would not be getting along any more easily in this house than she would. Suddenly, as she realised this, her mind swelled with sympathy for him.

After she finished her bath Nisa led her upstairs to the room that was to be hers.

A moment later Nisa called out from the terrace. 'Elder mother, the new daughter-in-law has finished her bath. She is waiting to wash your feet. She says she'll eat the food you left in the room only once she has done that.'

'Washing my feet can wait. First feed the daughter-in-law. I have not had my bath as yet. She can wash my feet tomorrow.'

'Sister, come and sit down to eat. You'll wash her feet tomorrow. Other chores such as preparing betel leaves, grinding sandalwood into paste, and sending neatly folded new clothes to people in the village can also wait. I'll help you with those tomorrow, and we'll send the things through Saniama. Today, we'll bring in the sandalwood disk and rolling pin, and the new clothes. If the sandalwood and clothes can be prepared tonight, only the betel leaves will be left for tomorrow. You'll not be overtaxed.'

Basanti had never heard of such things before, other than from people talking in Cuttack. She had never imagined she would have to stay confined inside the house with her lips sealed and do as she was told. She had not learned how a daughter-in-law should act. After a few exchanges with Nisa she said, 'Nisamani, I was brought up in a town with no one to advise me. I've never seen a village and never had a chance to learn what a daughter-in-law must do. Will you please tell me how to go about this?'

Nisa had heard all this before and responded immediately. 'Yes, you'll do as your seniors did, won't you? The chores are the same—preparing betel leaves, washing feet, clearing away leftover food, giving massages, folding saris, cooking, and so on. For example, what you need to do now is wait with a mug of water to wash elder mother's feet as soon as she has bathed. You won't eat until you have taken a sip of the water in which she has dipped her feet.'

'Except for cooking, folding saris, and preparing betel leaves, I'm a stranger to all these things. But you're here with me, so why should I worry? I leave everything to you.'

'Of course! Did I say you'd have to do this all by yourself? You wouldn't know how to, and, more importantly, would I let you do this on your own even if you did? But then, let me tell you something, you may have seen people being given a massage, though you may not have massaged anyone yourself. You can easily learn to give one if you try. Give elder mother a massage at least once a day.'

Basanti pinched the youthful soft cheeks of Nisa with her delicate fingers out of love and gratitude.

After this advice from Nisa, Basanti sent word she would like to wash Subhadra Devi's feet. If it were not for Nisa's advice, she would not have even remotely imagined doing this.

Nisamani is the daughter of Sarbeswar Babu, who played an important role in the marriage. Readers already know that he works in Mayurbhanj. He only returns home on holidays, and except for the remittances he sends, he does not bother much about home. His wife's name is Haramani Devi. The only people in his world are his daughter Nisamani and his wife. Although he does not expect much from this world, he has great confidence in his daughter—the love of his life. Greatly in favour of women's education, he not only allowed his daughter to study at the village school but also hired a private tutor to coach her. What's more, he employed lady teachers from the local mission in Balasore to teach Nisa how to darn socks and hook carpets. Nisa was a smart girl: by the age of 10, she had completed her upper primary education and learned how to weave.

Now the only thought of Sarbeswar Babu and Haramani Devi is how to find their dear daughter a suitable husband.

Nisamani is in her teens and good-looking. Unlike the others, she was not at all surprised when she first saw Basanti. Many of the village elders had thought they would never see the woman Debabrata had chosen to marry, assuming that since he had not married in a traditional way he would not dare bring his wife to the village, afraid of how the elders and his mother would react. So when they saw Basanti arrive, riding in a palanquin, they were taken aback by how courageous he was. Nisa, however, was more advanced in her thinking than the other ordinary girls, wives and elders, and was better educated. That Debabrata would bring his wife to the village did not at all surprise her. Rather, she found it normal that an independent-minded person like Debabrata would do that.

Lifting the new bride's veil and seeing her before the others had the chance, Nisa realised the new bride was indeed a paragon of beauty. She could see her inner beauty mirrored in her face, and the new bride's nature seemed to match her good looks.

The two young women, who had not previously met, fell into a long conversation. Contrary to what she had assumed, Nisa understood her new sister-in-law was actually quite affectionate and generous-hearted. She did not seem to wallow in self-glory or pride; nor did she act superior and slight others because she was highly educated—the very attitude that estranges people from one another, that turns near ones into 'others'.

Nisamani was very happy that in her friendless life she had now found such a beautiful and accomplished sister-in-law for a companion.

It did not take long for Basanti to discover how Nisa felt. When she got to know this loving younger sister-in-law of hers, Basanti's uneasiness, stemming from her sense of isolation, quickly vanished. She began to rely entirely upon this girl of

14, somewhat surprised at the discovery of her own insecurity. Probing more deeply, she found that the affectionate and loving attention she had received from this tender teen-aged girl from the very moment she set foot in this house had won her over completely, and her agitated, panic-stricken mind began to lean on this girl lovingly for support. Just as a scared child feels safe and strong in the lap of her mother, Basanti too felt within her a surge of similar strength as she relied on Nisamani at this critical, difficult, and strange hour of her life.

She could not help but notice the succour and support this young girl provided at a time when she was meeting with rebuffs and barbs from every corner. She derived strength from her companionship and love—much as a man in trouble in a foreign land derives comfort and fortitude when he comes across a compatriot and trusts him almost blindly.

Nine[*]

Though it was Debabrata's unhappy lot to be pulled this way and that by the many crises and hassles in his life, he never let himself forget that his most important duty was to ensure that Basanti was happy, and, of course, to take care of her. How could he forget this, when she was a soothing ray of moonlight in his life? How could he ever forget when he had accepted to risk his bright future and almost everything that he held dear? This sacrifice had brought him joy. His heart's beloved—with whom his youthful soul had envisioned a blissful union, enveloped in the magical qualities of a dream—was now at his side, in flesh and blood. Had he ever for a moment imagined that his sacrifice would yield results so quickly and effortlessly? At first, he had been astonished that his beloved had so easily become his. Innocent in the ways of the world, he had no idea how a young man should behave towards such a precious object. He had not expected to receive God's favour so soon, and suddenly gaining the object of his love had, because he lacked confidence, overwhelmed him with fear and misgiving. Would he have the strength to take good care of this person he had so desired? Would he be able to cherish his beloved for all eternity, be able

[*] By Sarala Devi.

to provide her with all she deserved? He was not able to satisfy himself he could; the ease with which he had won a creature as rarefied as Basanti had planted in his mind the seeds of doubt.

At first, when Basanti came to his house, Debabrata did everything he could to make her feel at home. He did not want her to be sad and miss her mother, or think she had been forsaken and become an orphan, or consider her fate was now to be one of perpetual slight. He did not know how far he had succeeded in this.

Fifteen days had passed since she had come to Similipur. Debabrata was seated on the terrace, a book in hand. He could not remember when his gaze had shifted from the book to the sky above as he went over the chain of events leading from the death of Nirmala Devi to the present moment. His life seemed to have changed dramatically in the blink of an eye, almost like scenes quickly shifting on a stage. Was he still the same Debabrata? Why did he no longer feel the same life force coursing through him as when he was a student? Why did he no longer feel the same joy bubbling up within him, the same torrents of thoughts and imagination racing through him? Yet, he truly was still the same person! Why had his poetic soul become mute, why did he feel so dispirited? He must surely have changed. He realised that under the barrage of onslaughts from the world his soul had been crushed. He heaved a long sigh of despair and wondered if he was doing right by Basanti. A feeling of deep self-loathing came over him; he was unable to forgive himself.

He looked within himself once again and could see there all the feelings he had for Basanti. What was he doing wrong then? Maybe somewhere in him there was something lacking, and that was making her unhappy. There seemed to be no reason as such for his mental turmoil. Maybe it was his mother's hostile behaviour and the spiteful attitude of neighbours, relatives, and friends that had disturbed his equilibrium. He felt distanced from everybody, a stranger, a rank outsider who had been cornered like an animal. He was a man after all, an educated man of means, but he felt undone by this subtle feeling of exclusion within his family, which affected him more than external social pressure.

The beams of the eleventh lunar day-moon bathed the terrace floor in a flood of silvery light. The dew-drenched flowers in the pots lined up in rows smiled radiantly. The stars seemed dim in the moonlight. The blue sky, peaceful and beautiful, seemed to empathise with Debabrata's grieving heart. The strong breeze, blowing in from afar, troubled the smooth set of his curly hair. While rearranging it he caught sight of a blurred figure standing behind the window in the room at the top of the stairs. Who could that be?

Acting nonchalant, he moved towards the landing. Suddenly he grabbed the bunch of keys tied to the end of the sari the shadowy figure was wearing. Peals of laughter rang out from another woman standing some distance away on the staircase. They dissolved into the air along with the sound of her footsteps as she ran down the stairs.

'Oh! What are you doing?' The words were followed by a feeble entreaty from the familiar creature. 'Please let me go. Let me go down and give Ma a massage.'

'Don't try to trick me. Why were you hiding? Were you afraid to come closer?'

'Please forgive me. I'll make sure I won't be caught again.'

'Fine. You've admitted your guilt; now, get ready for your punishment.'

'Whatever your lordship wishes. Any punishment you decide upon will be most respectfully accepted.'

'That's good. Now, come and sit. Let's talk.'

Letting a light smile crease her crimson lips, Basanti sat on the mattress.

'Who ran away laughing when I caught you?'

'Nisa and I came up to the roof to stretch our legs. Dhania had told me you had gone out on your bicycle. When I saw you I told Nisa that we should stand absolutely still and that she should make sure her bangles didn't jingle. When you turned towards us she knew you'd play that prank, but the imp didn't warn me. So she ran off laughing when I got caught. Will she spare me now? She's going to tease me to death.'

'Serves you right! Now you're going to get it from both sides, from my little sister and from me. You reap as you sow. I came up to the roof to lie down as I found it hot down below. I have been lying here for quite some time. Anyway, why don't you ever come up? Look at the beautiful moonlight! Feel the cool breeze! It seems like you're too caught up in your domestic chores.'

'Well, what else would you expect, now that I have a house to look after? Maybe you think that because I don't come up to the roof I'm languishing in the heat. You think that while you're enjoying yourself here we're frying down below. Well, you're wrong. My room also gets the breeze, and your sister and I read and gossip. You may be lying here like the ever forgetful Bholanath, with nothing to do, but I have a lot on my hands, from household chores to my own work.'

'What work is that? I know you're caught up in the drudgery of housework day and night. You won't listen to me. When you were at your place you used to go for a stroll every day; unfortunately, you can't do that here. Otherwise, what work do you have?'

'Oh, I forgot that for you reading books and writing for the newspaper doesn't count. Well, I used to go out for a walk when I had the chance. Now I don't; it's not possible, but I don't mind.'

Basanti smiled wanly and said nothing. Debabrata was cut to the quick when he understood his wife's innermost desire. A rending sigh from his anguished heart melted into the night air. Resting Basanti's head on his shoulder, he said: 'Do you think, Basa, that pretending not to see your situation makes me happy? Don't you think I understand that after leaving your home in Cuttack for mine you've constantly been at odds with your principles, your values, and your happiness—and all because of me? Hasn't your 'Deba bhai' seen how you used to get angry with your mother when she forbade you from going to the riverbank for a stroll? Doesn't he know what your pastimes are—reading, knitting, and hooking carpets—and how your Boula used to fill up your spare time? These eyes of mine have witnessed all this, haven't they?'

Basanti saw how troubled her husband was and, to ease his feelings, said in mock anger: 'All stuff and nonsense you're speaking now, raking up stories from the ancient past as if you've nothing better to do. I'm quite happy, quite satisfied. How could I possibly be sad? This is of your own invention, whatever it is. I don't remember things that happened ages ago. You only know how to unravel a whole spool to find a single thread.'

Debabrata knew what Basanti was trying to get at. 'No, Basa, no. Do you think I'm such a hopeless good for nothing? Don't you think I know how much you have had to sacrifice to adjust to these new surroundings? And all that just to make one person happy!'

'You'll never grow out of saying such silly things, will you?'

Drawing Basanti even closer, Debabrata said: 'Basa, I don't care about myself. My regret is that I haven't been able to make you as happy as I wanted. It's difficult for me to imagine that my hopes for us will reach full bloom at some happy time in the future.'

Basanti felt warm tear drops fall on her forehead. She looked up and saw that Debabrata's broad chest was inundated by streams of tears. She fondly wiped them away with the end of her sari. 'What's this!' she exclaimed. 'Are you crazy? Since when have you made crying a habit?' She tried to laugh but could not. Tears streamed from her doe-like eyes like a spring in the Himalayas, giving an outlet to the pain raging inside her heart.

What earnest attempts Debabrata was making for her happiness and comfort, Basanti thought. This living proof of how deep his feelings for her were made Basanti brim with a sense of triumph, gratification, and immeasurable happiness born of love. Deeply moved, she encircled Debabrata's neck with her arms and spoke with great tenderness. 'Listen, you're the same Deba bhai I knew before, but my arrival was like a stumbling block in your way. Because of me you've come into bitter conflict with society and with your mother. Before our marriage you hadn't actually thought much about whether you'd be able to come to terms with it. On finding yourself in a hostile situation, you must have felt bitter towards me. That's what I used to think when I saw how depressed you were. But now I see I was being unfair to you. Now I ask myself if God will resent the good fortune of a helpless woman like me, so singularly blessed with so much affection and tenderness. Deprived of a secure haven from the very start of my life, I now depend on you. Very often I'm afraid that this security will also elude me, that one day my wretched life will be without your life-giving affection. No, no, I couldn't live without your love. I don't have the strength.'

Debabrata was completely engrossed in the soulful and passionate utterances of the darling of his heart. He felt as if an angel had descended from heaven and poured ambrosia into his ears out of pity for his shattered, feeble, and persecuted mind. It was as if the Mandakini was surging through him, banishing all forms of weakness. The ambrosial touch brought back his youth; he felt reborn into the lost realm of youth known to him in his student days, discarding the frailty of the present. Embracing his beloved, overcome by emotion, Debabrata said: 'I'm so privileged to have you; because of you my life is a success.

Even if you feel you're lucky with a hapless fellow like me, I still think that I'm the more fortunate, because my youthful dream has come true and all the obstacles and troubles have been overcome. I'm beginning to believe this more and more today. I know that immediately after our marriage there was discord in our conjugal life; it was like a barrier on the path of our complete union. It is clear to me now that this was why my life felt dull and weak. The indomitable power and strength a man gets from doing something noble has always eluded me. I wanted to feel this through a deliberate effort of the will. For that I have fought hard with myself but have not been able to remove this half-heartedness. This has made you apprehensive. My indifference and absent-mindedness have caused you terrible pain.'

The hint of a smile lighted up for an instant Basanti's blood-red lips before fading away. Debabrata continued: 'Neither of us tried to understand the other. This lack of communication has not actually crippled our union but has put limits on it. That's why I felt myself to be devoid of strength, why I lost self-confidence and was full of self-reproach. I felt I was being accused of some unknown crime by society and by my mother. Now it's clear to me that my listlessness and passivity were the result of not having made you my own, earnestly and fully. Please forgive me, Basanti.'

Pressing her tender arms with great feeling and deep remorse, Debabrata went on. 'Will you please pardon my unpardonable crime? In not controlling my mind I haven't done the right thing, even if I didn't understand that. I may not have failed in my duty towards you, but my regret is I haven't tried hard enough to bridge the gap between us and reach an understanding. Please tell me whether you'll forgive me for the hurt my dilemma has caused you?'

Basanti broke into a smile. 'If I had had an inkling of the momentous discovery you'd make, I'd never have let you catch me. Nothing in my mind says you have hurt me. What am I to do if you work yourself into such a pitiable state and ask for my forgiveness? You express your regret to me for some presumed offence you've caused me, but I've never thought about you in this way. Whom shall I forgive then? Please know this: you stand forever forgiven in my eyes, come what may.'

'Please tell me plainly you've forgiven me.'

'You're talking as if you've killed a cow and are desperate to do penance.' In a state of elation, Debabrata suddenly kissed her. Blushing deeply, eyes lowered, Basanti darted downstairs, not heeding Debabrata's plea to wait. She went down and started to massage her mother-in-law.

The relationship between Debabrata and Basanti became consecrated under the canopy of the sky, making the moment auspicious. They realised how close they were to each other and felt this new-found intimacy could stand up to any outside force. Their attraction for each other had grown, and their reliance on each other was now based on even more solid ground. Not a trace of conflict troubled their souls.

Basanti was like the wild current of a river—fast, fresh, and flowing. Nothing that was empty or broken had any place in her life. She was of nature born; her soul had been conceived in freedom, in the freedom of a woman. From the very beginning her life had unfolded under this aspect. She had set her sights on higher things; her loving and eager mind knew no limits. But this did not mean she was aggressive. No. Restraint was an important part of her nature. She had never had to struggle to impose control on herself, since by nature she was remarkably self-controlled. The instrument in the deep recesses of her heart rang out new melodies in fresh rhythms everyday and resonated through her daily life of cares and duties. She never tired of her many chores—from work in the house, to writing, reading, and looking after her mother-in-law, to other work. Like the ever-smiling night-flowering jasmine in autumn she was always cheerful, basking in the radiance of her own being.

Since coming to Debabrata's house as his wife, Basanti had carried on a quiet battle against all sorts of odds. She had endured outmoded customs silently, putting on a cheerful face and doing as she was directed. Not that this left her indifferent. She wondered why she bent to her mother-in-law's every whim, when doing so clearly went against her own likes, her own thoughts and desires. She was not intimidated by her mother-in-law; she only wanted to spare Debabrata pain. And even that would not have counted for much if their relationship had been based on impurity, falsehood, and convenience. Her love for her dearest was deep; if he felt so much as the prick of a tender blade of grass it was as if she herself had been struck by a stone. She always strived to make Debabrata happy, to flood his being with the soothing splendour of peace, even if that meant sacrificing her high ideals. What sacrifices had he not made for her! When, after the marriage, Debabrata's family had invited their relatives to a feast in Similipur and they had refused to come because the bride was from a lower caste and had cut all ties with his family, Debabrata had boldly replied: 'Our house is not going to be swept away if no one comes. I'm at nobody's mercy, and I'll not flatter anyone. Let's see who's cutting off whom.' Hadn't her husband accepted the punishment completely and without complaint? Hadn't he tolerated all kinds of harsh words from his mother, staying silent only for her sake? Was there a graver or greater task in the world than to do right by a person like him, who was guided solely by his conscience and was so dedicated to his duty? She did not ever want to seem to be someone who was incapable of enduring far less than her husband just because she was personally affected. As a woman she was expected to show greater openness and tolerance than a man, she thought, and buoyed by this she continued to perform her duty with pleasure.

Subhadra Devi, however, bore a grudge against Basanti, not only for having taken away her son but also for the torment this caused her. Her anger rained down in torrents on the poor and innocent daughter-in-law.

Through sheer willpower Basanti endured her mother-in-law's hostility, and the hurtful and vile words that accompanied it, and went on about her work in silence. She did not think of herself as weak or lowly; rather, she felt that she was strong and that by tolerating the abuse she became worthy of her husband. This gave her great joy.

And precisely for this reason Debabrata began to harbour misgivings. He began to smart under the ill treatment Basanti was receiving from his mother. He was quick to realise that Basanti was enduring everything only for the sake of his own peace and wellbeing.

Debabrata did not, of course, fully understand that behind Basanti's calm exterior lay a tumult that rocked her mind from time to time, a tumult arising from her desire to efface herself, to brutally repress her deepest feelings. He could imagine what lay concealed in her heart. Her suffering was truly unbearable to him. The more she tolerated and sacrificed therefore, the more restless and impatient he grew and the more he began to reproach himself out of an anguished sense of his utter inadequacy.

Ten[*]

The two friends sat facing each other. Darkness crept into that silent corner of the house. A sombre ache was gathering in Basanti's stilled heart. The evening seemed to be passing in a dream. The pain was bittersweet.

Basanti spoke to Nisa, entwining her neck in her soft arms. 'Nisamani, I'm very happy today, a letter has arrived from my Boula, my best friend. But she's deeply hurt I haven't written in ages and has accused me of having forgotten her. Now tell me, could I ever forget my Boula?' Basanti's voice was choked with pain, her eyes were welling up.

'So you think she was wrong to wonder why you haven't written?'

Basanti kept quiet. Many memories from long ago, both bitter and sweet, were filling her mind today after a long time: the image of her mother on her deathbed, as well as that of Kalyani Devi drawing a motherless, helpless Basanti to her bosom with her caring hands. What proof of a mother's infinite loving heart they had given her! Then there was the closeness between her and her Boula, and the deep wistfulness they felt when they did not have a chance to meet. She remembered being lovingly

[*] By Suprava Devi.

chided by her mother for sneaking away in the morning with her Boula to gather flowers. And the memory of the painful parting from Kalyani Devi, who was like a mother to her, and from her best friend Suniti when she stepped onto the path to her unknown future, trepidation in her heart! How agonising that moment of separation had been! Doesn't her Boula know all this, doesn't she remember these things? Then why does she think Basanti has banished her from her mind? She probably cannot imagine that Basanti is no longer the free bird she once was, cannot imagine that she yearns to soar into the high heavens but has been forced into silence after knocking vainly on the cage door, her hands and feet in shackles. She is no longer a girl; she is a married woman. Basanti's heart, as fragile as a flower, has been deeply hurt by being so misunderstood by her Boula, and at that very moment another thought streaks through her mind like lightning. What about her husband? What if he too misunderstands her? Then where would the little Basanti be in this enormous world? Of course, she cannot bear to think of this. In the deepening evening, as it settles in that small corner of the room, the images from the past start to flit through the mind of Basanti, the village bride, like snapshots of a rural scene.

'My, my! Why pick on me for what your Boula has written? You aren't talking to me, eh? Well, why would you? I'm leaving tomorrow, and that will be for the best.' Nisamani tapped Basanti's tender cheeks lightly in mock anger.

Basanti acted as if this was news to her. 'Don't you like it here? You'll leave only if I let you, and pray tell me how will I spend my days without you here, Nisa?'

'Right, why are you using such sugar-coated words? As if you knew when you came here that someone by the name of Nisamani would be here to keep you company?'

Basanti smiled. Her smile was sweet like the tender rays of the rising sun, but also as pale as the light of the setting sun. 'Won't you come back?'

'Why wouldn't I? My mind will always be with you, busy wondering what my new sister-in-law is doing. Please remember this one thing: be careful to do all the chores for your mother-in-law. She's a village woman, and you're an educated woman from the town. She's bound to find fault with you. You shouldn't pay attention to her words.'

Basanti listened seriously to this advice from her little sister-in-law. The deep feeling of empathy in this girl's heart touched Basanti to the core. She felt unprecedented joy: someone else in this family besides her husband cared for her. Her soul felt tormented thinking about the imminent separation from this affectionate girl. Basanti saw herself as helpless for a second time since coming to her in-laws' house. Her husband was with her, but how could she convey to him the hurt her mother-in-law was inflicting on her by calling her an 'educated' wife? What would he think? She decided to endure everything in silence.

Basanti held Nisa's hands. 'All right Nisa....'

At that moment Subhadra Devi's voice rang out from another corner of the house, giving Basanti and Nisamani a start. 'My dear Nisa, will your whispers in that corner never end? Is there no work to be done?'

'Why, Badama,' answered Nisa. 'We have finished all the chores. The cooking's been done. There's nothing else to do, is there?'

'Yes, as if I have enough strength left to fold a paan and to do other things while the "modern" daughter sits in my house reading letters.'

Basanti and Nisa came out of the room only to find Subhadra Devi seated on a mat on the veranda, encircled by some well-known women from the neighbourhood: maid Saniama, Hema's mother, and the mother of Madana. These people were in the habit of going to any house to which a new bride had come. They set out to find fault with her, after finishing their chores and sending the children outside to play or using threats to pin them down inside to do their studies. Although Basanti did not know them, she had learned something about their nature and conduct from Nisamani. So when she came out this evening at Subhadra Devi's call and saw these people, she instantly knew threatening clouds were gathering, and a downpour imminent. Nisa was her parents' only daughter, the first born, dearly loved, and a little haughty as a result. She was annoyed by the way Subhadra Devi spoke curtly, for no reason at all, to her sister-in-law in front of people like Madana's mother. She felt like reacting, but when Basanti saw her face flushed bright red she understood what Nisa was thinking and dragged her inside the house on the pretext of getting paan. What was the point of protesting? Nisa was here today, but at daybreak she would be gone. What would happen then?

Subhadra Devi did not take this silent acquiescence well. There is a class of people who love to blabber and chatter all the time. They cannot stand people talking back to them, but they equally resent it if a person does not respond. Subhadra Devi belonged to such a category. Basanti and Nisa's silence did not please her at all. Nor did the inquisitive minds of people like Saniama feel satisfied.

Sensing Subhadra Devi's reaction, Saniama commented, 'Salutations to the daughters and wives of today. They don't care for anything. God, what has the world come to? See what has come of our Deba Babu's decision to marry a paragon of beauty.'

Madana's mother added fuel to the fire. 'It's your own mother-in-law who's calling. At least have the courtesy of coming and asking what she wants. But no, that doesn't happen. My God, the lady came, took a look, and made her exit. Shame, shame!'

Hema's mother expressed her sympathy. 'All right Deba's mother, you only have one daughter-in-law. If she doesn't attend to your needs, doesn't listen to you, and doesn't serve you, how will you manage?'

'Serving me, attending to my needs! Don't even mention such things. The wife of Deba has studied in a school. She knows how to sing and play instruments. Will such a daughter-in-law accept to be confined to a corner along with the cooking pots? Will she listen to me?'

Saniama moved a little closer, keeping her voice low—but not so low that she could not be heard by Basanti from inside the house. 'Any idea who has sent word to our new bride? She was reading a letter to Nisa Devi. I'm an ignorant fool, what can I understand? She quickly hid it when she saw me. God only knows who the writer of the letter is.' Having said this, Saniama looked this way very guardedly and prostrated herself by way of paying obeisance to the Lord.

'What sort of conduct is this on the part of a woman?' Madana's mother chimed in. 'What is all this about singing, playing instruments, and writing letters? This Nisa was born only yesterday, and even she has turned out like that! What times we are living in!'

'Nisa? Don't talk to me about her. She chatters all the time. God no, I can't deal with her. Let her go to her mother tomorrow. I'll be scolded by her mother for the bad things she's learning and doing.'

'After all, she's somebody else's daughter. Saantani, why should you bear the entire burden?' Saying this Saniama put an end to the discussion.

'Mother I'm famished, won't you give me something to eat?' Debabrata drew near and stood close to them as he spoke. Not even a thunderclap would have startled the noble-hearted visitors, such as Madana's mother, as much as this did.

Subhadra Devi eyed her son. 'You're never to be seen, dear. So to whom should I serve food? You ate a little something and went out in the hot sun and are returning after nightfall. Come on inside and sit down to eat.'

At this point Basanti made her entry with the paan. Her face was not covered in the needless pomp of jewellery; her natural bride-like restraint was her only adornment; her head was slightly bowed. The same people who a moment before had been engaged in criticising her conduct could not help but feel full of appreciation for such a goddess. Seeing their admiring glances, Debabrata too saw her with enraptured eyes and felt within him a surge of pride.

Hema's mother suddenly remembered her daughter lying ill at home. She took leave. 'I'm on my way Deba's mother. You stay. What troubles do you have now? After waiting for so long you have finally got goddess Lakshmi herself. Will you find another daughter-in-law like this in the entire world?' They all made their exit amid eulogies addressed to the daughter-in-law.

Eleven[*]

The morning rays of the sun bathed the room in their radiance. A mild breeze softly kissed Debabrata's fair brow and his sleepiness disappeared at its calming touch. He woke up not just from his sleep, but from a sweet dream which was etching with a magic brush a lovely image. His sleep interrupted, he returned to the world of reality. The realm of dreams had disappeared, and Debabrata found himself in the stark world of wakefulness. He went out on to the roof.

Four months had passed since his marriage. The day he had been waiting for with much anticipation and apprehension had come and gone. But had the marriage brought him peace and happiness? The very reason why he had hurt his elderly mother and why the flame of rebellion had been ignited within him and left him without a care for the criticism of society? His lifeboat, long at sea, was at last headed for shore, but suddenly it seemed as if an opposing gale was sweeping him out onto the vast, bottomless ocean. He could see no shore, only unfathomable water, waves upon monstrous waves. It was as if someone was telling him: 'Futile, all your efforts are futile.' His restless and impatient heart cried out sometimes, overwhelmed. Between

* By Suprava Devi.

the future he had imagined and his present plight there existed a gulf as wide as that separating heaven from hell. He had thought that he would set up a home in a far-off village, where the horizon bowed its head in benediction before the lush grain field and where farmers were engaged in producing food for the world, that he would spend his busy days as if living a beautiful dream amid motherly affection, wifely devotion, and the care of friends. He had married Basanti in the face of opposition from elders and relatives thinking her innocent laugh and charming demeanour would be like a balm for his hurt mind and make him forget his isolation. But the reverse had happened. His mother was busy finding fault with the daughter-in-law; the entire village was awash with criticism of her. Debabrata saw and heard everything. At times he protested vehemently, taking his wife's side, adding to his mother's displeasure; at others he kept quiet, fearing greater trouble, but feeling terrible pain in his heart for Basanti. A flower had bloomed. He had brutally picked it, but would he be able to keep it alive? The betrayer that he was, he had brought peace to a dying mother by taking charge of her precious gem, but had he really been able to provide Basanti with the care she needed? His mind was filled with these thoughts when his glance fell on Basanti, freshly bathed and starting on the day's chores. Seeing in Basanti the personification of a dedicated care-giver, he felt elated but at the same time was overcome with deep sympathy for her.

Debabrata came down and stood in the kitchen, where Basanti was preparing breakfast. He came in so quietly she did not realise he was there. 'God, how awfully busy! No time even to lift your eyes to notice that someone is in front of you.'

Basanti was caught unawares but tried to laugh off her embarrassment. 'Yes, when will there ever be enough time? One has to look the man in the face, and at the same time place the tray with snacks and tea at his feet.'

'Oh, you'd rather not. Fine, I'm leaving.'

'You're really bad. You love to tease me. Did I say I wouldn't?'

Exactly imitating Basanti's tone of voice, Debabrata replied, 'Then what did you just say?'

'Nothing. Mother is finishing her bath; she'll soon be out. Don't I have to attend to her needs? That's why I'm quickly finishing my chores. You know this, but you still want to tease me.'

'Basa, after coming to my house you've been facing many hardships, haven't you? Here are a few: bathing before the crow's first caw, cooking and feeding this precious husband of yours, not to mention waiting daily upon mother. And, if on top of all that, the husband brings guests home, then the chores multiply with more cooking to be done. You must be cursing me.'

'Is that what you would do? Curse? You're very good at shifting the blame onto me. Why do you talk like this? You say "coming to my house": is the house only yours, isn't it mine as well? If I get up before the crow's first caw, how does that harm you? In fact, I like to get up at first light.'

'You like that? But I know you were never in the habit of waking up early.'

Basanti handed Debabrata his tea and snacks. 'Yes, at home I was a late riser. But it was different in the hostel, where students aren't allowed to sleep until eight in the morning. In the hostel you had to get out of bed at six sharp and go to the dining hall for breakfast. If you didn't, then the head boy would give you extra chores. Do people come into the world their habits fully formed? It's experience that teaches us everything. Did I ever imagine living without my mother or could I ever have practiced that?'

Debabrata looked at Basanti's beaming face in astonishment. Who had taught the ways of the world to someone so innocent, he wondered. At the mention of her mother Basanti's face had gone pale and her voice was on the verge of breaking down. Debabrata tried to change the subject. 'Okay, Basa, have you given up singing and playing the tabla?'

'Why, I do play sometimes.'

'How come I don't get to hear it? ... I know people will sneer and frown, but is there any reason to be afraid of criticism if what you're doing is right?'

Basanti had never learned to be afraid of slander. She well knew how her parents had suffered for having chosen to live independently in Cuttack and having given their daughter a modern education. Her memory of the hurtful remarks people had made about Debabrata's taking charge of her affairs after her mother's death was still painfully vivid. It was against her nature to let herself be guided by the opinions of others. The lesson she had learned from the lives of her late parents was that it is beneath one's dignity to bow to injustice and vice. Would this same Basanti have given up her favourite hobby of singing and playing music out of fear of criticism? Stirred by her husband's words, she spoke up. 'No, I'm not afraid of what people will say; at least, I haven't learned to be afraid of that. Otherwise, I would have had to give up many things.'

Debabrata knew what 'many things' meant from the way his wife's face flushed pink as she said this. From her raised tone of voice he understood her deep loathing of injustice. The more Debabrata became acquainted with his wife's nature, the more his affection for her grew. Basanti, in turn, was feeling proud at the thought of her husband's loving heart.

Looking at Basanti, his eyes full of affection, he asked, 'Is anything else the matter then, Basa?'

Before he even asked this he knew it would not be easy for Basanti to spell out the what 'else'. The stark reality was that her mother-in-law disapproved of her and this truth would muffle Basanti's voice. Did that mean that Basanti was afraid to speak the truth? No. Rather, she was concerned it might hurt her husband.

'Basa, I understand everything, but I'm actually very weak. I feel powerless to speak up. My weakness pains me greatly. I rely entirely on you. You'd better forge ahead and let your weak husband just tag along behind.'

Basanti's winning smile eased her husband's pain. 'I had no idea you were weak. All right, your inability is forgiven. So much talk over something as trivial as singing and playing the drums!'

After having his tea Deba set off on his bicycle to see his friends. While on his way, he responded to Basanti's last remark: 'They're not trivial for me.'

Debabrata was gone. Basanti remained rooted to the same spot, reflecting on her husband's words, his endless concern for her happiness, his deep unhappiness over his mother's coldness towards her. Many of Basanti's hopes might have remained unrealised so far and her ideals might have been compromised at several stages of her life, but today she felt that her life had not been entirely futile. She was happy as she realised this, but her happiness was tinged with sadness: 'Why does he worry so much about me and make himself unhappy? Will I be a bother for him all his life?'

Basanti came out of the kitchen and saw Saniama picking the young shoots of the pumpkin creepers off the thatched roof of the husking-pedal shed. 'Saniama, is mother out after her bath?', she asked. Saniama was too busy. Thinking she may not have heard her, Basanti went to Debabrata's sitting room. Tidying up this room was one of her chores. She dusted her husband's books, cleaned the table, and got a supply of fresh flowers and leaves for the two silver flower vases. The vases were a wedding gift from her best friend Suniti.

Basanti returned to find Subhadra Devi on the veranda, shivering. 'Mother, what's the matter? Why are you sitting here?' Saying this, Basanti felt her brow, which was slightly warm. 'Mother, you're running a temperature. You had your bath and then came out to sit in the sun! Please come inside.'

Basanti insisted that her mother-in-law lie down on the bed. She brought her a glass of sherbet made with lemon and sugar and then began to caress her gently. Basanti always had a chest of homeopathic medicine handy. She wanted to administer a dose to Subhadra Devi at the onset of her fever but lacked the courage to ask her. She remained quiet, massaging her softly.

Saniama made a grand entry at this time. 'Saantani, why are you sleeping at this hour? Oh, God, your body's burning.' She said many other things too.

Subhadra Devi spoke to Basanti in a quiet voice. 'Is Deba not home? Has he eaten? Have you eaten something?'

Before Basanti could answer, Saniama retorted, 'The young Saantani served him tea very early, and he left on his bicycle a long time ago.'

'Saniama's here to look after me; go, my child, and have your food.'

Basanti was greatly touched by this first expression of love from her mother-in-law. 'No, mother, I won't eat anything now. Allow me to sit here; please don't say no.'

'Why won't you eat, Ma? Go and eat something.'

Hearing the word 'Ma' from Subhadra Devi's lips, the love-starved Basanti was overwhelmed. For four months she had been a bride in this house but had never been so fortunate as to hear one loving word from Subhadra Devi. This was the first. It was not that Subhadra Devi did not like her. In fact, during these past four months she had been charmed by Basanti's efficiency, her ability to care for others, her power of endurance, and, above all, her poise and grace. Although she had not said so, she must have felt that peace and well-being had reigned in her house since the daughter-in-law had taken charge. Basanti was stealing her way into Subhadra Devi's heart. Subhadra Devi could not, however, forget that Debabrata had married against her will. The more serious his offence seemed, the more she turned against her daughter-in-law. Besides, if Subhadra Devi ever began to display some affection towards Basanti, Saniama was there to return her mind to its previous state by recounting

Basanti's open conversations with Debabrata and his friends, and her letter writing. The women of the neighbourhood added fuel to the fire by gossiping about Basanti's other unpardonable errors: fondness for singing and playing music, administering homeopathic doses to a Pana woman's child, and sewing shirts for a Hadi woman's child who was suffering from a cold. For these and other reasons she found it difficult to show love for Basanti, and even at times to feel it, although she was not a bad soul.

When people fall ill they are generally sad and gloomy; Basanti's loving care came at the right moment. Subhadra Devi forgot everything; she looked up and saw by the bedside a dedicated woman taking care of her—a daughter. She drew her to her bosom lovingly.

Basanti was elated. 'All right Bou, I'll go and have my food if you'll listen to what I say. I'll go if you take this medicine.'

'All right then, do what you like with the old woman.' Subhadra Devi reached for the medicine as she said this, but a grateful Basanti raised Subhadra Devi's head as if she were a baby, gave her the medicine and wiped her face.

A few days later, under Basanti's care Subhadra Devi recovered after being down with fever for a short time. Things were back to what they had been before, and Basanti remained trapped in the same darkness. In fact, the gloom around her had thickened. She could not think what she had done to provoke her mother-in-law's anger and why she had become hostile again so soon after giving her the first glimpse of her loving heart. Later she discovered her mother-in-law had become displeased due to Saniama's exaggerated description of her conversation with her husband the other morning. Saniama had heard it all. Basanti's hatred for lies, ingrained in her since birth, reared its proud head and rebelled against such falsehood. Her feisty spirit could by no means accept this. She wanted to rise up in rebellion against such treatment, but the next moment her education and training persuaded her to ignore such a trivial matter. She also remembered Nisa's parting words of advice and certain experiences Nisa's mother had had as a daughter-in-law and which she had shared with Basanti. She had passed through much turmoil and tumult in her journey to where she was now. Basanti turned all this over in her mind, feeling terribly bitter. This then was the much-glorified married life! Did everyone go through this or was she the only victim? True, she was now much more secure, but had her life become as happy as she had dreamed it would? How had her high ideals, her new hopes been swept away, and to where? Thoughts like these began to surface in her mind as she sat in the dark. Frustration weighed down her soul. Compared to the present the remote past seemed to Basanti beautiful, sweet, and attractive, but wanting to return to that beautiful past was mere wishful thinking. A pair of eyes seemed to tear through the dark night of her soul and to burn bright like jewels. They were her husband's. Her heart filled with gratitude; the moroseness of her mood disappeared.

There was another reason why Subhadra Devi was bitter. This was Basanti's remaining on terms of friendship with Ramesh, Debabrata's bosom friend, his partner in his projects, who followed Debabrata everywhere like a shadow. In the world of the village this was something unprecedented. And not only in the village; even in large towns people would have found it difficult to accept that a woman could become friends with an unmarried man, and return his gestures of friendship.

When Ramesh came to Balasore as a volunteer for Utkala Sammilani, Debabrata brought him home. His simple childlike manners, his spirited and solemn tone of voice justly earned him regard and love. For this reason, when he bowed down to touch Subhadra Devi's feet, she too was touched by the humility of this good-looking young man.

If Ramesh had not acted as a priest and united the two souls to the sacred utterance of mantras, where would Debabrata and

Basanti have been today? That debt was beyond repayment. Could Debabrata be so ungrateful and act so narrow-mindedly as not to allow Basanti to exchange a few words with Ramesh for the simple reason that she was now a part of the world of the village?

He took Ramesh inside and presented him to Basanti. 'Basa, here's Ramesh. Would you be here today if it weren't for him?' Saying this, Debabrata looked at Ramesh and smiled, his eyes brimming with gratitude. Basanti's look expressed the same regard and love, and she greeted Ramesh with a namaskar. Seeing them feeling so obliged, Ramesh let loose a stream of words to overcome his embarrassment.

'Listen here, Debabrata. You've dragged me to your house. I was hoping to be fed something. Apparently, you've forgotten I'm from a Brahmin family.'

Debabrata and Basanti both laughed. 'Basa, today you'll be tested,' said Debabrata. 'It's not enough to have won a prize for your cooking. You have to give us a demonstration.'

Overjoyed with Ramesh's simple and ingenuous manners, Basanti went to the kitchen to prepare some snacks. She had received prizes for her skill at cooking while a student at Cuttack Girls' High School. She was indeed an expert cook and took great pleasure in preparing food and feeding people. Try as she might to find fault, Saniama could not help but praise the daughter-in-law's cooking. Nisa's mother could not sit down to her midday meal if it did not include at least one curry Basanti had made. Only Subhadra Devi had not until this day touched any food she had prepared. She complained that Basanti used to visit the houses of people from all castes in Cuttack. 'Even here she sits, stands, eats, and drinks with the white lady who comes to teach Nisa needlework. Will I take food cooked by her? Shame, shame.'

Basanti left the room, giving the two friends an opportunity to have a heart-to-heart talk after a long time. Debabrata was not aware at what point during their conversation he opened up and expressed his deep-seated anguish to his friend. Ramesh kept silent, unable to think of a word of solace. Anguish flooded his innermost being.

The two friends remained silent for quite a while. They looked up with a start at the sound of someone's soft laughter and saw Dhania standing before them with a plate in his hand and Basanti herself not far from the door. Dhania was all smiles. A bit embarrassed, the two friends dragged a stool closer. Dhania placed the plate on it and left. Ramesh surprised Basanti by showering her with praise for her tasty food. He returned to Cuttack by train the same night.

What about Basanti and Debabrata? Who has kept a record of the slander showered on them? Subhadra Devi made an exception this time by blaming her son more than the daughter-in-law. The daughter-in-law, after all, was a woman, a member of the weaker sex—how intelligent could she be? And then, she had gone to a school, had rubbed shoulders with Christians, had not learnt the ways of the village thanks to her upbringing in the town. But Deba, he had grown up in this village guided by his mother. He could be expected to know her deeply held values, sanctioned by tradition. His lapses were truly unpardonable.

The more Debabrata became concerned about Basanti's happiness and well-being, the more he helped to build an impenetrable wall between his mother and the daughter-in-law. Driven blind by his love, he failed to see that this wall might one day come crashing down on him and that an even taller and more impenetrable wall would be erected around Basanti, creating a barrier between her and her husband.

An afternoon in the month of Aswin, autumnal and indolent. Subhadra Devi was enjoying her siesta in her room; Debabrata was not home. Basanti was pacing throughout the house, moving from one room to another, unable to decide how to pass this indolent afternoon. How to spend her time was a thought that had never crossed her mind before. Her days at home had always flown by, with various engagements and much fun and laughter. Things were different here: mornings and evenings somehow passed, but not the afternoons; they seemed to drag. Basanti picked up Tagore's novel *Gora* from Debabrata's table and began reading it, starting from the end. This novel was dear to her, and despite having read it a number of times she sat down to go through it once again. Someone approached from behind and snatched the book from her hand.

'Who's that?'

Nisa broke into a peal of laughter.

'So this is how you read! I've been standing behind you for a long time, running my eye over the lines along with you. Do you really get so caught up in what you read?' Nisa sat close to Basanti as she spoke.

'What's made you so late?'

'Well, I just ate and ran out as soon as I finished. Mother was calling after me, but I didn't turn back. She'd have delayed me another hour if I had. You're brooding over something, sister-in-law of mine; you haven't heeded what I told you.'

'I listened to your every word, Nisa. You'd know that if you tested me. I could recite every word.'

'Well, tell me what you were thinking about?'

'Something.'

'Tell me what.'

'As I was reading this book, the thought came to me that like the characters in it we too could do something. If you would help me out, I would like to give it a try.'

'If you're willing to trust me with any project of yours, how could I refuse?'

'Nisa, I'm thinking of starting a school. You're free in the afternoons and so am I. It would be good to open a school for children. We two will teach, but how will we get the children to come?'

'I'll drag them kicking and screaming.' Basanti laughed at Nisa's flippant remark.

'May I share in your laughter?' asked Debabrata, coming into the room.

Basanti and Nisa were fired up by Debabrata's interest in the project. True, he brought wind to their sails, but he could not, in his heart, approve of their plan. He knew that far from being fulfilled, this fond hope of Basanti would feed his mother's discontent. But he did not have the heart to discourage Basanti; on the contrary, he encouraged her. Who knows, the plan might succeed. But where would they set up the school? There was no lack of space in this house, but they were faced with insurmountable barriers. How would he be able to battle the odds? He had no strength left in him. This seemed like a lifelong fight.

'Where are you planning to set up your school?' Debabrata asked. Nisa bailed her out. 'Why brother, in our house. I'll talk to my mother and I think she'll agree. And father will be home tomorrow for his holiday. We'll tell him, and he'll make the arrangements.'

Basanti and Debabrata were happy. 'No reason to worry then.'

Basanti had only seen Sarbeswar Babu at the time of her marriage but could not forget the glimpse she had had of his loving fatherly heart in that brief time. She had enough evidence of his deep affection for Debabrata. Basanti felt elated to know that he would be arriving home soon. Fatherless from childhood and having lost her mother in her adolescence, she had gained a second mother, but had also left her behind soon afterwards. She waited for Sarbeswar Babu's visit with keen anticipation.

It was after being away for a long time that Sarbeswar Babu came home during the Puja holidays. Seeing him Debabrata felt as if some sense of purpose had been restored to his otherwise directionless life. His weak and battered soul was buoyed by limitless energy and happiness.

Sarbeswar Babu was very upset to learn from Nisa how Subhadra Devi and the villagers were treating Basanti and Debabrata. He felt greater pain still when he saw Debabrata. Where was his always smiling, always beaming face? His loving and simple heart was cut to the quick in these advanced years of his life. Debabrata was more than a son to him. He told Debabrata to have supreme confidence in God and put his future in His hands. There was no other way. Though a little shaken inwardly, the old man smiled his simple soulful smile and asked, 'Why are you brooding, Deba? At your age I would have demolished mountains.... What do you say, Basa, dear girl? Deba, what reason do you have to be afraid as long as my dear little girl is with you? You may laugh no end now, but you will live to see your old uncle's words come true.' So saying, he patted Basanti's head in affection.

During the few days Sarbeswar Babu was at home nothing ever seemed to get done to his complete satisfaction if Basanti was not there. Everything seemed to come alive for him at the magic touch of this little angel. Nisa began to sulk over her father's appearing to care more about her sister-in-law than about her. When he learned this, Sarbeswar Babu pulled his only daughter to his chest, saying, 'Dear child, you'll set off for a stranger's home in a few days' time and make that your own and live there the rest of your life. Won't you bequeath this dear girl to me?' He said this and smiled in an attempt to make light of the grief he was feeling over his impending separation from his daughter. Only a father's heart can know how much anguish lay hidden behind that smile.

Twelve*

'Where are you Deba's mother, where have you disappeared?' Sarbeswar Babu called out for Subhadra Devi as he entered, his ever cheerful face made even more radiant by his warm smile.

'What a surprise at this hour! Do come in. Saniama, bring a mat and get some paan from the daughter-in-law.' Saying this, Subhadra Devi came out of the prayer room holding her prayer beads. Saniama spread out a mat on the veranda and placed on it a plate laden with some paan. Sarbeswar Babu sat down. Subhadra Devi too sat on the veranda.

'I had no idea you were around. After all, if you were, you'd be hopping from one lane to the next, from one house to another, but not even your shadow has been seen. I was feeling badly, thinking the man didn't even show his face before leaving.'

'No, no, I haven't been able to come, I haven't had a free moment. I've been away from home for a long time, you see, and things to be settled with the land and the estate, as well as sundry other chores have kept me fully occupied. Is it easy to sort all these things out? Today I had some spare time and thought to myself, well, let me go and see how Deba's mother is and what she's up to.' Subhadra Devi heaved a long sigh. 'Well,

* By Muralidhar Mahanti.

what's left for me to do in this world! My days are numbered;
I'm like a ripe mango waiting to fall in a gust of wind or to
rot after the first spell of rain. Doing well or doing badly, what
meaning does that have for me?'

'Shame on you, speaking such words of ill omen! Why are
your thoughts taking such a turn when you still have a long
time ahead of you? You have a full life to live with your son
and daughter-in-law and the faces of your grandchildren to see
before your time's up. Why are you in such a hurry?'

Subhadra Devi responded drily. 'What do my son or daughter-in-law care for me? Everyone thinks only of themselves.
Why would anyone be worried about anyone else?'

Sarbeswar Babu felt concern. 'Sister, why are you talking like
this? You'll not find the likes of your son and daughter-in-law
in six neighbouring villages, and yet you're talking like this!
Tell me what you don't like about your daughter-in-law.'

'Did I say there was something I didn't like? And how does it
matter what I think? Has anyone asked or consulted me? After
all, who I am to speak well or ill of others?'

Sarbeswar Babu understood that Subhadra Devi was not
really displeased with her daughter-in-law but that she still
had not forgotten the hurt Debabrata had caused her by marrying without her consent. She was still smarting from that.
Sarbeswar Babu felt sorry that such a minor matter had not yet
been laid to rest. A fire still seemed to be smouldering within
even if the flames had died down. He could see the sky was
overcast for Debabrata and Basanti.

He had come on a different mission, and at Nisamani's goad-
ing: to get Subhadra Devi's approval for Basanti's plan to start
a school. He was at a loss now about how to broach the subject
and attempted to lighten the mood. 'My dear sister, who has
made you so angry and upset? Do you have half a dozen children
that you can afford to think such unwelcome thoughts? No,
this doesn't become you. You have only one son, and is what he

has done so serious when you compare it to what today's boys are doing? He only married a girl of his choosing. So what? Shouldn't we be happy for them because they're happy? Do we have anyone other than them? All right, I'd accept your anger if your daughter-in-law wasn't worthy or if your son and his wife were neglecting you. No, sister dear, please forget all this for my sake.'

Subhadra Devi could see that Sarbeswar Babu was more inclined to blame her than to show her sympathy. She quickly changed the subject. 'No brother, you're mad to be imagining that I have taken these things to heart. I was only talking for the sake of talking.'

She moved to another topic. They gossiped for a while about the neighbours and the village, but Sarbeswar Babu's mind was not at all on what they were saying. He was simply forcing himself to keep on with it despite his mind being filled with other thoughts and worries. From time to time he would remember Nisa's request. She would feel let down if he did not get the matter straightened out, but he fretted over how to raise it and what the result would be. At last he decided to be open and direct. He knew that Nisa and Basanti were determined to start a school, and that a clear decision should be reached before he left again.

They were so fired up that even a small misstep could have dire consequences. Since Subhadra Devi would learn of the plan at some point, it would be better if he told her himself. Thinking over all this, he finally brought up the subject. 'Sister, I have a message for you from Nisa.' 'What is it?' Sarbeswar Babu continued haltingly. 'Nothing much. You know how close she is to Basa. She was telling me today, "Father, will you tell Badama to let her daughter-in-law visit our house in the afternoons when she's usually free. I could go fetch her myself."'

Subhadra Devi thought for a while. 'Your house is the same as mine, so why would I say no. But then, people would not take kindly to a new bride going outside the house so soon. As it is she has earned the displeasure of people for her complete lack of shame or discretion. She's making things worse by writing letters, reading books, and playing the tabla. People are criticising me for this. Tell Nisa to come and go as she's been doing. I won't let the daughter-in-law leave the house for some more days.' 'Yes, Nisa is coming and will keep coming, but Basa too needs to go there. The thing, sister, is this: Nisa and her friend have thought of a scheme in their simple, childlike way. You know what they're saying: that the girls of this village are unenlightened due to lack of education. We're whiling away whole afternoons, they're saying, that could be used to teach the girls the alphabet and to read books.' This was a jolt for Subhadra Devi. 'What am I hearing! This is all nonsense. They are girls from a Karana family after all, and there are certain accepted ways for them to spend their leisure time: weaving baskets, drawing jhotis on walls and floors, playing ludo or dice. But what's this instead? Are they going to become memsahibs and set up a school?'

Subhadra Devi's voice was rising. Afraid Basanti might hear what she was saying, Sarbeswar Babu spoke out quickly. 'Peace, sister, peace. What are you saying? Am I so much as hinting at that? They'll do all the traditional things, but in a slightly new way. They'll teach the little girls things they themselves are doing. Why are you panicking so much? Our Tima, Chuntia, and Kuni will go there to learn. Aren't they related to us? If one's a grandson, another's a granddaughter or a nephew or a niece. Wouldn't they learn from their aunt, sister-in-law, or sister in the normal course of things? Besides, Nisa's mother will be there, on watch, always.'

Subhadra Devi quietened down a little. She felt somewhat consoled, thinking that whatever happened would happen under the watchful eyes of her sister-in-law, whose skill in running the house she admired. 'All right, let her go if she has to, but through the alleyway and the fields behind the house and not on the open road in front of everybody. I have other conditions, but I'll tell these to my younger sister-in-law.'

Sarbeswar Babu had never expected to be able to convince Subhadra Devi so quickly and easily. He was euphoric and stood up. 'All right, sister, let me go now. I'll come again tomorrow. Where's Basa? I was hoping to see her.' 'She's in the kitchen,' Subhadra Devi answered, turning her face away. The picture that formed in Subhadra Devi's mind, a picture that went against her sense of propriety—of Sarbeswar Babu and Basanti engaging shamelessly in banter, exchanging glances and smiling at each other—soured her mood completely. But Sarbeswar Babu, with a simple child-like heart and happy beyond measure, thought nothing of going into the kitchen.

Placing one foot inside he called out, 'Where are you my dear child?' Basanti was doing some cooking; she came out, smiling. The end of her sari was firmly fastened around her waist, drops of sweat glistened on her brow like pearls, her face was flushed from the heat of the fire, she had a ladle in her hand, and her sari had spice stains in two or three places. She was a sight to behold. The old man gazed at her for a moment and laughed. 'Here's my mother Lakshmi.' The praise made Basanti blush. 'Uncle, what brings you here?' 'Did I just arrive? I've been here a while and was with your mother-in-law. Basa, you should know that your mother-in-law has allowed you to start your school.' Basanti could not believe her ears and thought the old man must be joking or kidding. 'Really, no, that can't be true.' 'No, dear, no. Has this old man ever told a lie? I see you don't believe me. Well, that's natural. But I'm not telling a lie or joking; it's the truth. I came today because Nisa insisted. I never believed sister-in-law would agree to this, but then, by some miracle, she did.'

Basanti was overcome with joy. She had not tasted freedom since the day she had found herself trapped in the suffocating world of the village. The small mercy of this simple permission assumed gigantic proportions for her. The uncharitable opinion she had formed of her mother-in-law, for being superstitious, disappeared at once. Overwhelmed with happiness, she said, 'Wonderful. So the school can start tomorrow.' Sarbeswar Babu smiled. 'No, you crazy girl, don't be so impatient. These things should not be done in haste. Many other things have to be considered. I'm leaving now, but I'll come tomorrow with Nisa and we can all sit down together and decide.' Basanti did not want to let him go so soon and asked him to eat first before leaving. But he made his escape after beguiling her with different stories. He could not wait to share the good news with Nisamani.

Thirteen[*]

Debabrata had been greatly preoccupied the past few days. A sea change had taken place in his mind since he had learned about the school Basanti and Nisa were intending to start. For the last four or five months he had been floating in a dreamlike state; he had quite forgotten that he too had something to do. The news of the school roused him from his stupor. He could not, of course, keep from heaping praise on Basanti for having set out to accomplish something so Herculean. At the same time, he felt annoyed with himself. The events of his life when he was still unmarried paraded through his mind. He recalled the enthusiasm of his college days, the inspiring leadership he had shown his fellow students, his energetic speeches at meetings and functions. How gratifying all that had been! He also remembered the brilliant future he had painted for himself while still a student. These prospects had given him a glorious feeling. Where had his aspirations and unshakeable excitement disappeared? He was astounded by the static and idle life he had been leading these last few days. His friends had expected a lot from him, but he was sitting here, his hands empty, even

* By Prativa Devi.

now when he had a chance to do something. What would his friends think?

These thoughts weighed heavily on his heart, and he lost interest in the pleasures and diversions of life. Would the strength, ability, and opportunity God had given him go to waste? No, he would not let his life come to naught.

Sarbeswar Babu's leave was nearly at an end. He had rejoiced at the news of Basanti starting a school and had strongly encouraged Basanti and Nisa. When he learned that Subhadra Devi too had given her approval he was very happy. It was decided to set up the school in an outbuilding on his property for the time being. Basanti and Nisa redoubled their efforts once they had Sarbeswar Babu's sympathy and support. Basanti had no time to pause and think about possible repercussions.

Before leaving, Sarbeswar Babu went from door to door with Nisa and convinced a few girls to become students at the school. At first, some people in the village strongly objected to the idea of educating girls aged 15 or 16.

In particular, they thought it inappropriate that grown up girls should go to school, trudging along the open village road. They were afraid that by learning to read and write a few letters of the alphabet these girls would become 'Christianised' like Basanti. But Sarbeswar Babu was a much-respected elder in the village; he had mastered the fine art of using sweet words to prevail upon everyone. So those who objected at first, later gave their consent.

Nisa and Basanti wanted the school to be inaugurated by Sarbeswar Babu in person, but this was not possible. Getting girls for the school and attending to all the arrangements took a considerable amount of time. In the end, Sarbeswar Babu had to leave as his holidays were over.

The school was now set to open. Nisa's enthusiasm had to be witnessed to be believed. She had finished all her household chores before the calls of the crows and the cuckoos. Having cleaned and tidied the room where the school was to be housed, she ran to give the news to Basanti.

Basanti was just as enthusiastic. She too had got up early to attend to her chores, as she had to finish up her work by 11o' clock so she could get to the school. The work in the house fell on her shoulders. On top of that, even the slightest inattention on her part, such as not placing exactly the right dollop of lime on a betel leaf, could end up turning her world upside down. She had to take extra care today. Her great happiness might make her slip up on something, earning her the criticism of her mother-in-law's friends. She felt trepidation at the thought.

Nisa embraced Basanti. 'My nuabou, my new bride,' she said. 'I've been up and about since the crack of dawn and what have you been doing? Cooking not yet finished? It's getting to be time.'

Basanti replied helplessly, 'Nisa, you know how much work I've got to do. Lend me a hand, and we'll finish in no time.'

Nisa tightened her sari around her waist and set to work. Together they completed all the chores and set out for the school.

It was starting with only 10 students, but Basanti and Nisa were not ones to despair. They threw themselves wholeheartedly into their task of teaching these 10.

They were certain that if they ran the school well and provided these girls with a sound education, then the number of students would increase.

Basanti and Nisa accompanied the girls to school and escorted them back home afterwards. This they did so that the students would feel encouraged. They also spent their own money on slates. Following Sarbeswar Babu's advice, they started off with reading and handwriting, moved on to sewing, and ended the lessons with morally uplifting stories and legends.

Because of Basanti and Nisa's hard work and encouragement
the number of girls grew day by day. Nisa managed to overcome the objections of parents and get them to agree to send
their daughters to the school.

The news of Basanti's opening a school created a stir among the
traditionalists in the village. The thin ray of hope that Subhadra
Devi had entertained, that through her example Basanti would
give up her bad city habits, had quickly evaporated. What
greater shame could there be than for a newly married woman
to walk openly along the village road? How would Subhadra
Devi be able to show her face to her neighbours? Alas! She rued
that evil moment of weakness in which she had given in to
Sarbeswar Babu and consented to the school. But had she ever
expected things to come to this? It was like an entire arm being
swallowed when only a finger had been offered. Deep remorse
seared her heart.

All of this was too good a subject of conversation for the likes
of Madanama, Saniama, Hemabou, and Parabou. The gossip
about Basanti, in all shapes and forms, spread through the village. Basanti's name was on everybody's lips everywhere, on the
side of the pond, in the afternoon get-together, at the evening
meetings. All this turned Subhadra Devi against Basanti. She
stopped talking to her, and she did not forget to give Debabrata
the occasional tongue-lashing.

It was not as if Debabrata did not realise why all of this was
happening. Although initially he had supported Basanti in her
project of starting a school, he had not been able to give it his
unreserved approval. Of course he did not regard Basanti's act
as sinful or unjust; he simply could not come to terms with
the fact that Basanti could so quickly take on such a serious
undertaking.

The slander against Basanti pouring in from all sides, cou-
pled with Subhadra Devi's insolent behaviour, made him feel
deeply resentful. He was angry she would act like this knowing

full well how people would react. He resented the fact she had not given thought to the disquiet her action would cause and the slight and suffering she herself would endure because of it. More importantly, she had not bothered to think about the effect all this tempest and tumult would have on him. He had gone through many a storm recently, so why was Basanti creating these fresh storm clouds just when the sky was clearing and nature was once again settling into peace? Debabrata had misgivings thinking about their far-reaching consequences. But, of course, he was unable to give voice to these thoughts. There was no way he could do that. After all, Basanti was doing nothing wrong.

He was greatly troubled by all this and decided that the best way to deal with the stress and his worldly woes was to throw himself into something new.

For a long time, Debabrata had been wanting to set up a library in his village. For this purpose he had collected books from the hostel. The question now was where it could be housed. Where could he find a room for the library? But how much of a problem could that be for the son of a wealthy man? If he so wished, he could easily have a building constructed. A plot of land near his house had been vacant for ages. If he were to build it there, the library would certainly be very useful. He mentioned this to some enthusiastic young men in the village, and they immediately agreed to join in the undertaking.

Their enthusiasm was a real boost for Debabrata; he could not put off starting construction on the building. He had been idle for a long time. How much longer could he persist in that state? How would he live out the rest of his days? He decided that until the building was ready the books would be kept in a room in the annex to his own house and that everyone could gather there in the evenings. A handwritten notice announcing this was circulated in the village.

The evening meetings at Debabrata's soon came alive, and the house reverberated with talk about books, essays being read aloud, and discussions on all sorts of matters.

But this was not enough to satisfy Debabrata. He decided to bring out a slim monthly magazine with the help of some like-minded youths. It was to be handwritten, everyone agreed, with contributors turning in their essays written out in longhand. Debabrata was made the editor. The group of young enthusiasts became engrossed in running the magazine, and each issue carried poems and prose pieces on different topics. Everyone hoped the magazine would soon come out in printed form, if only they could press on, keeping their hope and enthusiasm intact.

Debabrata also formed an association for the boys in the Upper Primary School of the village to promote physical exercise and sports. He went there after school hours and started to coach the boys in wrestling and games of various kinds. The boys were passionate to learn and became his ardent followers.

By immersing himself in all these activities Debabrata was trying hard to forget his worries, but the embers of discontent smouldering inside him were slowly being fanned into a blaze by his mother's sullen face and occasional vitriol, as well as by the slander and innuendo from others. There was no lack of disparagers, even among the youths who had enthusiastically joined him in his undertakings. They had many laughs at his expense, talking about Basanti amongst themselves.

Subhadra Devi was completely shattered by the behaviour and attitude of her son and daughter-in-law. Her daughter-in-law had already been on this slippery slope, but what had made her son lose his wits? His education should have prepared him to look after his estate and property, but he was doing just the opposite, caught up day and night in trifling matters with his motley crowd of youths. How would he be able to impose his will on his wife? Subhadra Devi's world was adrift on a boundless ocean.

Nothing escaped the notice of the intelligent Basanti; she was aware of what was going on in Debabrata's mind. She realised that he was not as free and as frank with her as before and that he was spending most of his time outside the house. But she remained calm and steady, shaking off any fleeting feeling of bitterness that arose in her mind. She believed that this unseasonal cloud would soon lift from her husband's mind and that he would then realise his mistake. His decision to take up these projects filled her with optimism. The hope that their union would become more complete through their commitment to public life fortified her heart, and she continued to perform her tasks, large and small, with determination.

Fourteen[*]

One afternoon, after finishing all the household chores, Basanti was leafing through a Bengali monthly when Debabrata came in, engrossed in a new issue of *Nababani*. His face, if one looked carefully, seemed a little serious. Basanti noted that but did not understand the reason.

Debabrata sat down near Basanti. 'Basa, there's an essay by you in *Nababani*.'

'Yes, I sent one in last month.'

While reading the concluding portion of the essay, Debabrata remarked, 'Everyone would agree the essay is of high quality, but I have a few questions about it and a couple of reservations as well.' Debabrata finished talking but seemed to have still more to say. Basanti remained silent.

Debabrata continued. '"The Place of Women in the World" is an apt title. It's indeed time to reflect on where women belong in this world. It's normal, of course, that differences of opinion on the subject should exist. But you know what, Basa, I had no idea your views were so far ahead of their time.' Basanti continued to remain silent, unable to make out whether his words contained irony, hurt pride, or wonder.

[*] By Muralidhar Mahanti.

Debabrata spoke again. 'Okay, consider this portion, which seems very radical to me.'

From the very beginning of human civilization our saints and, in their wake, a good number of philosophers, historians and litterateurs, have been trumpeting to the world certain so-called certitudes which only proceed from man's selfishness and lack of consideration. There is no end to the number of times that we have read in their essays platitudes such as "women are the better half of men", "women and men constitute two equal parts of the social whole", "women are responsible for the welfare of men, whereas men are responsible for supporting women", and so on. Writers or poets who have written about women, whether out of pity, love or hate, have considered women only as the daughters, sisters or wives of men. Why is the idea that women are subordinate so lasting and all pervasive? Why has no one imagined a distinct and independent identity for women, separate from men? There are often portrayals of men in splendid isolation from women. Are women born to be the slaves and servants of men? Don't they have any existence other than as the property of men? Have they been born to be the shadows of men, the daughters, sisters, and wives of men? The independent existence of women is ...

'Now Basa, please tell me what kind of autonomous life you would lead that has nothing to do with me. Please explain, I'd love to hear about it.'

Basanti replied softly. 'It's not that I would do it, but there should be a place for women outside the world of men. Unless there is, women's lives will not be full. At present, a woman's life makes up only a small part of a man's, is a minor interlude in the drama of his life. Everyone believes women do not have an independent status. Women have to break this myth. Only then can they emerge in their full glory.'

These words did not seem to go down well with Debabrata. 'Basa, look, these sentiments sound good and are easy to put into writing, but in reality they're probably not well-founded. Here's the first thing to consider: it's fanciful to think that women can protect themselves and survive without the support of men. At least that's my opinion. If you look at the physical differences between men and women you'll see that one is designed for work and war and the other for stability and love. These differences cannot simply be ignored. Other arguments could be cited, but they're not necessary here. Besides, imagine what chaos and confusion there would be if your principle of autonomy were allowed to prevail. Society, which has been held firmly together by the mutual love and respect of men and women, would fall apart and come to naught without this.'

Basanti forgot herself in the heat of the discussion. She spoke excitedly. 'Granted society would fall apart, but how would that matter? We do not need a selfish society like this one. Men are the kings, heroes, makers, and prime movers, and women are nothing! Women are just shadows, mere slaves, caretakers, subordinates, and objects of pity! We don't need a society like this one.'

Debabrata's tone became agitated too. 'Look Basanti, you might be interested in hearing my view on the subject. Well, my view is that men and women have an equal place and are support and sources of love for each other. They should grow equally. This is how the collective welfare of mankind will be made possible. But your absurd and far-fetched ideal of autonomy is not only detrimental to society and destructive of domestic bliss, it's also a contemptible revolt against the noble design of God. And to go around preaching that ideal is not only unjust, because it's false, it's also horribly shameless....'

Debabrata came to a sudden halt seeing Basanti's pale face. He understood he had hurt her cruelly, carried away in the heat of the argument. Feeling contrite and utterly ashamed, he held Basanti's hands. 'Basa, please forgive me. Foolish that I am, I've hurt you in the course of my self-absorbed chatter.'

Basanti forced a smile to crease her pale face. 'No, you haven't hurt me at all. What is hurtful in what you said?'

After this they tried to talk about other things, attempting to hide their true feelings from each other. But the simple, innocent, and transparent exchanges of an earlier time were gone. Some insurmountable barrier had been erected between them, and they began to feel and think differently towards each other. For the sake of peace in the family each tried to conceal from the other the change that had taken place. Debabrata now knew for certain that his view on the liberation of women did not match his wife's, and Basanti too knew how her husband felt about the question. She saw that far from being the liberal or liberated person she had thought he was, he in fact believed men should dominate women, to a lesser or greater degree. His speech was proof of this. Their opinions were opposed to each other.

*Fifteen**

A Fragment from Basanti's Diary:

I can't stop thinking about how so much was made of so little the other day. He did not use to be like this. I have seen him day in and day out: calm, gentle, and unassuming, he's the picture of affection and politeness. I haven't heard a rude word from his lips. Why then did he flare up? Is it criminal to publish an essay in a monthly magazine? If it is, I didn't realise that.

Memories from my adolescence come to mind. One day a highly excited Deba bhai dropped by our house. 'Basanti (we had known each other for only a few days, so he called me Basanti instead of Basa), have you heard about Snehalata's suicide?' 'No. What happened?' As he told the story of why she had killed herself and how she had done it by dousing her sari with kerosene and setting it alight, Deba bhai's eyes breathed fire and his fair face turned red with anger and hatred.

'That's our society!' He continued in the same agitated state. 'The groom's family asked hers for dowry far beyond what they could afford, saying they were due it for the huge favour they

* By Annada Shankar Ray.

were doing of saving her family's ancestral honour by accepting their daughter. Everywhere such demands for dowry are being made by families of the groom. The bride's father fell from the sky. He sat helpless, his hands on his head: if a daughter is not married off at the right age, 56 generations are condemned to hell. The girl could not bear her father's suffering and the insult to her own dignity; she got her reprieve by sacrificing herself at the altar of the false gods of society. Today this incident took place in Bengal; tomorrow it will be the turn of Orissa. Tell me, who should be called to account for this crime? The man or the woman?'

'The person who commits the crime of suicide,' I answered.

'Not at all! The person who provokes it. Society as a whole has to take the blame for this. And by "society" I mean the world of men.'

That day he started to explain things to me. 'If Snehalata had been taught that it was acceptable to remain single for life, and if society didn't frown upon a woman remaining unmarried by choice, then would she, driven to the wall by the groom's family's lust for money, have taken her priceless life? Women have to be given an education so they can carry on with ease without getting married, until they'll be able to provide for themselves.'

Not once, but many times, he said to me, 'The only way to improve the status of women in society is through education. Men too would benefit from that. If a mother is educated, her child will learn, and if a wife is educated, her husband will gain a companion. Do you remember the time-honoured shloka, "*Gruhini sachibaha sakhi mithaha priyasishya lalite kalabidhou*" (Housewife, yes, but also keeper of secrets, companion, one-of-a-pair, favoured student, adept in fine arts so numerous)? If women could be raised according to this principle of Kalidasa, how happy and successful men would be.' As he said this, his eyes grew large in delight.

Apparently, he is still the same person. I don't know if his views have changed, but he seems to show little concern for the work I have started inspired by him and in the hope of having his support. I have been at the receiving end of everyone's barbs since I started running the school, and the one person who could have turned all this suffering into happiness, by showing just a little warmth, has remained indifferent.

And that essay! In an essay for a monthly magazine I tried to convey the suffering of women. At one time he eagerly promoted this sort of activism. Has marriage changed everything? Fine! I understand I am no longer the ordinary, unknown Basanti Devi; I am now the wife of Debabrata Babu, the zamindar of a village, and any mention of my name is a slur against his person. Does he really believe that? Does he lack even a little courage to ignore criticism?

No, I'm wrong in the way I'm thinking. He has endured a lot by marrying me. Hasn't he had to put up with enough slander? How can I blame him? Maybe mistakes I have made have put him off, but what mistakes have I made without realising it? Should I ask him?

I have a feeling I have not taken enough care to make him happy. I must have neglected the person dearest to my heart, too busy either with household chores or with trying to do good. But then, what good are teaching school and writing essays, if not to secure his happiness? Would he truly be happy if, like 10 other women, once I've finished my household chores, I spend my time playing with shells, gossiping, and sitting like a doll, staring into his face?

I can't get to the bottom of it. The mind of man! He alone knows what he wants and when; as for me, I'm tired of trying to figure it out.

Mother-in-law is calling for me. 'Daughter-in-law. Where are you?'

I have to go; not a moment free, even to write!

Last night he came home very late. Maybe it was half past 11 or even midnight. Mother-in-law and I had waited for him without eating.

The expression on his face and the colour of his eyes instilled fear in my heart. I am still being tormented by a vague apprehension. His eyes were red like a hibiscus, his voice quite grave and heavy. I lacked the courage to ask any questions. Maybe it would have been good if I had. At times life makes you feel vulnerable enough to make you want to talk your heart out, but unless your mouth helps, you keep quiet. Yesterday I found myself in such a situation.

Mother-in-law is going around saying I have gone from using mantras to cast spells on her son to making him do things that result in his losing his health, vigour, and spirit, and in his remaining silent. According to her, I'm a witch of a wife who won't be happy until she eats her son alive.

So this is what was in store for me! What has he done to save my honour and esteem, when my only succour was his love, and to help me endure the disdain of my mother-in-law, the criticism of society, and the insinuations of the maids? Nisamani! Nisamani! If only you knew my hurt and anguish, you would think twice before encouraging me to go on with this school project.

When Nisa arrived, she was in such good cheer she was almost dancing. She is always alert and spirited. She lost no time in chattering away. 'Dear sister of mine, you cry and pine so much! Sister, what are these tears for? Has brother said something? Is his "Basa" losing her charm?'

Her words pierced my heart to its core. They gave me such a start that I shivered inside. How could Nisa have suspected what terrible hurt she had unwittingly caused me!

Concealing the fierce beating of my heart and forcing a smile on my face, I answered her with whatever composure I could muster. 'No, my eyes look swollen because I've just woken up.

Come and sit. No, not there, sit leaning against me. My little sister, how I feel like taking you onto my lap!'

She is only a child after all. How could she feel my suffering? Why would I let her know that 'Basa' has indeed lost her charm?

Oh, God, give me strength. I was born to have to put up with everyone's slights and loathing. Tears are rolling down from my eyes soaking these pages of my diary, the clear-eyed mute witness to my agony.

It is getting more and more intolerable day by day. Where has peace vanished. Everywhere there is silence, and everyone is acting as if in a pantomime. Mother-in-law has taken shelter in the prayer room. If anyone asks, she says, 'Don't ask me anything, go and ask the daughter-in-law.' Adding, 'I've had enough drama. Tell me when my death will come. Oh God, when will you save me?'

Mother-in-law sometimes calls me gently if she is pleased with me for some reason. 'I'm an old woman. Leave me to myself and my Gods and prayers. Between the two of you, you can look after the house.' If I cry, she says, 'Come, my dear. Am I so unbearable? I only get peeved with you when the whole world maligns you.' If I remain silent, she says, 'Well, it's not hard for me to understand. There's been a row between you two, hasn't there? Such things are normal when you set up a home together. Do you want to hear about Deba's father? Deba was four years of age at the time. Yes, it was in the month of Margasira. Don't remember what lunar day it was, maybe the ninth or the tenth day. Yes, as I was saying, Deba's father called me and said....'

The story she told me was quite long. The point of it was this: she and her husband had an argument over something or the other and did not talk to each other for two months. Finally, when the anger had subsided, they still did not talk but managed with hand gestures. One day, completely out of the blue, Deba's father addressed her as 'Deba's mother' and a 'yes' came out of her mouth in an unguarded moment. The freeze was thawed by the full-throated laughter lying bottled up in their hearts.

After telling the story mother-in-law heaved a long sigh. 'But then I know the ways of you educated wives. You people are good at taking control of your husbands and making them dance like monkeys. I know that educated and uneducated wives are equally unhappy.'

Anyway, the good thing is that she's not a stranger to the simple truth of the human heart. My mother-in-law's feelings are volatile like mercury. Maybe tomorrow she will crucify me, like she has done many times before, but for the compassion shown to me today, a million thanks from the core of my heart.

x x x

All right, let me put this to her. It's one thing if my husband slights me or if my mother-in-law alternately praises me as Lakshmi and damns me as a witch, but who are the maids and servants to cast aspersions on me? I can't forgive such an insult. No. I will be hard, cruel, and unyielding in the face of humiliation and injustice. I will assert my rights. I will not be weak.

If there is a rift between husband and wife, then the servants and maids also are divided into two camps. That's what is happening here. These people have somehow begun to sense the misunderstanding between us and have started on their games of winking and innuendo. 'Did you see? The same Deba babu and our Basa sister! As a couple they were once as inseparable as turtledoves ... now they ...'

They have a golden opportunity. When they go rumour-mongering with their vicious whispers, what reserves of honour can I dip into to hold my own? Other girls and daughters-in-law in the village were literally burning with envy at my good fortune. The day is not far off when I will see them smirking, pointing their fingers at me, and making up doggerel using my name. Oh, God!

Even Saniama quipped after biding her time, 'Heed my words, little Saantani. Go back to where you came from without making too much of a fuss. You've already damaged our babu's good name enough by casting your spell on him. Now leave this house quietly, my goddess Mangala.'

I turned red in anger but calmed down the next moment. How is she to blame? She may only be echoing somebody else. Forcing myself to laugh out loud, I said to her, 'All right Saniama, do you think you'd like the new daughter-in-law if your babu married again?'

Saniama paused to think for a while.

I kept drivelling senselessly but was unable to suppress the emotions rising up in my heart. 'Dear Saniama, curse me all you want for the troubles and ills I have brought with me, for having brought your beautiful world to rack and ruin. But won't you complain the same way about the new daughter-in-law? Granted, I have every defect; but will she have only merit? Or will you also one day call her Ma Chandi, telling her to pack up and go back by the road she came on?'

The words seemed to touch a chord in Saniama, and she was chastened. 'What will I tell you, Ma, about the stories many people are spreading about you. I'm a simpleton; what do I know or understand? I speak what I hear others speak. But do I really not respect you? You have fed me such delicacies and you have given my son a place in your school. How cruel of me to say such things to you! What a grave sin I've committed! Ma, please don't take it to heart. I'm just an old woman. I'm mad and have a loose tongue.'

How am I to deal with such people? One statement in front of me and quite another behind my back. They're in a hurry to vilify, but soften when they hear a sweet word. Then once again they lapse back into their herd mentality and resume their hateful speeches. They don't care to think and consider. You're done for if you set out to try to shape them into decent human beings, and you're also done for if you don't.

Fine.

Sixteen*

A Fragment from Debabrata's Diary

Every passing day convinces me that Basanti does not love me. I don't know why the thought always comes to me these days that I've made a mistake by marrying, that I've been cheated. What is it that really prompts someone to marry in total disregard for society? It would seem that it must be for happiness, for love. If one day he finds he has been surrounded like Abhimanyu and is being mauled and maimed by the arrows of scandal and ridicule, but without love to give him the strength, energy, and fortitude to put up with the suffering, because that love has evaporated, then what happiness will he fight for and what pleasure will he live for? It is different if he has married without love right from the start. Then it's easier for him to live like most other people and accept his lot, but I haven't tried to take the beaten path, which is why the suffering that others easily endure is becoming unbearable for me.

If I were in love with her, then I would carry on in the face of her apathy, forgetting all my woes. The happiness derived

* By Annada Shankar Ray.

from my love would outweigh the suffering that comes from self-sacrifice, but I have never loved her.

Haven't I though? No, I haven't. There was a time when I thought I did. That was before my marriage. By the time of our marriage I did not have such deep feelings for her, only a sense of obligation, a desire to fulfill a promise. Only a sense of duty misled me into believing that I was taking on life's battles and opposing society for the sake of love. The intoxication of that love has disappeared. Only the dull dryness of duty remains. Will I, with my unfeeling heart, destroy society and remake it? I do not have the strength for that.

I have been cheated, my heart and mind oppressed by the dull emptiness of a huge delusion. My mind tells me, 'Debabrata, you have kept your pledge like Bhisma, but your life has turned out to be more insipid and meaningless than his.'

Has it all been in vain? It must have. Cast out by society, expelled from my mother's heart at home and from my wife's mind, I would like to do something. But on the strength of what? This exhausted mind?

I feel like crying. Shall I? Let me. Let me cry on this moonlit night and let all my suffering pour out in the form of tears only to evaporate on the river bank. At times I'm reminded that I'm the spirited and energetic Debabrata, a man. What reason do I have to break down like this? No, Debabrata, this is not the time or the place to put up a façade. Look, the river is weeping in its cascading rhythm, carrying within her bosom endless tears of grief. The moon is weeping in its rippling beams, venting the anguish of loneliness and separation. You too should weep; you must.

All right, with my tears I'll wash away my grief.

X X X

No idea what time I got back home last night. I came walking in with the unsteady steps of a drunkard. Basanti had not gone to sleep. I had a strong urge to press her soft hands firmly in my grip and look her in the eye with fiery eyes and ask her once, only once, 'Basanti, please tell me the truth, do you really love me?' She would probably have answered in panic, 'Yes.' And then I would have pushed her away from me and spoken with fierce passion, 'No, you false woman.'

I am writing like a mad man. Shame on me! Basanti has never told me she does not love me. She has never knowingly hurt me. No, she has. I will convince myself that she has hurt me day and night. Be it true or false, I am determined to believe today that she has never loved me, that she married me out of a selfish desire for the good life. That is certain. Mother and daughter together set a trap for me. They singled me out as their victim. They feigned love and took advantage of me. All right, they have taken me for a fool and do not know how clever I am. I did not realise this until today because I am such a simpleton.

Basanti has never loved me. She has always looked to her own needs, has only thought of her own comfort. How is it that it took me so long to understand something that simple?

That essay against the male race she penned, doesn't that indict me indirectly? What other man does Basanti know, or has she come in contact with, that she would have so much spleen against the entire male race? Surely I am her target? Who else? She hasn't had a father since her childhood, no brother, and virtually no male relative. So who else can she be fulminating against? Could there be another man on whom she has taken out her anger because she loved him and sulked over him? This doesn't augur well. Does she love someone else? She must. Yes, she surely does; I'll say it a thousand times that she does. I myself have seen her write letters to Ramesh. But where's the harm in that? I asked her to do it, but then what made her do as I said? Surely she wanted to. Is it a crime to write letters? Yes, it is. Why would she write letters? What does she lack for? In her letters she must be complaining against me. She must be writing, 'I'm not happy in this marriage.' She must be saying, 'I'm suffocating in this house. This has happened because of Deba Babu.' There must be more along these lines, but I'm unable to think of more! Oh, I'm feeling so vexed. I seem to be becoming increasingly suspicious. Shame on me really, surely I didn't use to be like this!

Yesterday when I saw Basanti's face I felt as if she was trying to say something but was unable to form the words. As though someone was choking her. Poor Basanti! She's very lonely; no one cares about her: an irate mother-in-law, an indifferent husband, hostile villagers. As if she alone is to blame for having married me. Innocent girl! I'm only hurting myself by suspecting you. Why did you write that essay? That's when I began to distrust you. Alas, why were you in such a hurry to start your school? The only thing I wanted was for us two—husband and wife— to exist only for each other; I wanted that no force should be able to separate us, neither country nor society; I wanted your sole and undivided attention. Why did you throw yourself into social work, neglecting me?

I felt chastened. But I still could not convey my message: 'Basanti, I love you, you love me.' My innocent, blameless darling! What is her fault? She's doing what she thinks is right. How could she know that I'm suspicious of her for no reason?

Wouldn't everything be clear if I had a straight talk with her? But who would initiate it? She or I? I shrink within, lacking the courage to broach the subject. She must feel the same way. She's a woman after all.

If only I could once get her to understand. 'Basanti, the only thing I have against you is this: why have you poured all your energy into social work, ignoring me? Maybe my wish is selfish, but this is what would bring me happiness. I want you Basanti, I want you all for myself. I come first, the world afterwards. My love for you far exceeds what the world can ever give you.'

X X X

My head has gone haywire again. At times it's clear to me that I'm not quite myself. At other times I feel I'm being oppressed. It's like I'm being tortured from all sides, and while I gasp for air as I swim in a bottomless ocean, others are enjoying the fun. But at times I come to myself. Everything then seems a figment of my imagination. Everything seems as it was before, with people loving and respecting me, the village elders giving me a wide berth because of my importance, and, more importantly, the magistrate shaking my hand. My mother's anger is born of her love. I should not be so stupid as to think that Basanti has to proclaim her love for me. I should be able to know everything from her looks of longing. Can anyone really say 'I love you' to the face of someone he loves? Why then should I resent Basanti? Only seasoned lovers hide the bitterness of their hearts under a rhetorical display of love. It's the empty vessel that makes a lot of sound. The vessel that is full is silent.

X X X

No, this will not do, these ruses and stratagems will not work. For how long will you go on deceiving me, Basanti? I know you have stopped loving me. You would be happy if I died, wouldn't you?

How hard you try to avoid me! If I were not clever, you would really completely deceive me! You yourself see how you have deliberately kept busy only to keep away from me.

She does not have time to see me during the day. Meeting with her is well-nigh impossible as she busies herself with the household chores right from the break of dawn. What were you doing? Answer: 'Chores still not done, I'm still at them.' What are you up to now? Answer: 'Picking flowers for the deity.' What are you going to do? Answer: 'The cupboard has been infested by termites. Has to be dusted and cleaned.' Many chores, not a moment to rest. Well, wouldn't the maids and servants be able to attend to these things? Does she have to do everything? If you ask her, she'll say, 'Will they be able to put their heart and soul into the work? Can they take personal care of things? They're more likely to misplace and mishandle things.' She has no respite in the afternoons. She's happy if she can leave me behind in the name of her school. And there she'll spend her time until evening amid a bunch of uneducated and primitive village girls, teaching them to read, to hook carpets, and to sew and will not return home until I go out on my bicycle alone and bored. What pleasure does she take in those things? I have a feeling she simply wants to torment me.

Nor is Saantani to be seen after dark. Come on to the rooftop, sing a song, play on the harmonium, gossip, or hear me read from a book. Nothing doing. She relieves the maid and applies herself to the service of the mother-in-law, giving her a foot massage. Or makes the curry herself, relieving the Brahmin cook. If there's nothing else to do, then there's always the Ramayana to be sung to the group of maids. Who has asked her to do all these things? God knows what grave crime she would commit if she sweetened her husband's lonely life by giving him a little love! But no sighting of Saantani until the poor husband dozes off to sleep after spending considerable time tossing and turning in bed until midnight. It seems her work is not over until she personally makes sure all the relatives and all the maids and servants have eaten. Isn't all this merely a pretext? The truth is she does not have the time or the mood to talk with me. My claim on her is nothing; it is always the world that comes first.

Who is it you are trying to fool? Debabrata is simple, but he can also be shrewd. I see all, I sense all. I will act the day things get out of hand.

Seventeen[*]

Basanti sat in the sitting room upstairs. The window in front of her was open, and the lamp, as it flickered, gave off a faint light. It was midnight. A hushed silence had fallen over the house. Debabrata had gone to visit a relative and not yet returned.

It was a night in the rainy month of Asadha. The noise of the village had died down long ago. Outside, it was drizzling and flashes of lightning intermittently lit up the window pane. Dark and dense banks of clouds were woven into the fabric of the sky. Fireflies flitted through the mango trees on the property, and jackals in the crematorium on the edge of the village howled shrilly, heightening the sense of foreboding and announcing a bleak day ahead.

The dim light in the room fell on Basanti's face. She was lost in thought, her locks dishevelled by the gusts of wind. She frequently wiped her brow with the end of her sari.... 'Oh my god! What about the letter I was supposed to write to my Boula?' Saying this, she shut the window, raised the wick of the lamp, and drew her chair closer to the table. On the sheet spread before her she began her letter after four long months.

* By Sarala Devi.

My beloved friend! I received your letter long ago. Your eyes must have run dry waiting for my reply. You must have been hurt, perhaps even, given the ways of the world, thinking ill of me. But what else could I do, dear friend? I don't have the heart to tell you a lie and say I haven't had a free moment to write these past four months. The truth is I haven't been in a frame of mind to write a letter. And you well know I don't like to write to a friend just for the sake of appearances. What is there I can tell you about myself? Oh! There's nothing worse in this world than a life of drudgery. I'm sitting here penning these lines to you after midnight, and I feel as if the sharp and pointed sword of impending doom suspended above my head will at any moment pierce my skull. I have probably never been so worried about the future. Everything hangs on the will of God, on whatever He decrees. Do I seem to have become completely fatalistic? You mentioned the change in my life. Lives change every day, the hour that passes is lost forever: there's another day and then another hour. And sister, change is inevitable for a person who is helpless and weak, who cannot put up resistance. Not that change is always for the better; it can also be for the worse. Well, let me leave that for now.

Yes, my Boula, my flower! Many a storm has buffeted this poor life, and many hopes and much trust have crumbled to dust. The only thing that survives is ambition: forever hungry, but completely powerless. It races on day and night, night and day, in the vain hope of being realised. But alas, there's not even the slimmest chance of reaching the horizon shining in the distance. You asked about the changes in my life. Things are bound to change, my friend; who has the power to prevent that? Friend, think of yourself, aren't you changing? Of course, in many ways you're still only a girl and so far change has not left its mark on your body and mind. The hopes and fancies of heady youth, with its usual fun and laughter, have transfigured your reality into the delusional fantasy of some imaginary magician. Do you know what the real world is? The burning rays of the afternoon sun during a scorching summer, the hot parched earth. These are now part of what I am experiencing. True, the cool shade of youth with its hope still insulates me, but I feel I am being singed by the fire raging on this barren fringe. The charm of living is on the wane. You might think your Boula is very selfish. Well, she would admit that—a hundred times over. But doesn't the self come before the world? Don't we all pursue what our hearts desire before we begin to live for family, society, and country?

Debabrata could be heard coming up the stairs, and Basanti was not able to continue her letter in such a free and easy manner. She signed off with, 'More I am keeping for later. Write back, and accept my love and regards. Yours.' Panicky, she folded the letter, placed it in an envelope, and sealed it. As she was putting it into the writing case, the letter fell to the floor with a mild thud. By then Debabrata had reached the threshold of the room. Seeing him Basanti quickly picked up the letter, put it in the case, and locked it. She winced, realising there was no reason to have locked the case.

Debabrata could not help but notice how hesitant and anxious Basanti was when he came into the room, or her panicked look as she put the letter in the case and locked it. He wondered, of course, why someone who never bothered to lock her writing case had suddenly felt the need to do so.

... And rushing to do it when she saw him? What could have gotten into her? When have I ever shown any curiosity about her private letters? What meanness has she ever seen in me that has made her act with such secrecy? There's no reason for her to think like this. In my innocence I have believed her worthy of trust, I have unconditionally offered my love to her, I have never opposed her, her slightest sorrow plunges me into gloom—and yet she acts towards me like this? Why does she think I'm so petty and mean? As if I were a robber who has come to steal her peace and happiness. As if that was my sole desire in life.

A sigh forced its way from deep inside him, causing his large frame to tremble before dissolving in the air. He had no desire to say anything. He only felt awkward and uncomfortable for having suddenly come into the room.

He put away his kurta, shawl, and shoes and went into the bedroom. He was so disturbed by this small incident that he forgot to change his dhoti.

Once in bed, he kept brooding over the events of his life, his relationship with Basanti, and much more. It seemed to him it was he who had made the greater sacrifice of the two, suffering bitterly on account of her. But what had he received in return for all the sacrifices he had made, for all the suffering he had undergone? He was not a god; he could not offer self-less devotion to the woman he had married in the face of great opposition. Like everyone else in this world he expected something in return for what he gave. How had Basanti fulfilled her end? He spoke aloud. 'Intolerable. I don't have the strength to endure this anymore.' His eyes began to burn, and while tossing and turning he dozed off at some point. He did not tell Basanti to come to the bedroom. Was this deliberate or did he simply forget, who can say? It is as if this small incident had made Basanti irrelevant for him.

The night followed its natural course and made ready to usher in the dawn with all its offerings. The earth began to pulsate with life at the touch of the new light. Why do mornings, each the same, always bring new mysteries?

Usually Basanti finishes her morning ablutions by the time Subhadra Devi leaves her bed. Why then wasn't she to be seen today, although it was already late? While sweeping the floor Saniama asked, 'Where's the young Saantani? Why isn't she up? She's usually had her bath by now.' 'Go and wake her,' replied Deba's mother. 'Why is she still asleep?' Saniama called out as she went up the stairs, 'Saantani, your mother-in-law's been up for a long time and is attending to her chores. You're still asleep.

Come, your mother-in-law wants you.' When she entered the bedroom calling out all the while, she found no one there. The servant had made the bed and swept the floor. Unable to understand, she paused to catch her breath and then went to another room to look for her.

The door to the sitting room was closed, but not bolted. Saniama pushed the door open. The daughter-in-law was asleep in an armchair, her head to one side, her hair dishevelled. Saniama stared in utter surprise. 'Bohu saantani, bohu saantani.' Basanti awoke with a start and arranged her clothes. 'Saniama, have I slept too long today? What's mother up to?' She felt a profound sense of regret when she saw Saniama's surprised look. She quickly went downstairs and was taken aback to see her mother-in-law busy chopping vegetables. While going past her on the way to have her bath, Basanti's steps faltered. Since coming to the house she had never been caught so unprepared. She could not help being angry with herself. The thought of how Saniama would go on gossiping about how she had found Basanti, and what her mother-in-law would think, made her want to dissolve into the dust.

'Saantani, have you heard what your daughter-in-law's been up to?' 'I've no idea. What's going on?' 'What else, stuff and nonsense! Your daughter-in-law was sprawled in the armchair in the drawing room. She hadn't washed, her hair was in a mess. When I called her, she muttered something that went over my head. Deba Babu wasn't in his room; the room had been tidied up.' 'I don't understand anything. Maybe they've had an argument. Who can read their minds? Who can say? I have to put up with everything because I'm too generous. Who on this earth has ever brought home a daughter-in-law that's as much of a gem as mine? Oh, God, no! Please don't open your mouth to anyone, not to a relative or to a neighbour. If what happens inside this house becomes known outside, we'll be ridiculed and have to hang our heads.' Oozing sympathy, Saniama answered,

'Saantani, what standing do you have left in the village that a matter as small as this would make you lower your head any further?' 'You're right, dear. A thief's mother cannot cry, even out of shame. If she cries, then it's behind closed doors. My fate is to blame, but who else do I have to run to with my complaints?' 'When I woke up in the wee hours the other day, I felt like having a paan and went to my room in search of my betel case. I looked up and saw their bedroom plunged in darkness, but there was a light on in the Bohu saantani's room and she seemed to be reading some book. I didn't look closely. I thought perhaps she had gone to her room to get something. But, no, she was up to something else....'

This last part of what Saniama had to say fell on Basanti's ears as she was coming back from her bath. She burned from head to toe with humiliation. From the way her mother-in-law and Saniama sat facing each other she had already guessed what they were talking about.

She knew her mother-in-law's nature but had not expected she would stoop to speaking about her in such a demeaning way with someone of so low a station. Her mother-in-law might put up with such talk about her from a maid, but she could not accept it. Her blood began to boil.

On another day she would perhaps have put up with such an insult, calling on her presence of mind and capacity for tolerance, but she had a headache from not having slept the previous night. A searing pain singed her eyes, turning them black. She found it hard to walk, to support the weight of her own body. And there was another reason too. Although she kept trying to get used to the climate of hostility, her mind, unable to be reined in, was growing more and more restive. She did not realise that Debabrata's odd behaviour was responsible for this. For all these reasons she was not able to simply let this insolence pass. Her mind began to be violently agitated by a futile anger that had no outlet. She said to herself, 'Why, why do I have to do penance like this. I haven't committed any sin.' But outwardly she remained calm and spoke in a measured voice. 'Mother! You have every right over me, and as a mark of my respect I have never answered you back. You can say anything you want to me, and I won't mind. But for someone so lowly to show me such contempt to your face! I may not have much self-respect, but surely you are not lacking in it. Doesn't this hurt your reputation too? Am I not connected to you?' Saying this and without waiting for an answer, she went upstairs to change her sari.

Deba's mother was rendered helpless and speechless with shame and anger by her daughter-in-law's impudence. She could not stomach the insult hurled at her in the presence of Saniama. It was as though both Saniama and she had bit the dust. How could a person who never ever lifted her head to put a word in edgeways, despite being called names and being snubbed, speak so harshly to her very face? And in the presence of a mere maid! She should at least have learned to restrain herself in front of someone of such inferior status.

'Why are you crying over such a trifle, Saantani? Why are you shedding so many tears for nothing?' Saying this, Saniama started to wipe away Saantani's tears. She melted in sympathy and began to weep too. 'That is written on my brow, my foolish girl. Will I take a trivial thing to heart when I have endured so much more? It's like in the saying: "The tricks Kanhu has been up to will be remembered until my dying day".' After putting the vegetable basket away and sweeping the floor, Saniama continued in an aloof and indifferent voice. 'No oil on the hair and no comb run through it for months. What a sorry state your hair and skin are in!' When Saniama moved to give her an oil massage, Deba's mother declined, saying it was already late and the chores still had to be done. Then she suddenly headed to the pond for a bath after applying a mere daub of oil on her hair.

It must have been almost half past eight in the morning. At around this time every day the assembly of gossipers would begin their session at the edge of the pond, the buzz of their voices rising to a peak and then subsiding, finally dissolving into silence. The daughters and wives would have finished their baths and left before daybreak; those who showed up after this group had left were the leading members of the assembly.

Today it was the turn of Mukuta, or Auntie, as she was known to everyone, to give the sermon. The subject was Nisamani. 'That girl's been pampered by her parents, and right from the start she's been full of herself. Since she's begun associating with the daughter-in-law from Cuttack she's become a know-it-all. Showing respect to her betters and behaving like most other girls in our world—no, don't expect that from her. If you utter a cross word or two to set her straight, or tell her how to act, does she take it lying down? No, she kicks up a row and sends you scurrying for cover wilting from shame.'

Dama's mother: 'These days everything's topsy-turvy. No one has a thought for anybody else; even little urchins don't think twice before giving you a mouthful. We've done our days as daughters and wives, we've seen our grandchildren—no one has ever been able to find a blemish on our character. In our time we were discreet and timid. That's all been done away with now.'

Rami's mother: 'Whoever brings Nisi home as a daughter-in-law is done for.' Dama's mother: 'Well, if she appeals to the person who brings her home as his wife, what else does she care about? What does it matter if the neighbours approve?'

Auntie: 'How true! Whose approval does a daughter-in-law seek these days? Only the son's. In this day and age it's much better not to have a mother-in-law, a father-in-law, a sister-in-law, or an elder or younger brother's wife. And even if they are there, who bothers with what they want? Everyone's selfish. Can't you see the difference between what our village daughters-in-law once were and what they've turned into? Now, they think only of themselves.'

Rami's mother: 'There was a time when we stayed hidden behind the door for five or six years, and our mothers-in-law never heard so much as a murmur from us. When there were festivals or weddings, the milkman or barber would arrive with hampers from our father's house, and any letters they brought with them we hid in the kitchen. Where was the post office then and did anyone think of mailing letters? Our world didn't extend beyond our fathers and brothers, or at the most our neighbours. If we wanted to read aloud a line from some book, we'd only do it behind closed doors. Now everything is done right out in the open.'

Auntie: 'Why tar all the girls in the village with the same brush just because one girl or daughter-in-law has turned out badly? Now that you've sent your girls to school, you'll pay the price. My, my, earlier they wouldn't so much as utter a word when you glared at them. Now, will they even listen to you if you ask them to run an errand?'

Dama's mother interrupted her. 'Does the moon or the sun ever see them once they've filled their bellies? Saying, "It's time for school, sister Nisi will scold me, sister-in-law will badger us", they fly off like kites, as if someone's house is on fire, and no one catches a glimpse of them.'

Auntie: 'Earlier, one of them might have been a problem; now they've all gone astray. "No light has entered her own home, but our slick sister Padi frets at the darkness in the homes of others." No matter how much a girl learns, it'll all come to fire and ashes.'

Rukuna's mother, even though she was part of this older generation, had earned standing in the assembly because she had some learning and knew a bit of weaving and sewing. She tried to take charge of the situation. 'That's all very true, but then learning to weave the new patterns in new styles is certainly a good thing.'

Rami's mother: 'Are we dumb, blind or deaf that we lack the little intelligence needed to tell what's good from what's bad? Who can't recognise good as good?' For a long time there had been some veiled tension between Dama's mother and Rukuna's mother. Dama's mother saw her chance to show off. 'We should see to our own affairs. Why should we give ourselves headaches worrying about those of others?'

In the meantime, Deba's mother had reached the pond. Even if she had not heard the discussion right from the beginning, from the last words that fell on her ears it did not take her long to guess how it had begun. Her grim expression dampened the spirits of the gossipers and the assembly fizzled out before long. The presence of Deba's mother soured the sweetness of the gossip, bringing the lazy languid bathing to an abrupt end.

Deba's mother commanded respect from everyone—from the members of the assembly to the ordinary women of the village. This was not, of course, because she was generous; it was because of the hope for some personal gain from associating with the mistress of the only zamindar family in the village. Everyone came to consult her over even a trifle. No one dared to speak directly to her face and if it was something she would not take kindly to, then silence was the only option. There's no knowing why everyone's sympathy for her had increased a hundred-fold recently, as she had been ostracised since the day of Deba's marriage. The villagers had expected to be witness to an exciting display, but this eluded them, as the contest between Rama and Ravana, with daughter-in-law and mother-in-law taking the parts, did not play out as expected. Having failed in this, their hawk eyes tried to find other faults. The day Basanti's school started, their desire was fulfilled 100 per cent.

Seeing Deba's mother's serious face, the married women of the village began a game of knowing winks. They returned to their houses, understanding that their pond-side assembly could not last much longer.

Deba's mother usually took seven or eight minutes to bathe. Saniama, who had come to the side of the pond with a change of clothing, could not help asking, 'How many hours will your bath last today? Why don't you come out? This new-season water will give you a cold and fever.' 'I still have a lot to endure in this life. My life isn't as insignificant as the tip of a needle; it won't be so easy to snuff it out.' Saniama had hoped to hear exactly this. 'Did you see that, Saantani?' she asked. 'What doesn't this ear have to hear, what doesn't this heart have to bear?'

'My brow is burnt, what does it matter what I hear? There's a lot more the ear will hear and the heart will bear as long as I live. Those who have never opened their mouths in front of me feel free to talk against me because they think I'm weak. Good or bad, she's our daughter-in-law after all. When her father-in-law was alive, he was able to make the tiger and the deer drink at the same ghat. Since his death the house has lost its glory, and the villagers have started riding roughshod over us.' 'Why think about that, Saantani? Destiny seems to have conspired with the belittlers. If she had done as you said, would they be able to go on about her lapses, and would we have to steel our hearts and listen? Who has the cheek to speak to you? But then who will listen to you? Does anyone think that what you have to say is worth even the dust under their feet?' 'Like son, like daughter-in-law. Neither has done as I say; I can't speak to either. These are shameful times. Don't our sons prefer to wait upon their wives rather than take care of old fools like us? Not much longer for us now—just waiting for our days to end—we're only saying this for their own good—it's they who will have to listen to things—because we live exposed like a tree stump we find it hard to hear people speak ill of them God knows why we don't die. Has our time of suffering ended?' Saniama spoke as if to Basanti. 'Alright you've done a bit of reading and writing, but why have you collected a bunch of girls and made yourself an easy target for our enemies for no reason at all?' 'I told her, tried to reason with her, even chided her, but she didn't pay heed to anything. What am I to do, Saniama? However foolish we may be, haven't we lived in the world longer than they have? ...'

While they were talking Dhania arrived. 'Saantani! The little Saantani has sent me to fetch you, worrying herself sick over your delay. Please come soon.' Deba's mother asked anxiously, 'Has Deba had his food?' 'The cook has finished cooking and is sitting idle,' Dhania replied. 'Deba Babu was looking for you. After eating he left for Braja Babu's house for a game of cards about an hour ago.' 'And the daughter-in-law?' Saniama, noticing that Saantani was cooling down, wanted to heat things up a bit. 'Oh, she has sent you! Because she can't have any food or water if she hasn't seen her mother-in-law. Maybe that's why? Is she really concerned or only putting on a show?' But Deba's mother felt pleased at her daughter-in-law's words and said, 'All right, I'm on my way.' Offering a palmful of water to the sun, Deba's mother made her exit.

Basanti always provided comfort and care for her mother-in-law. She had expected to do the same today, but the incident in the morning had cast a shadow over her usually cheerful face. Her silence and the pallor of her face made her seem sombre. Nisamani's face had also paled, even if she did not know or understand what had happened. As on earlier days, today too Basanti performed her duties, washing her mother-in-law's feet and bringing her fresh clothing.

Deba's mother had already started to soften. She felt even happier when she did not see any change in her daughter-in-law's behaviour, despite having expected that today there would be some. She asked Nisa, 'Dear! I took so long today. Who can have given her food, what could she have eaten? She's not new here anymore and should help herself to her meals. I might have told her that 1000 times, but she has never listened.' 'Elder mother,' answered Nisa. 'I have just arrived. How would I know if she has eaten or not?' 'How can today be an exception when that has not happened in days, months, and years? When has she ever eaten if she wasn't offered food? Her face has lost its colour; she probably hasn't eaten.' Basanti spoke bashfully, making a face, 'No, mother, an hour's delay won't burn my belly. I'll eat after you have finished your puja.'

The words she had spoken to her mother-in-law in the morning troubled her. She ruefully thought, 'Why did I let this little thing rattle me today when I have put up with so much? After all, she's like anyone else. Is it her fault if she wasn't careful like me? She won't stand for a word of backtalk from her son, with whom she's so indulgent. Because she felt hurt the other day, she kept quiet. If she had kicked me, I would not be feeling this badly now. Shame on me! How uncivilised, how impolite I am! How I hurt her with my loud mouth! How it must have hurt her! All my training, learning, and discipline acquired over the years has gone down the drain. It seems to me, my conscience is a false ally.' On top of all that, the affection her mother-in-law had shown her heightened Basanti's shame and regret. She shied away from looking her mother-in-law in the face. She said to herself, 'I will fall at her feet and ask for forgiveness. My sin cannot be forgiven otherwise.'

Eighteen*

Basanti went upstairs after finishing her chores. Although she had been very efficient in carrying them out, she could not help feeling that all she had done was drudge and slave throughout the day. Her mind was clouded like an overcast night sky.

When she tried to understand the events of the past two days she felt perplexed but had at least some sense of why Debabrata had reacted so strongly. Although she felt guilty, she was extremely reluctant to face him. Her feet wanted to move but remained frozen; her mind yearned to reach out but stayed inert.

Hearing the sound of his sandals on the stairs Basanti felt nervous and pretended to be absorbed in a book she picked up at random. Her heart beat wildly at the idea that Debabrata was about to enter the room. For the past two days she had remained aloof and secretive. The thought of confronting him today, and of how that might turn out, led to mixed feelings of confidence and doubt. To cover this up she sought shelter in a book.

During the past two days Debabrata, too, had been avoiding Basanti and had spent much of his time outside the house. The feeling that the fault was mostly his for having nursed a

* By Sarala Devi.

grievance against Basanti created turmoil within him. He felt hesitant to even cross the threshold of Basanti's room when he thought about how embarrassed he would feel to go to her, start up a conversation, and look her in the eye.

He paced in front of her room for a good five to seven minutes and then took a deep breath, convincing himself that Basanti had no idea what was going on in his mind. But he was clearly deluding himself if he thought his hesitation would escape the notice of sharp-eyed Basanti. Finally, he said, 'There's no water in the pitcher in my room. Is there any in yours?' He felt embarrassed about the awkward signal he was sending of a man dying of thirst and jumping out of bed to quench it barely 15 minutes after having his meal.

'Yes, it was filled this evening,' answered Basanti. She took the silver glass from the shelf and handed Debabrata a glass of water.

Debabrata, of course, was not thirsty at all. Seeing his plight as he forced himself to drink down half a glass, Basanti tried to save the situation. She spoke quietly. 'Don't bother. Why do you drink so much water? That's not good for you.' Debabrata knew all his stratagems had failed. Feeling embarrassed, he set the glass down on the table.

Basanti opened the paan case and handed two leaves of paan to her husband. Happily tucking one in his mouth, he offered her the other. 'Why two for me? Why don't you have one?' Basanti accepted the paan, shyly looking away.

After pacing about the room for a while Debabrata sat on a chair next to hers. He immediately felt as if a load had been lifted from his chest, as if these brief exchanges had put their relationship on an even keel. Basanti stood up and leaned against the chair. The light in the room shone radiantly on her face. What exceptional beauty was embodied in the easy and delicate fold of her sari with its finely wrought silk border, the unkempt curls falling over her temple, the betel juice that had dyed her lips, and the deep blue of the little dot shining on her fore-head! Her hand was resting on the arm of the chair. Debabrata saw that the gem-studded ring his mother had given her when unveiling her face still adorned her ring finger. He had seen it many times, but today it seemed to glow even brighter. She was not dressed elegantly, she did not use any cosmetics; like every other day, today too she was in her ordinary clothes, wearing the usual ornaments. But Debabrata's wide eyes spoke of his astonishment at the sight of such exquisite beauty. He blurted out incoherently, 'Basa, your fingers are so delicate. The rings fit your fingers in a way that is yours alone.' Basanti's face turned crimson, as she felt the intimacy of Debabrata's hand on her own. The warm shiver of an electrical charge coursed through her body right from the tips of her fingers. Withdrawing her hand from the arm of the chair, she said in a tone of mock anger, 'You still aren't able to stop yourself from falsely praising oth-ers. That's not good.'

Embarrassed somewhat, Debabrata tried to change the sub-ject. 'Why don't you sit down? You're punishing yourself by standing like an accused in the dock.' Basanti sat down. 'Yes, that's the right word, "accused"!' Debabrata understood what Basanti was hinting at and felt slightly contrite. 'Point taken; please forgive me. Who will forgive my mistake if you won't? Don't you think my behaviour these last few days has also hurt me deeply? In fact, it has hurt me much more that it has hurt you.'

Basanti had stifled her rising emotions, thinking that feel-ings had no place in a relationship based solely on convention, in which no empathy existed and where gestures of affection were only attempts to placate the other person. In such a situ-ation expressing what one felt merely demonstrated what a low opinion one had of oneself. At Debabrata's words her pent up emotions began to dissolve in a flood of tears. The unpleasant way Debabrata had dealt with her over the past two days, the treatment meted out to her by everyone in the house, beginning with her mother-in-law's servants and maids, began to flash before her eyes like scenes from a movie. Overwhelmed by a rising wave of tears, she cleared her throat. 'The destiny one is born with is that person's alone. Who else will share it? If my destiny wasn't cursed, would I be the cause of everyone's unhappiness?'

This sudden turn in the situation baffled Debabrata. He had no idea what he could say to Basanti. He felt deeply miserable at the thought that he had made her unhappy ever since he had brought her here, that he had not been able to give her the happiness or peace owed to her, that he had not even felt prompted to make an effort in that direction. Finding no ready words to console her, he started to wipe away Basanti's tears with the folds of his dhoti. After a while he said, 'Basa! I'm terribly unlucky. My studies and learning are utterly valueless. I'm worse than an animal. So fallen and base is my nature that feeling a sense of shame about it is not enough. Basa, why did you make the fatal mistake of falling in love with such a poisoned fruit? I'm unfit to ask for forgiveness. I've only caused you pain. Utterly selfish that I am, I've taken you for granted. I'm completely unworthy of you.'

Basanti had never thought he was soft-hearted. Debabrata's words of regret were like thorns pricking her very heart, but she found it next to impossible to contain her pent up feelings. She wanted to speak out. 'No, you've traded everything in order to make me happy, there's nothing wanting in your sacrifice, you're the presiding deity of my life. Why do you think yourself poor or mean? No, I'm the one who is unable to make you completely happy. I'm powerless. Why do you grovel in the dust, seeking forgiveness? This indeed is my greatest punishment.' Up until now Basanti had been weeping out of a sense of hurt pride; now her tears began to flow untrammelled, expressing remorse over her incompleteness, inadequacy, and vulnerability.

The sight of a shaken Debabrata plunged her into the depths of sorrow. How much her momentary lapse had hurt her dearest! She was deeply pained by the remorse she was feeling. Using all her strength, she spoke firmly but in a calm voice. 'You're unhappy because I'm suffering, but it's nothing. Why give it so much importance? The glory of patience and endurance is a woman's alone. Compared to the suffering of many women in the world my lot is much happier. Like Goddess Lakshmi, my wish is to satisfy everyone, and my failure to do so gives me pain. The sorrow I've caused you by my agitated state of mind will stay with me as long as I live. My love for you survives still, despite my being so unworthy. This is my greatest glory.'

Looking wistful, Debabrata seemed to lap up Basanti's words. When she paused, he pulled her close lovingly, losing his eyes in hers.

Basanti, my queen, please, for my sake, forget all the troubles I have caused you. You've talked about endurance; God's undeclared purpose is probably this: shakti will counter force, shakti exists in the world to withstand force. Our hearts go out to women for the suffering they endure, and despite which they remain cheerful and continue to perform their duties. A woman's life is perennially full of peace, serenity, and beauty, despite the reverses of discrimination, sorrow, danger, the hassles of life, and the troubles. She is like the still and deep ocean in whose caring and giving bosom we seek shelter at every moment. But, Basa, whatever a woman is, a symbol of shakti or of anything else, she is certainly not born to suffer the tyranny of a man. And a man who bends a woman to his indomitable will can only pass for a scoundrel.

Basanti smiled slightly at these last words and kept quiet. Knowing Debabrata the way she did, she could not rule out the possibility that he would contradict his own words the very next morning.

Nineteen[*]

A midday in winter. Basanti was upstairs, exposing her books and magazines to the sun as well as soaking in the warmth of the sun herself. Absent-mindedly she turned the pages of one of them. Seeing Braja approach, she stood up and started to move back inside the room, asking as she did, 'Hello there. Didn't you have a nap this afternoon?'

Braja, a distant relative of Basanti's through marriage, had recently had to give up his M.A. because of irregular attendance at classes. Smiling, he responded, 'Yes, failing in that attempt "at the present juncture", "for the time being at least" I am here.'

Laughter rippled like quicksilver through Basanti's voice. 'Oh, I'd forgotten that "samprati"—at the present juncture—and "apatatta"—for the time being at least—are our new imports.' Sitting down and still laughing, Braja started to rifle through the books and notebooks. In the course of their conversation he suddenly asked, 'All right, sister-in-law, tell me what's your goal in life?'

Basanti remained silent for a while, tearing up a piece of paper. 'I don't have any particular goal,' she replied.

[*] By Sarala Devi.

'I find that hard to believe. Why, even some people with no education set themselves goals. You're well educated, why haven't you?'

'You may not believe it, but I'm telling you the truth. I haven't yet been able to decide what my goal should be. But I do have certain beliefs about the sort of life a woman should have. Do you want to hear them?'

'Yes.'

'Well, you people seem to believe there's no purpose to a woman's existence, don't you?'

'I don't understand.'

'The plain truth is that in the eyes of men there's no special purpose to a woman's life. She's supposed to want the same thing as her husband, her dharma is supposed to be the same as his. Isn't that so?'

Braja sat in silence. Basanti continued, smiling, but with a touch of sarcasm. 'What purpose or goal could you expect a woman's life to have when as a person she counts for nothing and scribes and writers of the scriptures repeatedly advise her to dissolve herself in the self of her husband?'

Braja did not say anything.

'All right, let me put it like this: in addition to laws for women, the writers of the scriptures have formulated laws for men. But do you think the Hindus of India follow these to the letter? Are you willing to accept today that Shudras—the lowest born—exist only to serve the three higher varnas, that to do this is the sole justification for their lives, that they are forbidden to touch the vedas, etc? If such laws from ancient times are true, and if no one has the right to question them, then how can you and your friends stand up and protest against them? Doesn't that mean that the old values are crumbling day by day and that even if you try to keep only their essential elements you'll be out of step with the times? You're all for breaking our ties with the government, but what justifies that? Doesn't that simply mean you're unable to accept the political order as it exists? But haven't the pundits and priests of the past always taught us to pay the king the devotion due to him as the representative of God? Why don't you totally obey this religious edict? It would seem the uneasy murmurs of protest being heard from the depths of India don't bode well for you, Braja. What position will you take? You're well educated, which is why I want to get you to use your power of reasoning. You know that women didn't have any role in composing the shastras or in framing the social codes. There's been tremendous opposition from society, from time immemorial, to self-expression for women, which is why women have been confined within the four walls of a house, like frogs in a well. Whatever you might say, I could never support this system, which you consider to be ideal and eternal. My small and limited understanding is that in an ideal society men and women should join hands and work together. Neither should have precedence over the other; every effort should be made for them to be equal partners. Any social system in which such equality does not exist is headed down the perilous road to chaos and strife. History will bear witness to this.'

After a short pause she resumed. 'The primitive instinct of men, when given power, is to see to their own self-interest. And women have always been subjected to their arbitrary behaviour. Others, if they want to, can valorise this passivity of women as respectful restraint, delicacy, and humility, but not me.'

Braja pretended to be sympathetic. 'But what other choice is there? It would seem that God has not inscribed the word "independence" on the brow of Indian women.'

'In that case Indian women are destined to remain mired in ignorance. Look Braja, in no society today that claims to be advanced and civilised have men offered independence to women on a silver platter. You know what sacrifices the suffragettes in Europe made to achieve social independence. Is independence so cheap and valueless that it can be had for the asking? To obtain it the oppressed have to strive hard and use all their might. It's true that in this country too, like every-where else, there are some liberal-minded men, but aren't they like a puddle the size of a cow's hoof compared to an ocean? I seriously question the judgement and far-sightedness of people who would cite the example of this miniscule group and pro-pose forbearance, saying "one day the time will come". Women have to rebel, have to overcome the passivity of centuries, prove their worth, and rise up against oppression.'

'But all this means that many more women first have to be educated.'

'Certainly. Without education women will never be worthy of full independence.'

'Okay, one thing. Since you're asking for complete indepen-dence for women, you should also argue that women should not become mothers, since motherhood stands in the way of their cherished goal of freedom.'

'That's a delicate point, Braja. Who says that motherhood goes against independence? Women have never rejected their duties as mothers; on the contrary, they have experienced great joy and gratification in fulfilling them. But motherhood does become a burden if it's not freely chosen. In a situation where a woman is subjected, that pure feeling becomes perverted. But how can motherhood be an impediment if it promotes the development of a woman's personality? Society has given procreation precedence over the person, and this has robbed motherhood of its glory. Motherhood finds its fullness and sense of bliss only when womanhood has been nurtured to full expression and vigour in a wholesome climate of freedom. Viewed this way, motherhood is never the antithesis of com-plete independence.'

'Such talk from you sounds like a sermon.'

Basanti felt a little hurt. 'I spoke because you wanted to hear me. I didn't want to inflict a lecture on you.'

'What you're saying makes me think you're projecting your own hopes and desires onto all women.'

'Very well then, if that's what you want to believe. I wouldn't want to try to persuade you otherwise.'

'So, is your cherished goal to gain complete independence?'

Basanti answered coolly. 'Yes, it is.'

'Have you set your heart on an extreme kind of freedom that will upend the life of our poor Deba bhai?'

Basanti remained calm. 'If I had, wouldn't his world already have been upended, since I've been espousing this ideal for such a long time?'

Braja became agitated. 'You'd better take a close look at the path you're following. Day-dreaming and star-gazing have dire outcomes.'

Pausing a little and breaking into a taunting smile, he continued. 'I had no idea you were such an extremist.'

'An extremist? Yes, you could say that. It goes against my nature to downplay what my conscience and judgment consider to be right and to take the middle of the road for fear of being socially ostracised. That way I'm a pure individualist.'

An intriguing smile traced its course on Braja's lips. He got up from his chair and remarked, in a voice laden with irony, 'I'm off now. I'll be back another day for another lecture.' This uncalled-for insult hurt Basanti and she did not respond. Braja made his exit.

Just a short while after Braja left, Debabrata strode into the room. Noticing his unusual seriousness, Basanti was alarmed. He blurted out, 'I was on the veranda and heard your lecture. Complete autonomy is your goal in life; what you're wishing for is freedom from the beast in the shape of man. That's your deepest wish, isn't it? If you'd shared this with me earlier, you wouldn't have lost anything. All right, I won't let your act of betrayal spoil the rest of my life.' Saying this, he made as if to storm out. Basanti wanted to stop him and tell him, 'Please hear me out before you get angry. I only want that freedom whose mantra you have inspired me with.' But, feeling inhibited, she could not speak. The next moment she heard his voice downstairs; he was yelling for Dhania.

Twenty[*]

The day was well advanced. The scorching rays of a silent midday sun were fading but there was no sign of Debabrata. He had vanished since yesterday. The last words he had spoken still reverberated in Basanti's ears: 'I won't let your act of betrayal spoil the rest of my life.' Try as she might, she was unable to fathom what he had meant. Without being aware of it, she was shaking, as if afraid for some unknown reason, and was turning the pages of her diary, sighing deeply from time to time. While turning the pages lackadaisically, her eyes fell on the events of one particular day:

Deba bhai had been absent from Cuttack for days, off to some place with his group on a famine relief mission. One day, when I was seated on the rooftop, he came up behind me and covered my eyes. Knowing from his touch who it was, I said, 'Please let go, Deba bhai.' I had thought I would be cross with him, but this incident changed things and that didn't happen. 'Where have you been for such a long time, Deba bhai? Why didn't you stay there for good with your bohemian friends? How is it you've remembered to head my way after such a long time?' Deba bhai

* By Sarala Devi.

smiled and said, 'Basa! The bohemian way of life hasn't taken hold in India. And for everyone in this state, educated as well as uneducated, this idea is somewhat alien. You might know the word, but even you don't know what it means. An Eastern version of bohemianism is well-nigh impossible in a country that won't even allow members of the opposite sex to mingle as friends, where the very thought of that constitutes a terrible threat to people's moral intelligence. Believe me, I would like to return to the age of Kalidasa. How could he have composed such vibrant and beautiful poetry unless the society of his time was more appealing than ours?' This led to the subject of modern women and their liberation. I said, 'One hears of many educated women in other provinces of India who have gone to school and graduated. They must be enlightened, mustn't they?'

Deba bhai responded. 'Enlightened independent Indian women? Pray tell me where they are. That's just wishful thinking, because your experience is very limited. The women you think are liberated haven't tasted even a drop of independence. Do you think people become free simply by wearing shoes and socks? If that was what it meant to be independent, then "the liberation of women" would not be worth one paisa.' 'Okay then, do you mean to say that even Christian and Brahmo women aren't liberated?' Deba bhai spoke firmly, as he struck his hand with his fist. 'Yes I do. Please don't get me wrong, I'm not casting aspersions on any community. Nor am I in favour of criticising for the sake of criticising. But in my opinion, what Brahmo and Christian women, and a few women of the Hindu community like you, have obtained in the name of independence is false. On the contrary, it's Hindu women from the lower social stratum who have a kind of independence that equals or maybe even surpasses yours. These women are able to eke out a living without a man's support. They have the same right to earn a livelihood as their male counterparts. They come and go wherever they like: the bazaar, the riverbank, the fields. You'll be surprised to hear this, but women from the untouchable class support their husbands and raise the children if their husbands are drunkards and squander away their meagre earnings on drink. But what atrocities do the husbands visit on them on the slightest pretext! Would you say that you and your friends and the women you're talking about are more evolved than them? Not at all. You wouldn't be able to manage for a moment without the support of a man. Whether in the Brahmo community or your new Hindu community, men everywhere think of women only as property. You can't do anything except by a man's leave. You are probably not much different from those you write off as dyed-in-the-wool conservatives, maybe even worse. Men have you under surveillance 24 hours a day, which only shows they don't trust you. And when you think they do, they're only pretending. So tell me Basa, how are educated modern men, who brag about belonging to the new age, different from the men of ancient times? All right, let me give an example. Supposing you go out on our own without anybody's permission, move around town freely until midnight, and then return home. What would be the reaction?' 'My parents would be angry and shout at me.' 'But would they do that if you were a man? Today it's the father who gets angry; tomorrow it'll be the turn of the father-in-law or the husband. That's your plight. Can that be called independence?'

'Couldn't there be a good reason for their getting angry? Aren't there all sorts of things to be afraid of, some well-known and others unknown, when a young woman ventures out here onto the street on her own?'

'In every country there are things to be afraid of, but the women of Europe and America don't pay attention to those dangers. Don't you know how freely and uninhibitedly they move about on the streets and in the trains? Should we call it independence if people who claim to benefit from it can't look after themselves? Its meaning is incomprehensible to me.

In fact, there are many women in the Christian and Brahmo communities in this country who can be said to have made quite a bit of progress on the road to independence. But let me remind you of the English adage, "One cuckoo does not a spring make." The point is that real liberation of women does not exist in India, be it in the ancient society, or the new Hindu community, or the Brahmo community—this is true everywhere in India, no matter what appearances might suggest. You have to learn to look at the whole picture. There is the possibility for women to be liberated in the Christian and Brahmo communities, but only the possibility—it's not yet a reality.'

'Deba bhai! The unrestricted freedom you're talking about can exist in Western countries. That sort of thing won't thrive in the climate of the East. It's bound to lead to disorder and indiscipline instead of to peace and order in social and family life as required by the Indian tradition.'

What you say is true. That may happen during the first phase of liberation, but how can that be true of later phases? Japan is in the East and has already put it to the test. Western religion and social codes may differ from those in India, but aren't people the same everywhere? Can there be any difference between the nature of women here and the nature of women there? Besides, compared to our country, life in theirs is more orderly, even though the extremely stressful life there does not give people a moment to stand and stare. Haven't you heard how the pressure of work is turning men into machines day by day? Everything in that world—starting with industry, commerce and factories, to the daily rituals of eating, dressing and travelling—goes like clockwork. If you look closely, you'll find women at the root of all that. Is there a parallel in our country and society? Everyone in our country is a slacker, everyone is undisciplined.

'Deba bhai, you seem so open and accepting of the liberation of women. Tell me, if you marry, will you give your wife the ample freedom you're talking about?' Deba bhai became agitated. 'Basanti, I object to this idea of "giving," and I always will. No one can give independence to another person. It has to be taken by force by asserting oneself.'

After remaining silent a while, he continued. 'But I can say this much. If my wife-to-be wants to act independently, then I won't interfere in the least in anything she does, won't put up the slightest resistance. She'll be protected from evil by her own conscience. I won't allow myself to exercise my "husbandly" control in the name of my "duty" towards my wife. I feel ashamed having to explain myself. As long as I haven't shown this by my actions, isn't lecturing the same as playing a battle scene on the stage?'

Lowering my face and smiling, I said, 'All right, if I live I shall see whether this is what you truly believe or are only paying lip service to.'

Deba bhai answered, smiling playfully, 'Yes, of course you'll certainly see, because in the coming days no one will have as good a chance to see me as you will. Maybe you know this, and I'm certain of it.' I left the rooftop and came down, making a face at him as I did. Deba bhai made his way to my mother.

Basanti put down her diary and compared in her mind that incident with what had happened today. Her life seemed to her like some baffling illusion spun by a famous magician. Only one question kept on echoing in the depths of her deeply troubled mind: Is the Deba bhai of that time the same person as her husband Debabrata?

Twenty-One[*]

Evening came, and there was still no sign of Debabrata. Basanti was in the habit of bathing more than once a day, even in winter. But today she skipped her evening bath and did not do her hair. She changed her clothes and came into the room, sitting near the light. The postman had delivered a letter before sundown. The letter was long and the light at dusk poor, so she had put it in a box without reading it. Now she took it out. Her bosom friend Suniti had written after many days.

My dear Flower,

I have been noticing for some time now that your letters have been reduced to a trickle and my replies have been as short as your letters have been long. That's why I feel you might have taken something amiss. A short letter, unlike a long one, leaves room for misunderstanding. Brevity makes it difficult to determine the writer's intentions. All of this is troublesome, so what am I to do? You know very well I'm incapable of writing long letters. Today, however, I went back over all of yours. That's why I've sat down, pen in hand, to speak of a few things. This letter will likely be very long.

* By Sarala Devi.

I can well understand that day by day you're becoming fatalistic and more morose, that you're growing disenchanted with yourself. This is clear from the negative thoughts your letters reflect. I can see very well that you're finding it difficult to be your own self and follow your natural way along the path of life. There's something standing in your way that you're unable to cope with.

What a change from our childhood! We used to spend our days at peace, but now it seems that the hassles and turmoil of domestic life have cast a shadow over your always lively and cheerful mind, which used to flit about like a colourful butterfly in spring. But don't think that I haven't also changed. The world's constantly in flux: the miracle of adaptation that takes place constantly in nature keeps creation alive. Do you think my life's full of joy because, unlike you, I haven't been battered and crushed by worldly woes? You're mistaken. Does the suffering of man always have to be connected to the world? It can be without basis—a suffering that comes from existence itself, a pain that's bittersweet in nature!

Maybe God wants man to know the pain of living in the world, and especially the pain of attachment. Wherever you look, you see an endless sea of sorrow. Is there a shore, sister? If we focus only on our personal life and its sorrows, we will be thwarted in our purpose. But it's also true that any talk about embracing the suffering of the universe is merely talk, unless it has a basis in a person's life, in a person's hardships and needs. What I want to say to you is this: please don't focus on your own grief, troubles, and requirements. Try instead to rise above them and empathise with the suffering of humanity. If you can do this, your burden will be significantly diminished and you'll feel a surge of power within you. My feeling is that suffering and sorrow of the highest magnitude enriches the soul. Anyone who has realised this great truth has probably been bloodied and hurt badly, but has stood firm and unflustered in the face of the deprivations and troubles of life.

'For the world's more full of weeping than you can understand.' Your own experience will explain to you the deeper meaning of these verses by a Western poet. What's the use of always being gloomy, my dear friend? We ought to be prepared to embrace whatever comes. That is true heroism. Struggle is a part of life. Without struggle life may be peaceful and beautiful in a philosophical sense, but in my view such a life is drab. A person living such a life places the self above all else; she's impoverished indeed.

Call it what you will, fate, destiny, the unseen or the unforeseen, I won't accept it even if I am subjected to the worst crisis and suffering. There's no point in waiting for the day when man will be dispirited and weak, no use at all in dreaming about the future. It's best to live in the present. I think it's our duty to take the sorrow along with the joy, to take the rough with the smooth. The right thing to do is to rely on one's life force at every step of the way and to accept its indications as benedictions. Humanity has a chance to flower in the face of adversity. Accomplishment may be measured by wealth, honours, glory, and fame, but the greatest accomplishment of all is to pursue happiness by defeating the forces of adversity using one's inner reserves of strength. Of course, this is an uphill task for ordinary mortals like us, isn't it? Just pray to the Almighty:

The day grief overpowers
And delivers the message of the storm clouds
Allow me to share that dark night of grief
Singing all the while.

You will see what a surge of happiness you will feel.

You say you lack the strength to bear such a heavy burden of failure. You're human and, what's more, a woman. Why are you giving up so quickly, my dear friend? I find it hard to believe, whatever you may say. I don't have the strength to comfort you in your distress. Sometimes, like you, I too sink into gloom, but when I sing to myself the songs that give me succour in times of trouble, my mind swells with joy. Hope inspires me to go on.

I used to write off the desire for happiness as a poet's fancy, but new experiences have led me to the firm conclusion that this is not so. This desire is a proven truth of human existence. How wonderful, expansive, and endlessly beautiful is life! Where is the limit to nature's exquisite artistry? This question has stirred many a soul since the day of creation. But why hasn't anyone been able to get to the root of the enigma? All our thoughts have failed to take the measure of the ultimate mystery that eternity is. If you see things as separate and fragmented, the flaws, cracks, and limitations will appear magnified, but if you look at life in its totality, taking a cue from nature, then you will see how beautiful it is and how miraculous is the manifestation of the eternal in it!

Pessimism seems to loom large in our life, but in truth it is not that important. The pessimist will naturally wallow in misery, regarding as real the opposite of what the optimist holds true. In your life, at this point, the dark side of the universe dominates your vision. Do try to be an optimist. Suffering is blessing in life; accept it as a gift from the maker.

My dear Basanti flower, I have read your essays. Didn't Deba Babu once take umbrage after reading your essay on the plight of women? Didn't your crime consist, according to him, in drawing people's attention to the social injustice that's hidden behind willful blindness and mere glibness? The patch covers the wound, but does not heal it. For that, treatment is necessary. If in the process you suffer criticism and calumny, I firmly believe you'll wear them gloriously like precious ornaments adorning your head. Those of our brothers who are not afraid of resolving the problem that you wish to raise before the nation will definitely come forward in response to your call.

So much about you. Now let me say a little about myself.

I'm an idealist, and I die of shame every time the practical man boasts of having achieved the most by doing the least, with scant regard for the means employed, because this to me spells the death of the idealist.

The more experience I gain, the more my responsibilities multiply. In a situation where ideals are forever undermined by opportunism, it's an uphill battle not to give in to the lure of convenience. But it's all the more necessary not to do so. Once I read the shloka on the first page of your diary: 'Consciousness is not attainable by the weak.' Do keep that in mind at all times.

My idealism will always remain intact, even after confronting the naked, fierce, and stark face of reality. I may stumble against life's obstacles at every step, but I will love the world. I do not share the pessimism of those who have eyes only for the suffering, deception, and vices of the world. There is only one form of heroism in the world: to see the world as it is, and to love it. I increasingly feel this statement by Romain Rolland contains great wisdom. My hope is that you too will be blessed by such a realisation. You may disagree with what I have to say on some points, but my solicitude and concern will always be there to raise your spirits. We need not achieve something extraordinary nor be someone great, nor is there need for regret if we come to nothing. The important thing is for us to be good and just. People have many different pursuits: some excel in work, others in worship, and still others in their studies or other fields. Whatever I may be in the eyes of the world, I'll always strive to be true to myself. My head should not hang low when I explain myself to myself. I have written a lot today. Farewell.

Affectionately yours,
Boula Flower

A new wave of hope and joy surged through Basanti as she finished reading the letter. She felt her sentiments echoed in Suniti's. She got up from her chair, went up to the roof, and started to pace back and forth, feeling deeply satisfied. Her heart felt much lighter than it had for many days. What a feeling of relief!

Twenty-Two[*]

The day Braja came to his house Debabrata was feeling very low for some reason and had sought refuge in a siesta after his meal to try to temporarily escape his worries. But to no avail. Had Braja come by earlier the dreary afternoon hours could have been filled with relaxing conversation, but he arrived very late. Debabrata kept tossing and turning on his bed all through the afternoon. At times he missed not having someone with him, at others he was filled with inexplicable anger. Unable to understand his own reactions, he kept staring blankly at the ceiling. In a vain attempt to ease his torment, he carried on a dialogue with himself. 'Have I been unfair to her? Certainly not. I haven't failed in my duty as a husband. I can't cite any witnesses other than my conscience. But has she been able to accept me the way she should have? No, instead she has made wrong assumptions, become upset, and then blamed me for the state she was in. She must think her ties to me are simply fetters and grieve over that. Why would she, who loves to think and act of her own free will, not be thinking her husband is being kind to her and taking care of her only as he would a slave, only out of a sense of duty? Over the past few months I have noticed

* By Sarala Devi.

that her thoughts are inclined that way. She remains aloof and distant. Her face becomes pale the moment she sees me, as if she has almost stepped on a snake. I may not notice a great deal, but at least I can see if a person's attitude changes. Will tying more knots in a frayed string make it stronger? That's like a poor man mending a torn and tattered shirt to make it last longer.'

He had to stop brooding over this. He began to pace on the veranda in a state of utter agitation, unaware that Braja had arrived and was engaged in conversation with Basanti. While pacing about aimlessly he caught sight of a torn piece of blue paper in the wastepaper basket in the corner. Curious, he took it out. He recognised Basanti's handwriting. This was what was written on it:

'... as if the air has been poisoned, my joyful dream shattered—I'll not continue to live. I'm writing this letter to you in the hope that you at least will understand that a death of the mind is much more dreadful than a death of the body. You might think I'm as happy as a princess, but maybe not even someone living in a hut would envy me. I can't possibly believe this prison is any better than a Government jail. Please come and take me away from this hell hole. Save me! I'm appealing to you because I have no one else to rely on. But don't you already know this? I await your reply. If this last hope leads nowhere, there'll be nothing left but to try and draw the curtain on this miserable life of mine. There's no other...'

Debabrata did not even realise that the letter had slipped from his hand. He stared vacantly into space, as if in the thrall of a ghost. The earth under his feet seemed to have given way. Coming somewhat to his senses, he thought, 'Well, I wasn't wrong, was I? She's continued to play act with me in the name of social convention, although she has taken a lover in secret. God! Basanti... a woman without character! Oh, no, what am I imagining?' He kicked away the piece of paper. A moment later he picked it up again and stared at it. 'This is definitely her handwriting. Addressed to some saviour. I may not believe it when the whole world speaks against her, but how can I not believe my own eyes? How I wish I had gone blind before reading this!' His mind could not function any longer, and he went and sprawled out in the armchair. That was when the words an agitated Basanti was uttering to Braja in the next room began to resonate in his ears.

'A radical? Yes, you could say that. It goes against my nature to downgrade what my conscience and judgement consider right and take the middle of the road for fear of being socially ostracised.' Already riled up, Debabrata became even more embittered with Basanti. 'How base this Basanti is! She has no qualms about hiding her own unseemly thoughts and ugly ambition under words such as "judgement" and "conscience". Shame on her!' Filled with disgust, he stepped inside the room moments after Braja made his exit. What happened next, the readers already know.

The fire in the kitchen at Debabrata's house had not been lit since his disappearance the day before. Attempts to find him had led to nothing. This morning the servants had managed with a mouthful of watered rice, but neither Deba's mother nor Basanti had touched a morsel of food or sipped a drop of water the whole day. Now the day was done, and still there was no sign of Debabrata. The clock struck midnight. The starved household had embraced sleep out of sheer exhaustion with the exception of Basanti—who was wide awake. Panicking from time to time, she would look out the window into the street or fling herself onto the bed. Suddenly, she heard the sound of a carriage racing along the road, tearing through the night's utter stillness. It came to a halt in front of the house and soon somebody could be heard calling 'Rama', 'Rama'. No answer. Then 'Nidhia', 'Nidhia'. Nidhia did not come. Dhania, asleep, was woken up by the master's shouts. He called out 'yes' and ran to the front of the house carrying a lantern. There he saw the carriage. Debabrata called out from inside, 'Go and call the young Saantani.' Nonplussed, Dhania continued to stare and did not move. Debabrata spoke to him sternly. 'Have you gone deaf, you fool? Didn't I tell you to call the young Saantani? Move.'

Dhania had never seen the master in such an angry mood. At these threatening words he beat a hasty retreat. The threats, faint in the distance, fell on Basanti's ears. When she got up to find out what the matter was, Dhania arrived. 'The master's calling for you,' he told her. A dazed Basanti followed Dhania without a word. Her heart began to pound, anticipating some unnamed danger.

Seeing Basanti, Debabrata spoke from inside the carriage, 'Come here!' Basanti went and stood timidly near the steps of the carriage. Debabrata took her by the hand. 'Get in and sit down,' he ordered. Without a word she got in and took her seat. As Debabrata pulled her in, she could feel his sweat-soaked hand trembling violently.

Any desire to make sense of what was happening had left her. She sat quietly on one side of the carriage. Debabrata told the coachman to drive. The carriage started to move quickly. Dhania was left standing, lantern in hand, like a fool. Once the carriage had gone beyond the village limits, Debabrata told the coachman to halt. The carriage stopped. Debabrata cleared his throat and said gravely, 'Basanti, today you have obtained your release from me. You may go wherever you like. If you languish in my prison-like home you will end your life, and I want no part in the crime of killing a woman. I also don't want to give your saviour the trouble of taking pains to come for you. It's better you deliver yourself to him. I've had enough of a lesson and have been put through an ordeal because of you. No more. I didn't know you were a woman without character, but God saved me yesterday by opening my eyes. I am breaking my ties with you; I am free from all obligations. You have no place by my side from this moment forward.'

He was about to turn his back to her and leave but thought of something. He felt in his pocket. 'Yes, you might need money. It's my duty to see you're provided for when I let you go. Here, take this.' He took out a thick envelope containing a wad of notes. Then he said to the coachman in Hindi, 'Drive the carriage to the station.'

Basanti was stunned; she could not utter even a word. The two horses sped like arrows. In the faint light outside, she could make out that Debabrata's face had become white and bloodless like a corpse's. His eyes seemed to light up for an instant before losing their lustre. His body seemed ghostly, lean, and dark. He was disappearing into the night as he tottered along the narrow lane hedged by thorns. Like the moon about to sink at daybreak, Basanti's sweet face took on a deathly pallor. Regaining her senses as if awakening from a dream, she heaved a long sigh and wiped the beads of sweat from her face and body. 'Me, a woman without character? Let us see!'

Twenty-Three*

The soft and mellow Phalguna sun was waning. Churning up a sea of dust, a carriage bearing four young women was advancing slowly along the road in Darghabazaar. Judging by their clothes the women were educated and modern. They were all seated quietly, but one was casting her eyes about anxiously.

Suddenly one of the others asked, 'My dear Suku, why is your dear friend—your Golapa, your rose—so on edge today?'

Sukumari smiled. 'Don't you know, sister Mira? Someone's beau is to arrive today.'

Mira wanted to know more. 'Really?' she asked. Sukumari was about to add something, but she caught sight of the look on her Golapa's face. The usually playful eyes of her dear friend were filled with reproach. 'No, I said that in jest,' said Sukumari. 'My Golapa was saying his work isn't finished. How could he leave Puri before it's done?' This did not satisfy Mira. She looked at Sukumari's bosom friend. 'Relax, Suniti. We're not asking for a share in your prize. Why so much secrecy?'

Suniti spoke up, her tone one of exasperation. 'Really, sister Mira, how can you believe anything my sweet devil Golapa says?'

* By Sarat Chandra Mukherjee.

The fourth woman in the carriage was slightly older than the other three. At Suniti's words she heaved a sigh and addressed Sukumari, 'Suku, this is one of your bad habits. Why do you always go after Suniti? She's only a child after all. Don't you have any sympathy for her plight?' After a while she resumed, 'Who knows what sorrow lies dormant in someone's heart? What need is there to poke repeatedly at the place that is sore?'

Everyone was driven into silence by her words of reproach. The carriage came to a halt in front of a small building in Petin Sahi. Suniti got out with her books and notebooks and started to walk away, casting a sarcastic look at Sukumari. Sukumari called after her, pleading, 'For my sake Golapa, please don't be angry. I'm begging you. I spoke without thinking.' Suniti did not answer.

All the women were teachers at Cuttack Girls' School, some new and some experienced. Suniti was among the recently appointed. Sukumari was Suniti's Golapa. Earlier in the day when they were walking in the school's garden during recess, Suniti had remarked, 'You'll see, my Golapa, he'll surely show up today.' 'How do you know? Has he written?' Sukumari asked. 'No, nothing like that. That's what my heart's telling me. I can feel his presence all around me; it's as if someone's whispering in my ear, "he'll come".' As she was saying this, Suniti's whole being was filled with a strange excitement and her face lit up with a smile. She pressed Sukumari's hands strongly. 'Dear Golapa, he's certain to come today. Can the prompting of my heart be wrong? No, never.' 'All right, let's make an astrological calculation,' said Sukumari, and she promptly sat down to do it. The stars predicted he would arrive. Suniti smiled mischievously. 'Golapa, you sweet devil, you're rigging the calculation to make it coincide with what I want. If he doesn't come, then tomorrow I'll box your ears.' Sukumari too smiled slyly. 'No, my dear, you won't have to wait until tomorrow. You'll get a pair of ears to box today, a pair of elephant ears.' 'What did you say, you little devil?' As she said this, Suniti chased after Sukumari as if to give her a dressing down, but just then the school bell sounded. The two friends went off to attend to their duties. That day Suniti was unable to concentrate on her lessons. Seeing their teacher in a playful mood, the students set to gossiping. The head mistress of the school, a memsahib with a fiery temper, noticed what was happening when she passed by the classroom. She called Suniti outside and spoke to her harshly. 'Okay, you'll soon be leaving this school and going somewhere else, but your students won't be leaving with you. They have to write their examinations and pass. Do you understand?' By then, Suniti's cheerful mood had abandoned her. When Sukumari, unaware of this, raised the subject dear to Suniti's heart, Suniti became irritated with her.

Suniti got down from the carriage and started to walk towards her house, trying not to be seen. She tiptoed into the house. The thought of arriving unannounced and by surprise made her heart beat rapidly, but when she came into the sitting room she found the chairs empty; there was no one there. She sat down in a pensive mood, the urge to cry rising from deep within her again and again. After some time, she called out 'Mother, mother' impatiently, but Kalyani Devi was not home. From another room the old woman caretaker answered. 'Dear girl, mother's gone to Makrabag. Joseph's daughter-in-law has given birth to a son, but he's unlikely to live. Mother's gone to see him. What a sweet child!' A beautiful image of a child materialised before Suniti's eyes. She forgot her own disappointment for a while and began to think about the baby. After seeing it she had often wondered about when she would be blessed with one.

Evening came. Suniti wrote a letter and sent it to be posted. 'Dearest, I am not writing to oblige you to remember a creature as insignificant as me, and thereby waste your precious time. You wrote you had fever. If only you could let me know how your health is now. I hope that doing so will not put your valuable national work in jeopardy. You most certainly will not think it necessary to give your attention to anyone who is crushed under the chariot wheels of your work for the nation, but remember, I am not dead yet. Your unfortunate, Suniti.' The caretaker put the letter in the post; on her return she told Suniti that Kalyani Devi would be late as the baby's condition had worsened.

Suniti sat in the garden with her harmonium. The small garden glistened under the rays of the 10th-day moon and the flowers in bloom seemed to be laughing. Suniti thought to herself, 'He did not arrive during daytime. Will he come by a night train or bus?' Sitting on the small raised platform in the garden, she called out, 'Nutu, Nutu, Nutu ...' A puppy lying on the veranda came running and started to whimper, indicating his displeasure at the harmonium having taken his place in Suniti's lap. Suniti stroked his head and asked, 'Nutu, want to hear a song?' Nutu's protests became louder. Feigning anger she said, 'Stop it Nutu, don't disturb me while I'm singing. Listen quietly.' Saying this she started to play the harmonium. Nutu buried his little head between Suniti's small legs and silently enjoyed the music.

Suniti sang a Bangla song: 'The breeze has whispered into my ear that you my dearest will come. You will come and end my heartache with your sweet touch of love. Your arrival has been declared to me by the sun, the moon, and the whole of the natural world, you my dear will come.' When the song came to an end, Nutu raised his head and looked at Suniti. 'Did you like it, Nutu?' she asked. Nutu stared vacantly at Suniti. As she placed the harmonium on the ground, Nutu leapt into her lap. She held him with both hands. 'Nutu, your feet are dirty. You're becoming cheekier day by day, soiling my clothes all the time. If you do that again...' Saying this, she gave him a mild tap. Feeling her comforting touch Nutu closed his eyes. Suniti shook him a little and asked, 'Tell me, Nutu, won't he come?' Nutu kept on staring at his loving mistress helplessly. Crushing

Nutu to her bosom, Suniti said, 'Don't worry, Nutu, he'll come, surely he will. Maybe not today, maybe not tomorrow, maybe not ever in this life, but some day he has to come for sure. Don't worry, Nutu.' Nutu kept whimpering, his face fully hidden, as if to say, 'I'm merely thinking. But you have nearly worn yourself thin thinking. Why then don't you comfort yourself with the thought he'll come?'

Suniti put Nutu down and picked up her harmonium. 'Listen to another song, Nutu,' she said. As he had done before, Nutu hid his face between her legs without protest. Suniti sang another Bangla song: 'My pleasure lies in waiting for your footsteps upon this road. The rays of the sun are withdrawing after setting everything aglow, the shadows are dancing, the rain is coming, spring is coming. My pleasure lies only in waiting for your footsteps upon this road.'

The small garden seemed to come alive to the rhythm of the music. The evening breeze began to gently shake the trees and creepers, as though they were eager to feel the touch of some unknown guest and were echoing Suniti's song: 'Our pleasure too lies in waiting for someone's footsteps upon this road.' The moon and stars began to smile in the sky; the vast expanse of sky resplendent in the moonlight seemed to laugh out loud: 'Our pleasure too lies in waiting for someone's footsteps upon this road.' Seeing her feelings mirrored in the surrounding nature, Suniti began to sing ecstatically: 'My pleasure lies in waiting for your footsteps upon this road.'

Two hands suddenly reached from behind her and covered her eyes. She stopped singing, overwhelmed with happiness. A startled Nutu saw that a tall young man had placed his hands over his mistress's eyes and was smiling. He found this sort of insolence intolerable, and barked in protest. Putting the harmonium down, Suniti pressed the hands of the young man as she said, 'Shame on you Nutu, don't you recognise people?' Nutu fell silent.

They were meeting after three long months. Suniti had planned that the next time they met she would sulk, not speak to him, etc., but the pleasure she now felt made these promises vanish into thin air. Putting slightly more pressure on the young man's hands, Suniti said, 'Let go.'

The young man removed his hands from her eyes and asked, smiling, as he lowered himself onto the platform, 'Whose arrival makes you feel so happy? Who's that fortunate person, Suniti?' She did not reply. She sat, hiding her blushing face in his lap. The enchanted young man ran his fingers through her dishevelled hair.

Readers know this young man. He is Ramesh Chandra Mohapatra, Debabrata's friend. He had been introduced to Kalyani Devi's family through Basanti and Debabrata. Kalyani Devi was impressed with his sincerity and good character, and regarded him as a son. She allowed him to associate with Suniti. In the course of time the conversations between Ramesh and Suniti took on a different tone; for Suniti he was successively 'Mr. Mohapatra', 'Ramesh Babu', 'Ramesh', ending up finally as 'dearest'. Kalyani Devi was not unaware of the gradual unfolding of their love for each other. She observed it and was pleased about it. She was a committed follower of Jesus, but the narrowness of communal feeling found no place in her heart. Readers have already seen how she overcame any sense of discrimination to become Nirmala Devi's closest friend.

The affection Ramesh and Suniti had for each other soon attracted the attention of the neighbours; after a while, everyone understood they would marry. The leaders of the Christian community turned against Kalyani Devi. Reverend Simaltan came to her house and asked her, 'Is what I'm hearing about Suniti's marriage true?' 'Yes, by God's grace, my darling will soon marry Ramesh,' she replied. Padre Sahib became agitated. 'The Lord God will never be pleased with such a marriage. You know Ramesh is a heathen. He hasn't heard the enlightened word of Jesus. He'll never be able to go to heaven. His soul's condemned.' He was about to utter something even worse, when Kalyani Devi interrupted him. 'Padre Sahib, I've often told you I don't believe in such things. If what you say is true, that people who do not have the benefit of the word of Jesus are condemned to eternal perdition, then many great men mentioned in the Bible must be rotting in hell. Between the time of Adam and Eve and that of Jesus innumerable people on the face of the earth never heard of Jesus. Even after the advent of Jesus many people have not heard His name. Will all of them go to hell? It's misguided, Padre Sahib, to believe that the large number of honest, religious, and fair-minded men and women in this vast country would rot in hell, while for the small number of Christians like us, no matter how wretched, the door to heaven would open of its own accord—isn't all this simply preposterous?' Kalyani Devi's quiet manner and reasonable argument made the Sahib even angrier: 'You know very well that if Ramesh isn't a Christian the marriage can't be performed in my church.' 'I do know that very well,' answered Kalyani Devi. 'Not only not in your church, the marriage can't be performed in the religious institutions of any other community either. I won't try to persuade Ramesh to convert to Christianity, nor will I ask Suniti to give up the Christian religion. Let them remain as they are. The dusty road the Lord God has chosen as His refuge after being turned out of your religious institutions will be where I will seek the dust from His feet, holding the hands of Ramesh and my daughter. That will be their marriage.' Padre Sahib could not keep his calm any longer. Leaving in a huff, he said, 'Satan will be the ruin of you before long.' At the Padre's curse Kalyani Devi looked helplessly at the photograph of the crucified Jesus on the wall, thinking, 'Lord, why do people behave so terribly despite taking your name?' The photograph seemed to come alive. The serene and compassionate gaze of Jesus fell on Kalyani Devi's face, and she could see blessings streaming from His eyes and hear words of encouragement repeated over and over, 'No need to fear, Kalyani.' The next moment it seemed to Kalyani Devi that Jesus's gaze had turned slightly upwards, as if He was beginning to say with folded hands to someone, 'Father, father, forgive them, for they know not what they do.' From that day Kalyani Devi felt stronger, and she decided that despite enormous odds Suniti would marry Ramesh. The people of the Christian community were already acquainted with the firmness of her resolve. She was ostracised from that very day thanks to Padre Simaltan's 'kindness' and denied access to the church in Petin Sahi. From that day no one ever came to collect from her for Christmas or other Christian festivals and she never received invitations to social festivities.

After Basanti left for her mother-in-law's Suniti passed her First Arts examination and became a teacher at the Girls' School. Ramesh remained in the service of the country as before. Because of this, he was frequently away from Cuttack for long periods of time. For the past three months he had been in Puri on famine relief work. Today, he had come back.

Suniti asked, 'Where are you put up?'

'With a friend in the college hostel.'

'Oh, it would seem that our house has a bitter taste for you.'

'No, why? In fact, I have some work there.'

'Work be praised!'

Suniti heaved a sigh. Ramesh smiled.

'Are you keeping well?'

'Do you still have fever? Is your health all right?'

'My health? Very good. Don't you see how I'm gaining weight with every passing day. Even Yama, the God of death, will lose his appetite.' Suniti was in a mood to go on, but Ramesh covered her mouth.

They fell to talking about Debabrata and Basanti. 'I haven't had a letter from Boula for nearly two months,' remarked Suniti.

'Didn't even get a reply to the one I sent.' 'The same with me,' replied Ramesh. 'I've been going around the countryside near Konark for two months with no chance of meeting anyone from Balasore. I've written, but there's been no reply. I've no idea how they are.'

Kalyani Devi got back around 9 p.m. Ramesh touched her feet. As she patted his head, she asked, 'Are you well my son?'

'Yes, Ma, I'm fine.'

Kalyani Devi had them sit on the platform. She stood behind them and stroked their heads lovingly. All were silent. After a while large tears began to rain down on their heads in benediction. Ramesh kept on sitting silently, taking Suniti's hand in his. The next moment Kalyani Devi was overcome with emotion and drew them close to her. Bringing their heads to her bosom, she showered them with her blessings. The sound of a song in someone's tremulous voice came floating in from a distance:

> This union God
> You have arranged
> At an auspicious hour.
> With your calming touch
> This enchanted heart
> Has tasted a new life.

X X X

Kalyani Devi gave a letter to Suniti. 'The postman delivered this after you left for school today. The handwriting seems to be Basanti's. Read it to see what she has to say.'

Suniti and Ramesh read the letter. There was no way of knowing where it had been posted. The name of the place was not given, and the postage stamp was the Railway Mail Service's. The address given in the letter was a private box number at the newspaper. This is what Basanti had written:

Boula of my life. Forget, please forget, your unfortunate friend. I am presumed untrustworthy and my name is supposed to make all chaste women cover their ears. Do you understand?

I have been turned out of the house for over a month now because I am not to be trusted; I'm in the street today. All the signals that the street makes to a woman—I am a witness to all of those, Boula. I am at my wit's end, trying to fathom how strange I am, how strange this world is!

You don't need to know where I am; maybe no one needs to know. I will receive your letter if you send it to the address given below. If you would not consider yourself tarnished, if Ramesh Babu would not consider it improper for you to keep in touch with a woman of loose morals, then please write. Yours Boula.

Box 3561
The Statesman,
Calcutta

Ramesh and Suniti were both stunned. Debabrata had turned Basanti out of the house thinking she was untrustworthy! Unbelievable! Ramesh spoke in an agitated voice, 'No, no, that's impossible!' Calmly Suniti answered, 'Nothing is impossible on the part of the cruel male race.' Unperturbed, Kalyani Devi smiled a little when she heard all they had to say. 'No need for you people to become so worked up,' she said. 'No need to be worried even if Basanti has really had to leave her house. They will come together again. Good has come into their life in the shape of evil; there's nothing to fear.'

Twenty-Four*

As the whip fell on their backs, the two horses hitched to the carriage jumped and moved forward. The coachman wiped his hand and carefully pocketed the sweat-soaked five-rupee note Debabrata had given him. He snapped the whip twice more. The two horses, which were almost half dead, hardly reacted to their master's unjust treatment, thinking that 'big people act big', and kept to the task at hand. Their master, seated on the carriage box, was thinking the same thing, as he relished the feel of the tattered currency note between his fingers.

As his fear increased under the darkness of the night, his whip landed on the horses' backs harder and more frequently. His mouth, gone completely dry, was purged of the habitual sounds of 'haw haw' and 'cluck cluck' used to urge them on.

Debabrata did not look back even once before the carriage carrying Basanti disappeared beyond the village limits. He could feel the lashing of a terrible whip falling on him. He had neither the energy nor the will nor the time to look back, the little capacity to feel he was left with giving him no choice in the matter. He was like the two horses, which lived only to

* By Baishnab Charan Das.

run. He was trying his best to get as far away from himself as possible, but still the whip fell where it always had.

Debabrata walked unsteadily, straining to drag his unruly legs forward. To him, though, it was as if he had traversed heaven, hell, and earth, the three worlds in an instant, as if he had moved with exceptional speed! Like the two horses. But try as he might, he could not leave the coach or the whip behind, as if he was bound to them forever, with the strongest of ties. The whip seemed to be pursuing him at a speed faster than even that of the Earth in its orbit.

He did not know when Dhania had turned up, lantern in hand, walking beside him but keeping a safe distance. He was about to pass through the gate to his house when the noise of Dhania opening it brought him back to his senses. He stood there without stirring for God knows how long, his legs refusing to move. Poor Dhania had a thousand questions on the tip of his tongue, but was unable to voice them. After a while he spoke with great difficulty. 'Babu, when will the carriage come? Will you wait here until ...?' 'Shut up,' answered Debabrata, as his blood-shot eyes settled on Dhania for an instant before he began walking quickly toward the house. Dhania was now barely able to keep in front with the lantern.

Once inside Debabrata went straight upstairs. As he was closing his bedroom door, Dhania arrived, saying, as he tried to come inside, 'Babu, the old Saantani has not eaten anything.' Debabrata wanted to rid himself of Dhania and told him to get out. But Dhania stood there helplessly with folded hands. 'Babu, let me bring the old Saantani here for a moment.'

For a time Debabrata did not answer. Then, moved by some thought, he asked, 'Well, Dhania, how long has it been since mother hasn't eaten?'

'Since yesterday, neither the old Saantani nor Ma Saantani has taken even a drop of water. They've been waiting for you.'

Debabrata thought of something else. 'All right, tell me, what was the young Saantani doing these past two days?'

'Sitting and shedding tears. I saw that with my own eyes. Also writing something. And the old Saantani was talking in secret with sister Nisa and others.'

'Yes. All right. I ...'

'Babu, have you eaten anything? I would guess not. Nor has any of us. Ma Saantani served us food as she does every day, but what good could that do, sir, when I only felt like crying.' Dhania was able to say as much as this only because Debabrata had become distracted. Then Dhania began to sob like a child. Debabrata looked up, startled. He suddenly felt like laughing and did so, out loud. This cheered up Dhania, and he added, 'Sister Nisa said she'd quarrel with you when she saw you and that she'd take Ma Saantani to her house and keep her there, that she'd not let her come here. Has she really gone there?' Debabrata's laughter suddenly came to an end. As he was talking Dhania had raised the wick of the lamp on the small table near the head of the bed. Debabrata's eyes fell on the table and on a full-length photograph of Basanti, in a sandalwood frame. From a distance it seemed like the image of a goddess. A divine aura surrounded her face, and her beaming eyes were lifted as she advanced towards him with the promise of some far off magical realm. Was this the same Basanti that he—barbaric, mean, and cowardly that he was—had rejected like a worm crawling underfoot and banished far away on a pitch-black night, alone and helpless! In an instant the stark reality of his arbitrary act became real to him. Could this goddess be tainted, be without character! Yes, that was the heart of the matter; the earlier reserve reasserted itself in his mind, pushing the momentary softening aside. But he was also irresistibly drawn to the photograph. He stood transfixed for some time, staring at the picture. Then suddenly he lurched forward, picked it up and pressed it to his chest, as he burst into a wild fit of sobbing.

'Deba, what's wrong, my son?' Deba's mother asked anxiously, as she came into the room. His sobbing continued with renewed vigour. As the old woman stroked his head and back to soothe him, she asked, 'Where has my daughter-in-law gone, my son?' Having shed many tears, Deba sat leaning against the bed. He wiped his reddened eyes and said, his face lowered, 'Mother, don't ever speak to me about her. She's not here; she has gone back to where she came from.'

'What are you saying! Tell me everything. What inauspicious talk this is! Ram, Ram, may Goddess Durga protect her from harm. My girl is with child!' Debabrata stared at his mother without blinking. He knew nothing of this. He was filled with deep self-loathing and felt within himself an aching void. This turned him to stone. Deba's mother moved closer. 'Why don't you say something?' Sensing anger in the elderly woman's voice, Debabrata looked up. Her panic-stricken face was clouded with doubt. Her eyes were shining fiercely, with an energy he had not seen since his father's death. Afraid, he remained silent. Finally, with great difficulty, his face hung low, he spoke. 'I have turned her out, have driven her away.'

At that, it was as if lightning coursed its way, from tip to toe, through Deba's mother. 'What did you just say? Turned out the daughter-in-law? What has she done wrong? How could you do this, you the grandson of the great Saantara?'

'Mother. Don't say anything more. She's untrustworthy, a fallen woman!'

'A fallen woman? My daughter-in-law's a fallen woman? What are you saying? All right then, you can fend for yourself. I'm leaving this house this instant.'

'Mother!'

'Mother! All has turned to ashes! You're calling me "mother" after all this! What an irony that you were born of me!'

'Mother! Why are you blaming me?'

'I don't know anything. It's you who have decided who's to blame and who's not. Just tell me where my daughter-in-law has gone, and I'll go after her. Alas, a two-month baby in her belly! What can she be doing in the dead of the night. You wretch. You no longer have any shame. It's my fate written on my forehead. You have made this place unlivable for me!'

Debabrata stood there woodenly and listened to all of this. This unexpected resistance from his mother immediately dissolved his tender feelings. His heart, which had begun to repent and soften, hardened in a moment and once again became a barren place. He told his mother about the earlier events. After listening to everything Deba's mother stood up and slowly moved towards the door. She shouted to Dhania. 'Bring the manager here! A palanquin with two bearers is to be made ready in an hour. Move quickly!'

Debabrata was inside his room when he heard her order. He understood what she was intending, but did not utter a word. He understood his mother's nature very well. It was because of injured vanity that she had not opened her mouth to speak on any matter since the day of his marriage, but Debabrata knew how strong she was, knew she had been able to manage the large estate smoothly and for a long time by herself. He also knew the awe and respect she inspired in her account-keepers, servants, labourers, and among people in the village. Seeing how she was reacting he remembered when his father had been around, a time his mother had shone in her full splendour. Today, when he saw his mother as she once had been, he felt fear but also delight, for he had never approved of the way she had played the martyr purely out of self-pity. Sighing deeply, he thought to himself, 'If only mother had always been like this, if only she had always taken me in hand.'

Debabrata had not believed his mother would actually carry out her threat of leaving home, but when at dawn Dhania informed him that the bearers were ready with the palanquin and that the old Saantani would set off after her bath, he was dumbstruck. The next moment, however, a feeling of coldness and cruelty overtook him. In some corner of his mind he felt perverse joy. 'Let it all go. I have led Basanti out by my own hand. Mother will leave now. Let her. Very well.' His mind took pleasure in contemplating total annihilation.

He gave free rein to his thoughts.

Fine. I too will have my revenge. I loved Basanti and she tricked me. She has ruined my life, squandered my happiness and love, and gone away after cruelly crushing my tender feelings. Doesn't she have to atone for such a sin? If justice has any value in this world, if truth must prevail, then she will surely receive her retribution. I did so much for her; indeed, what did I not do for her? And she has paid me back like this! Was my life meant to be a playground for people to play their games of deception as they wished? What harm have I ever done to anyone? Why would everyone dupe me? Why would everyone play with my heart? No, no one in this world truly feels or cares for any other person. Look at my mother, if she had one iota of love for me, would she have turned Basanti's life, nay our married life, to poison? Isn't she the real cause of Basanti's betrayal? Definitely! If only she... Today she has done an about-turn and reprimanded me because I have thrown Basanti out! Everything has been blamed on me!

No, I won't look anybody in the face, I won't listen to what anyone tells me. Let's see how the world will trap me now. I have nothing now that I can call my own. Fine, let everything go. I will accept all criticism, insult, and calumny, and not react. Surely I have that much moral strength! Why should I be afraid? And what possible sorrow could I have? Yes, I admit I feel some resentment. Won't I... Will I be so untrue to myself? Do I know myself so little! No, I will banish this weakness from my mind; I will be vigilant day in and day out against floods of tears and tempests of sighs on account of that temptress, that scandalous creature.

Oh, my Basanti! Basanti of my life! What have you done? To think you are untrustworthy is like a hammer striking my soul! Tell me, please tell me just once that you are not unworthy of trust, tell me just once that you are mine, that you belong to me! That would not lessen your independence; that would not make you less of a woman.

The temptress is laughing. Independence is dear to her heart! But then, how is love contrary to independence? Can love ever be an obstacle to independence? That's impossible! I may steadily go back to mean, small, and ignoble acts, but as long as I do them out of love I am sovereign, not subjected, great, not small! If Basanti's heart had tasted the joy of the freedom that comes from love, then she would not have coveted the external form of freedom, which does not last. All otherworldly forms of bondage fall away before that ultimate freedom to celebrate the triumphant reign of love in the heart. No, she is partial to lawlessness, an extremist; the independence she favours is only another name for anarchy. What education has she received? Only some slick manners and the rules of etiquette! The education of the heart is alien to her. How can someone who finds liberation in confinement, power in servitude, virtue in self-sacrifice, make out the significance of love? I am blind. If I were not, I would not have pinned such hopes on her. I would not be in such a hopeless situation today by erecting such a huge scaffolding on her love for me. But Basanti was unreliable. How was I to know that right from the beginning, and until now, that temptress was deluding me by taking other lovers? I have done the right thing by driving her out. What would I have gained by being an obstacle on her path to happiness and by thus inviting suffering for myself? It is better that she is on her way out! I will not brood over this any longer; no, I will stop being weak!

x x x

Saniama went to the ghat at the crack of dawn on the pretext of brushing her teeth. In the course of her conversation she circulated news of the events of the previous night throughout the entire village, giving them her own particular interpretation. Of course, she only talked in confidence to another person—meaning to anyone who crossed her path—and only after swearing them to secrecy. Hardly an hour had passed before the rumour had spread from one end of the village to the other, that the daughter-in-law of the Saantara family—the educated daughter-in-law, the one who had started up the school; dear, yes dear, that very same person—had eloped with someone the night before. Who knew what she took or what else she had done? There must be something more buried beneath all this. The few who knew Basanti was expecting a child exchanged knowing glances and went around saying that all along they had expected such a thing would come to pass. Someone said she had gone to Cuttack, someone said to Calcutta, someone said to her father's house. Father's house or wherever—there was a babu who had appeared. She was supposed to have gone off with him. Some people claimed not to have merely heard this, but to have seen it with their own eyes.

This was when Saniama arrived at Deba's mother's house and began her usual gossip, in her habitually fawning manner, even before stepping inside. 'Ma Saantani! What can I tell you? I've been to the pond. What I heard at the ghat! Was this written in your karma? Did eyes have to see this, did ears have to hear this? Everyone's feeling sorry for you. I gave them a good tongue-lashing. Why wouldn't I? Should I back down out of fear? Has our daughter-in-law committed theft or adultery? Rotten brinjals all of them! Don't I know them, don't I know just how chaste so-and-so's daughter-in-law is? What a thing to say, when all their own dirty linen is out in the open! And they point a finger at us!' Deba's mother was prostrating herself before God at the end of her prayer. She was about to leave, but the moment she heard Saniama's voice she stood there stock-still, listening as if she was paralysed. She flared up as she heard

Saniama's words dripping in sympathy and flattery. From the day Basanti had spoken up in protest after remaining silent for a long time, Deba's mother had begun treating Saniama's words and those of the other women of the village as poison. The terrible blow to her familial pride today added fuel to the fire smouldering within her. As it is she had been boiling with futile anger because this sense of pride had been hurt. Saniama's false words of sympathy were simply intolerable for her. She immediately stood up, picked up a broomstick and gave chase to a scared and surprised Saniama. Deba's mother spoke only after landing a blow or two on her back.

'You're so insolent—so cheeky—that you dare speak to me with a straight face, you fool! What do you think, that the house of Saantara has no master, that you're a spy here? Come closer and I'll pull out your fangs, come! You give yourself a lot of importance, don't you! You've ruined my bright gem of a daughter-in-law, and now you've set out to throw ink in my face. Traitor, leave my house at once, off with you!'

Saniama was petrified. When Saantani raised her hand to strike again, she ran away as fast as she could.

Dhania arrived. 'Saantani, the bearers have been fed. Will any clothes need to be taken...?' Deba's mother flared up and chased Dhania too with the broomstick, 'What's this talk of going I hear, you rogues? The freeloading slackers can't wait for me to leave so they can roam like bulls here. You people expect me to leave just like that, don't you? I'll first squeeze each one of you like a minnow and take out your grey matter; only then shall I leave. The rice you eat for free in the house of Saantara has gone to your heads. All right, just wait you fellows, I shall see what you're capable of.' A scared Dhania was slinking away slowly. Deba's mother called out again in a commanding tone. 'Hey Dhania. Go and tell the manager I don't need the bearers and the palanquin now. I won't go. Deba Babu may need them to go to the station. Word will be sent. Are you leaving or are you just going to stand there and stare?' Dhania barely escaped with his life.

The manager came out to check on what should be done, as he was unable to understand the order. He shouted from outside the house. 'Ma Saantani, should the bearers leave?' Deba's mother, awash in rage, came running to the main door. 'What else would they do? Rescue my seven generations? Everything has to be explained to you more than once, doesn't it? I'll shake you out of your lazy habit of sitting with one leg over the other, just you wait; everyone has become swollen headed ...' The old manager, unable to fathom what was happening, was left speechless.

At this point, hearing the commotion from his room upstairs, Debabrata presumed his mother was about to leave. He hurried down not wanting to miss her and hoping to stop her from leaving. Seeing her state of mind, he said in a tone of surprise, 'Mother, what's the matter? Are you really set to leave?'

'My head's the matter! Everyone seems to have their heart set on my leaving, and if that's true for the master, how could it be any different for the servants? How was I to know this...'

'Mother!'

'Don't you say one word to me, I'm warning you!' Saying this, Deba's mother stormed into her room and shut the door.

Debabrata remained standing there, momentarily silenced. His mother's reaction had driven from his mind any thought of stopping her. Cut to the quick, he heaved a sigh and slowly withdrew, but he did not have to go far. He had barely climbed two or three stairs when his mother came out of her room in a rush and called out to him in a stern voice. 'Deba, listen to me.' Debabrata turned back. Without letting him come closer she said, 'Look, Deba, I thought I would leave, but now I'm thinking I shouldn't. You think your life would be a lot more enjoyable without having anyone to answer to, but as long as I live I will hold you to account. Your mother's not dead, she's alive. Remember, I'll not tolerate your whims and fancies as long as I am living in this house. Who will take responsibility for this sin? I am telling you. If you want me to live, then go and bring my daughter-in-law back. If you don't, you'll be guilty of the murders of a woman and of a mother. Whatever is in store for the daughter-in-law will happen! If you don't leave this house today, I will hang myself in front of you!'

Debabrata had come downstairs. He was stupefied. Still gathering his wits about him he replied, 'All right then, I'm on my way. You stay here!'

Deba's mother gave a dry smile. 'Are you mad? Do you think I'd let you leave just like that? Come, touch my feet and promise you'll do nothing behind my back, promise you'll only track down my daughter-in-law and bring her here, or get me her address. Promise me this by touching my feet. Or else, neither you will stir, nor will I! I will hang myself here in your presence!'

Debabrata was stunned at the sight of the resolute will inscribed on his mother's face. Suddenly his whole being was overcome by surging sobs and gasps, which threw him at his mother's feet.

Twenty-Five[*]

The coachman was filled with curiosity: what would this beautiful young woman, all by herself in his carriage, do once they reached the railway station?

The horses halted near the station gate. By then day had nearly broken, but Basanti did not get out or utter a word. When the coachman saw she was not in any hurry to get down, he came and stood in front of the door. Basanti stayed seated, propped up in one corner.

She was lost in thought. From the moment she had got into the carriage she had seemed to be under a spell. All along the way she had been thinking, her eyes blankly staring, but her thoughts had no end. She had reviewed her situation. Her complete helplessness now made her even more vulnerable than had Debabrata's barbarous treatment yesterday. Where would she go? As long as she stayed in the carriage she was safe. For two or three hours within its confines she could enjoy the freedom she had yearned for. The sense of security the small enclosure provided and the relief it brought were new to her. Then the carriage set off again, leaving behind the trees and the creepers, the hedges and the thorn bushes, and the houses on either side

* By Baishnab Charan Das.

of the road. It just pressed forward, with no prodding from her panicked heart. As she sat in the carriage a wish sprang to her mind many times, a wish to be carried along forever. Its slow steady rhythmic pace calmed the frantic beating of her heart on that lonely quiet voyage in the early hours of the morning.

She sat there in silence, wondering what to do, where to go. She was no longer able to dream her tender innocent dreams, buoyed by the beaming star at dawn! She had long forgotten the art of picturing the face of the beloved in the pale white brow of the half moon and the curled lip of Venus! Her insecurity, youth, and insignificance had become starkly real to her and she did not know where she could be safe. Cuttack was out of the question; how could she show her disgraced face there? There was just one place in the whole world left for her. Earlier she had wanted to go there, but only after giving advance notice, not without warning like this. Many times in the past she had tried to write to her Binod bhai. A few times she had actually written but had then torn up the letter. Suddenly she remembered having penned a letter to him only three or four days earlier, but that too she had torn up and thrown away. Alas! If only she had put the letter in the post instead!

No, she had no one else to fall back on, no one other than Binod bhai. But then she recalled events in her life prior to her marriage, before she had even met Debabrata. How Binod Babu, a cousin of hers, had let her understand he loved her and would be happy to have her for his wife. Intuitively she had understood, but she had made it clear he had no hope. And so a disappointed Binod had left Cuttack for Calcutta to pursue his studies. After that they had not been in touch. On the day of his marriage she had received a short letter from him and a photograph of a girl. Binod had written that he had married this girl and that her name was Basantakumari. At the end of the letter he had added, 'If ever you are in difficulty, Basanti, don't think of your Binod bhai as a stranger. This is all I ask.'

His wife, Basantakumari, had also written the other day. Basanti could suddenly see her girlish handwriting. 'How shall I address you, Basa? Everyone calls me Basa. Basa and Basa—no, that would not work. Well, I will call you "I" and you will call me "A"! My dear "I", I wish I could meet your husband; see the two of you together. I have heard everything about you. But please don't ask me from whom. All right then, tell me, what games do you like to play? There's no one else here; all I do is read. Do you know how to write all the letters? Please don't find fault with me. I have been asked to practice writing by writing letters to you. O.K.'

From this letter Basanti could imagine her young sister-in-law. Her girlish script gave Basanti great pleasure, and curiosity made her feel greatly drawn towards this 'A'. Of course, she had not replied to the letter; a battle had been raging in her mind at the time. And yes, after receiving this letter she had torn up the one she had written to Binod bhai and cast it aside. At the moment they were residing in Burdwan. At what address? Well, where else if not at the main hospital, where he was a doctor! Would they mind if she turned up at their house? No, why would they? Of course, it would have been better if Binod bhai had first received a letter from her, but now that was not possible. What time was there to write a letter?

Without leaving the carriage Basanti found out from the coachman that the train carrying the mail to Calcutta would depart at seven in the morning. She sent a wire to Binod bhai, saying she would be coming by that train.

As soon as he received her wire Binod Babu made ready to set off for Calcutta.

'Where are you off to in such a hurry?' Basantakumari asked.

'Calcutta.'

Binod Babu was in the habit of travelling to Calcutta at odd hours like this, and so Basantakumari was not surprised. Still, she made a face and stood near the window with her back to

Binod Babu, who was about to leave. Afraid he would be late for the train he was in a rush. He had not reached the door when Basantakumari, in an injured tone of voice, spoke to him from behind. 'All right, go.'

Binod Babu turned around. Smiling playfully, he placed his hand on her shoulder and asked, 'Angry?'

Basantakumari detached herself in mock anger and turned aside, as if in a huff, veiling her face with the end of her sari.

Today, Binod Babu had forgotten the strict rule imposed by Basantakumari that when he was about to set off there should be something from her sweet lips to accompany him on his journey. No exception to this rule had been made for a long time, and Basantakumari had never relaxed her injunction. Distressed at having forgotten, Binod Babu spoke words of endearment, calling her 'Basaa'. Basantakumari did not respond. Binod Babu could not leave without this formality being observed, even if he knew it was getting late. He understood how Basantakumari treasured this ritual and how much this love-lorn young bride of his would suffer if he neglected this rule laid down out of love. And so he drew her closer, more fondly and eagerly, and said, 'No, my dear, Basanta, I'm getting late for the train. I'll bring you a nice gift from Calcutta this time. Come, give me my pocket money for the journey.'

'Yes, last time you brought me a parrot, which didn't survive for even two days. Looks like it'll be a mouse this time round.'

Basanta's anger finally dissolved. She lifted her wistful eyes towards Binod Babu, and indicated with a child's sense of eagerness how large a mouse she wanted. As he took this chance to extract his pocket money, Binod Babu said, 'A mouse? No, my dear, this time I'll bring you something far better.'

'What? Tell me what.'

'You'll see.'

Binod Babu left. Basanta stood and watched until the carriage disappeared into the distance. Suddenly she thought of

something and turned around. 'Oh, I haven't finished the necktie, and six months have already passed. Shame on me! He'll
make fun of me. No, I'll finish it by the end of the day.' She
quickly took out her knitting basket and set to work on Binod
Babu's necktie. Not even five minutes later two kittens came
and started to play between her legs. At first, she did not take
kindly to this, but after five minutes she had the kittens on her
lap while she kept on with her knitting. The mynah called out,
'Basaa!' Pretending to be angry Basanta shouted at the bird and
chastised it fondly. 'Shush.' Again the mynah called out, 'Basaa,
Basaa, Basaa!' Again Basanta said, 'No, this mynah will be the
death of me! Get away from here. Why are these two kittens
out to get themselves killed?' While speaking solemnly to the
mynah she came running out onto the veranda. With her face
close to the cage, she asked, 'What, what, what?'

'Radhakrushna, Ra ...'

'Hush. Say, B-i-n-a-B-a-b-u. The words were probably lost
on the mynah, because Basanta spoke very softly. Turning its
beak sideways, it stared attentively, as if it wanted to hear the
words again. Basanta was a little irritated. 'How can I say his
name aloud, you imp? All right, say B-i-n-a-B-a-b-u, B-i-n-a...'

'Shush,' said the mynah. Anxiously, Basanta turned around
to see if someone had come in. Pretending to be angry she used
the border of her sari to cover the cage and darken it, waiting
to see what would happen. The mynah cried out in protest,
'Babu, Babu, Babu!' Basanta uncovered the cage. 'All right,
I'll get you back for this, just you wait....' The mynah made a
harsh grating sound, as if in pain. Basanta paid no attention and
went to the kitchen, where a moribund house bat was kept in a
bamboo basket. Basanta picked it up lovingly, speaking words
of comfort. 'No, dear, sleep.' The bat cried out shrilly. 'Oh, dear,
I've forgotten to give the poor thing milk.' Saying this, she got
some milk from the maid. The two kittens were after her all the
time, climbing over her back and head.

Basantakumari spent the entire day like this. Evening arrived, but she had completely forgotten about knitting the necktie for her husband. After sundown she occupied herself with the arrangements to be made for cooking, and left the two kittens on their own.

'Basanta, do you see who's here. See what I've brought for you?' Basantakumari stepped out of the kitchen in a hurry. She had made up her mind not to talk to him because he was so late returning. And if the gift he brought from Calcutta did not appeal to her, then the silence would last all night! But hearing the sincerity in her husband's voice, her resolve simply melted. She came running and was with Binod Babu in an instant, her unwashed hands, upraised, her head uncovered, beads of sweat on her face glistening like pearls. Suddenly she noticed a figure standing a short distance away, leaning against the wall—the figure of a woman. A surprised Basanta was left speechless. She stared at her husband with questioning eyes.

'Try to guess who she is. I've brought her for you from Calcutta. Saying this, a smiling Binod Babu made to leave. Basanta stepped closer to him and spoke in a low voice, 'You'd better stay. I can't speak Bangla very well.'

'She's an Oriya, not a Bengali.'

'Is that true?' Basanta ran back in, washed her hands and, taking Basanti by the hand, led her inside her room. Until then Basanti had been feeling somewhat strange and out of place. Moved by Basanta's simple and unassuming manners, she hugged her joyfully. 'Nuabou ...,' she said.

'What, what makes you think I'm a bride? I'm only a girl, my name is Basanta.'

'I thought your name was "A".'

'My God, how do you know that name? Have you seen my "I"?'

'I am she.'

'Really?'

Raising her large eyes Basanta scanned Basanti from head to toe.

Three or four days passed. Basanta seemed an extraordinary creature to Basanti. Her simple and ingenuous way of behaving, her playfulness, her motherly care for little creatures—everything about her seemed exceptional. And the sense she got of a sharply intelligent mind lurking underneath all that girlishness attracted Basanti more and more towards her. One day Basanti said to Basanta, smiling, 'Nuabou—no, sorry, "A"! I have something to ask you.'

'What?' Basanta looked at her, her large eyes raised. Basanti warmly took her on her lap. 'I shall put you to the test today.'

'Test? No, dear, no—I'm not up to any test. If I make mistakes, you'll tell the whole world. No, no.'

No, I'm not talking about that kind of test. I'll only ask you a few questions and you'll give me answers.'

'Go ahead. Ask.'

Basanti asked her a few questions—about her goals in life, about why she loved Binod bhai, about the meaning of love, and so on. Basanta delighted her by giving simple and natural answers to these complicated questions. Basanti was most impressed by the way she revealed her mind in answer to one of her questions: 'Do you like a person who praises you or a person who criticises you?'

Basantakumari answered with ease. 'I quite like it if I'm praised or criticised for good reason. I'm put off as much by praise that's uncalled-for as by unfair criticism.'

At the end of the question-and-answer session Basanta suddenly said, 'My dear "I", there is something I want to ask you.'

'What is it?' Basanti looked at her inquisitively. Basanta began somewhat haltingly and apprehensively. 'Tell me you won't parry or spar with me but will give me a straight answer. All right?'

'Why don't you ask your question?' Saying this, Basanti raised her expressive eyes and drew Basanta close. Basanta blushed. 'Well, you love Deba Babu so very much and he has the same feelings for you.... Oh, no, your face has become pale. That's why I didn't want to ask you. What prompted me to ask was ... if you two love each other, then how could he have let you go and how could you have left so easily.' Having said this, Basanta threw a cautious glance at Basanti, who had paled. Basanti was overwhelmed by this unexpected question. She seemed nonplussed for a few moments and then said, 'What point is there in crying over the past?'

'The past? What do you mean the past? How can there be a trade-off between a husband and a wife, how can things between them become the past? I have a strong feeling you love him even now. Yes or no?'

Basanti stayed silent. Basanta continued. 'All right, forget that. Tell me if Deba Babu loves you.' Basanti did not know what to say. Hadn't she asked herself this very question? In her heart of hearts she knew Debabrata loved her more than his own life. And she knew how deeply she loved him. She was left speechless. She had not really given much thought to what Basanta's simple question now opened her eyes. It seemed strange to her that such an impossible thing could have happened despite their love for each other. Truly, how could such a thing have happened? How could Debabrata have imagined she was a woman of loose character? That was impossible unless there was some reason. Why had she not yet understood? Until now she had believed that Debabrata could not bear her company and had found some excuse to desert her. It now seemed to her she had been wrong.

No, it couldn't be. What possible reason could she have given him to malign her? None whatsoever. And how could he ever doubt her character?

Basanti's mind rose up in revolt against him again.

Basanta went on. 'Again, what made Deba Babu turn you out of the house? And how could you just get up and leave in a huff. I can't make anything out of this at all. It could be that the rot had already set in. Or else why would he have reacted so harshly and how could you simply have accepted what he said and stormed out?'

It was becoming clear to Basanti that this misadventure had come about not through an absence of love, but only through a false sense of pride, out of a serious misunderstanding. Was she free from blame? Had she fulfilled her duties towards Debabrata?

Basanta spoke once more. 'I think you may not be too happy with me, but believe me, I would not have acted the way you did. I would not have sat down to eat unless I had cleared up the slightest hint of trouble brewing in our life. You two have suffered the fate that befalls two people who part ways without thinking. You are to blame for that. You seem to ... Oh, no, you have started to sob like a child!'

Basanta drew Basanti's face to her chest and tried to stop her from crying, but the result was just the opposite. Basanti realised how deeply she loved Debabrata. Basanta's words made her feel that she loved him twice as much as before. All her anger and hostility towards him had vanished in an instant. A half-opened bud of tenderness was all that was left of the past, and it now waited to be brought into full bloom by the gently wafting breeze, the stirring leaf, and the song of the cuckoo. The breathtaking scent of that bud was making Basanti ecstatic; the force of that love was flooding her whole being.

Twenty-Six[*]

It was between seven and eight in the morning. Suniti sat perched on a chair in her little garden, and the soft sound of music could be heard from not too far off. Suniti went to the gate. Her old friend Fakir Sahib was making his way towards her house. Fakir Sahib was a Muslim from Baghdad who had made Orissa his home for many years. Blind for a long time now, he lived by begging. A small boy took him from place to place, leading him by the hand.

Standing in front of the gate, the Fakir started to play. Suniti called him into the sitting room and offered him a chair. 'Master, please sing a new song today,' she asked. The master said nothing, but a beaming smile brightened his flowing grey beard. As he played, he sang an Urdu song in earnest: 'Oh, my love, I am neither a poet nor a singer. How then will I describe your sweetness and beauty? I am an abject beggar today, but had I been the emperor of Samarkand and Bukhara I would have given up those kingdoms for you. I would have repaired to the deep forest with you. There at your touch roses would have bloomed on thorny plants and wine would have flowed from palm trees. I do not know what kind of place is Firdaus, but I

* By Sarat Chandra Mukherjee.

would build it wherever I am only if you were with me. Won't you see me again? Will this waiting never end?' While he sang the old Fakir, who was past eighty, was overcome with emotion. Tears streamed from his eyes. At times, totally oblivious to his own self, he seemed to be staring off into the distance in delight. Suniti was spellbound as she listened to the old Fakir's love song. Her mind was etched with the image it evoked of a lover eternally waiting.

The musical interlude lasted for some time. Then Suniti said, 'Master, it's getting hotter by the minute. Please do not go anywhere. Have your meal in our house.' The Fakir made no reply but continued in silence. His blind eyes seemed to shine brightly. Suddenly the young boy who was escorting him and who had been looking outside spoke up: 'Welcome, Babuji.' Suniti went out and saw Ramesh standing quietly on the veranda. Her face lit up spontaneously at the unexpected sight. Saying nothing for some time, she only looked at him and continued to smile. 'Bah, a fine person you are!' said Ramesh. 'A gentleman is standing here and all this lady is doing is smiling.'

Suniti laughed a mischievous laugh. 'Oh, a gentleman indeed! Who asked the gentleman to stay standing here?'

'Wouldn't it have been impolite to barge into your house and interrupt the music?' Ramesh then made his way inside slowly, with Suniti following.

'When do you think you'll leave for Boula's house?'

'Suniti, it's Debabrata Babu's house, not Boula's anymore.' They had learned Debabrata had concluded, because of some letter, that Basanti was not worthy of trust and had her turned out of his house. The incident had affected Ramesh deeply. Suniti understood what Ramesh meant and stayed silent for a while. Then she asked,

'Please tell me when you're leaving.'

'I'll take the daytime train today.'

'Please take me with you.'

'Are you mad? What would people say?'

Brooding, Suniti answered in a voice choked with emotion. 'I don't see why you're so afraid of what people might say. Don't you know that people are a-hundred-tongued when it comes to criticising?'

'Oh, my God, you have started to argue. There's no time for that, Suniti, the train will leave soon. I just came by to see you. Where's mother?'

'Forget that, forget all your tricks. The train doesn't leave until quite late. Why don't you sit down?' Suniti made Ramesh take a seat. Once both were seated, the Fakir Sahib resumed his singing.

From near the gate the mailman called out, 'The mail is here.' Suniti ran out and collected a letter. She saw that it was from Debabrata and addressed to Ramesh. Debabrata had sent the letter in care of Suniti and scribbled a message in an upper corner: 'If Ramesh Babu is not in Cuttack, please forward it to where he happens to be.'

Ramesh read Debabrata's letter.

My dear brother Ramesh,

You probably have come to know about everything. To the very core of my being I am feeling what a criminal I have been. I'm unworthy of forgiveness.

I thought she was a thorn in my life and that if I got rid of her my path would be smooth. But this is not what has happened. I drove her out of my house, but have I been able to drive her from my mind? The fool that I am, I cast her out without realising how inextricably woven into my life she was. Since she left, her tear-soaked eyes have kept dancing before mine. In my dreams she looks at me piteously and asks, her voice apprehensive, 'Dearest love, am I untrustworthy?' Unable to stand that look I have tried to keep myself busy with chores. I have tried to mask the pain in my heart by doing so, but without success. Wherever I look I see Basanti pacing about in front of me, assuming a thousand different shapes. 'Did you really believe I was not worthy of trust?' I have not been able to find an answer to that question.

Those who were the most vocal in criticising her when she was with me are the same people who are heaping praise on her now she is gone. 'My son, such a daughter-in-law, pure gold; she's one in a thousand. You're such a good boy. Even in our wildest dreams we could not have imagined you would do this.' The deceitfulness of these people makes my blood boil, but my feelings of guilt are also growing.

The most difficult person has been my mother. At first she was in a tearing rage, but for the past few days she has taken to her bed with intermittent fever. At times she becomes delirious. 'Basa, come, apple of my eye, my daughter-in-law, come my dear child, come into my arms. Don't go to that wicked person.... Come sit on my lap.' This astounds me. These people seem to be missing her much more than I am. The same Saniama who was unable to bear the sight of her is crying day and night. Brother Ramesh, I'm simply unable to express in words the scorpion sting in my heart for the past few days. But God does not think I have suffered enough. Without Basanti, this house seems like a cremation ghat. One day, while moving about this haunted house like a man possessed, I found a couple of torn-up pieces of paper. When I read them I understood they were connected to that other fragment, the one that had led me to believe Basanti had betrayed my trust. From these pieces I understood that the letter I had thought was a love letter from Basanti was actually addressed to some dear relative of hers. Her letter began in a sentimental vein—'Have you forgotten your sad sister so quickly'—and went on: 'I can find shelter with no one other than you. The person who had made me proud by giving me a place in his heart has now taken to spurning me day in and day out. He is treating me as if I am not even human. Who else will come to my rescue and support me?' Below this was written, 'Your younger sister Basanti.' You can imagine how much my remorse has grown after reading this. I have been thinking about this constantly, but cannot come to a decision. I never knew Basanti had a brother. Did you know she had a brother or such a close relative?

When I think of the beastly punishment I have inflicted on a blameless soul like Basanti my entire body goes cold. I don't know where she is and have no way of finding that out. But brother, I still feel she is not angry with me. It seems to me as if she is always praying to God for my well-being. Her greatness, which has increased a hundred times in her absence, stings my conscience again and again and makes me miserable.

Suniti Devi will definitely hate me when she learns of this. Yes, I am an object of hate. I know that my unacceptable behaviour towards her friend is unforgivable. Please ask her only this: will she not forgive me if I do penance for my sin by spending the rest of my life in the endless fires of remorse? Ramesh, won't the two of you ask for mercy for me from God? I have full confidence that even if He will not listen to the anguished appeal from my impure heart, He will surely listen to an entreaty from the pure hearts you two possess.

Farewell, brother Ramesh, farewell. We will probably not meet again. What does it matter if we do not? The life story of a friend like me will stay written in your memory as only a sad dream.

Your wretched friend,
Debabrata

Ramesh felt stunned after reading the letter. His eye lingered on the last part. He was startled despite himself. 'We will probably not meet again': what could that mean? Was Debabrata thinking of committing suicide? No, no, that couldn't be. Was he so weak? Ramesh thought about it. Well, who could say? Nothing is impossible on the part of a person who can desert a wife like Basanti under the influence of misguided emotion.

Taking Kalyani Devi's blessing, Ramesh set off in a hurry. While fastening the tiffin box to his cycle Suniti said, 'Be sure to write me the moment you arrive at their house. I will wait for your letter the way a chataka bird awaits the rains. That night many tears flowed onto Suniti's bosom, as she sang mournful tunes on her harmonium, thinking about her Boula.

Twenty-Seven[*]

Debabrata called in leading doctors and surgeons from Balasore to consult on his mother's treatment. They concluded that her illness was due in large part to stress and anxiety and that every effort should be made to raise her spirits. A short stay in a healthier climate would instantly bring improvement, they said.

Deba's mother had fallen ill a few days after Basanti left and had taken to her bed after frequent bouts of fever led to a seizure. The sturdy, strong, and healthy figure she had once been seemed to have disappeared into the mattress. Her earlier aura was gone. She was a pathetic figure to behold.

The day dawned. Deba gave his mother her medicine, aired her linen, and sat next to her, running his hand across her forehead. 'Mother, you've often said you'd like to go with me to Puri and Bhubaneswar. Come with me. I'll take you away from here and we can visit Bhubaneswar for a month. That would be good for your health. Staying cooped up in this stuffy room is bringing your spirits down.'

Subhadra Devi frowned, her face pale. 'What pleasure would I get from going on pilgrimages and performing rituals piously?

* By Sarala Devi.

Or, will Bhubaneswar send me directly to heaven? Is it because death is near for a sinner like me that you're worrying so much? If that's the case, then all I have had to endure will be finished and I'll be saved from all of you. But my days continue on endlessly! If I have to die, I'll rot to death here.' This silenced Debabrata. He did not have the courage to continue suggesting a change of scenery. He hoped only to spare no effort on his mother's care and to make certain day and night that she was not reminded of that person whose absence had brought her such misery. But does a pat on the head take away the ache in the soul? Basa's tearful eyes and those of his mother, sad and angry, haunted him; they stared out at him from walls and fences, in doorways and on thresholds. He kept his feelings to himself and threw himself into taking care of his mother, into bringing her comfort.

The past few months had seemed like an eternity to Debabrata; his life had lost all balance—as if his spirited talk, his light-hearted banter, his handsome good looks had been infected with black blight. He took no care of himself, his hair was dishevelled and he went without shaving for days on end. His eyes were sunken; their shine had faded. He had become a mere vestige of a man, now hopelessly cursed. An enormous gulf separated the Debabrata of yore from that of today. He did not leave the house, did not speak to anyone unless forced to. He knew why he was suffering, but what he had done in a fit of extreme emotion now filled him with such remorse that he was incapable of setting the situation right. Until today he had not been able to decide what he should do to be happy and find peace. Seeing his mother's condition worsen day by day he was being pushed to the limit. One question weighed heavily on him: 'Have I been able to do my duty towards my mother? Because of me she has not had even one day of happiness, while dedicating every day of her life to my care and comfort and expecting nothing in return. I am neither a worthy son nor a deserving husband! I am simply worthless!'

The more aware he became of how ineffectual he was, the more his disdain for himself and distrust and hatred of his earlier male bravado increased. He only found some relief in being able to spend every moment devoting heart and soul to his mother's care. Amidst the encircling gloom of grief this was the only bright ray of light.

Time stands still for no one; two months passed. His mother showed no signs of recovery. Debabrata realised there was no reason to think she would live much longer. In the meantime, he had not been able to find any trace of Basanti despite frantic efforts and enquiries. His mother was not ready to believe this though. The thought she might soon die sent a shudder through him. Frightened, he lacked the courage to keep thinking about this and focused instead on salving his conscience. But how could he fool himself? Deluding oneself is not easy.

At times he even thought of setting out to find Basanti, even if that meant risking his life—but the very next moment his resolve would flag as he remembered his mother, abandoned and under the dark shadow of frightening death. How much longer would she survive? It was difficult to believe she could last more than 15 or 20 days. If he set out in search of Basanti while his mother was still alive, it would be as if he were sending her to her grave even before she had died. All his care and hard work would have gone to waste. And if his efforts to find Basanti failed—and they were likely doomed—then his loss would be doubled.

If his mother was not still alive when he returned.... With this thought churning inside his head he paced his room, turning his mind to something else when Dhania handed him a telegram. He eagerly read the wire and learned that Ramesh was announcing his arrival. Dhania acted as his master's right hand these days; the usual line separating master and servant had long been erased, without their even realising it. Debabrata constantly attended to his mother, while Dhania took on the tasks of receiving people and seeing them off, of supervising work inside and outside the house, and of managing everyone's affairs. Despite this, he was still feeling troubled on account of his young mistress. When Deba Babu was in Cuttack he had often been sent to her with books and letters, and had never left without receiving something for his efforts. When the Saantani scolded him or when Deba Babu got angry with him, she would comfort him and secretly give him money, shirts, clothes, and so on. At times the Saantani would discover this and remark, 'this Dhania boy's head has swollen to 10 times its size because of our daughter-in-law'. After coming to the house with his 'Basa apa' he had become attached to the household and to the family. He started calling her 'little Saantani', realising a servant should not address her in her in-law's house as 'Basa apa', as if she were his sister. But their relationship and affection for each other continued. It is in times of adversity that a man learns who his true and compassionate friends are. Dhania had been tested against the touchstone of grief and danger and come out unscathed. For Debabrata, he was now both a servant and a co-suffering, sympathising friend. He was the person who wiped the tears from Debabrata's eyes, the person who shared Debabrata's happiness. The concern shown by servant Dhania brought a million times more solace and trust to Debabrata's shattered heart than the show of sympathy from the people who felt obliged to call on him.

Afraid to upset him Dhania asked with considerable nervousness, 'Sir, who sent the telegram?'

'Ramesh. He says he's on his way.'

This filled Dhania with hope. 'He must be coming with some news about the little Saantani. Why else would he send a telegram?'

'Who can say?'

Master and servant were plunged into a state of confusion, between hope and despair.

On learning from Dhania about the telegram, Deba's mother was certain Ramesh would be bringing news of Basanti. A great load seemed to lift from her mind. For quite some time she had not taken an interest in household matters, but today she called people to her, made enquiries, and heard their grievances. His mother's new cheerfulness was disturbing for Debabrata: he was afraid she would become even more demoralised if Ramesh had no news. The shock might affect her heart, even kill her. His mind was totally focused on his mother; he could not think any more.

The moment he was anxiously waiting for finally came. Ramesh set foot inside the house, and immediately Deba's mother learned everything. She was shattered, but the news affected Deba less as he had prepared himself. Despite all his efforts, Ramesh had not been able to find any trace of Basanti. But he was hoping for a breakthrough soon. This last part he made up, on Debabrata's advice.

Deba's mother's eyes had dried up from shedding so many tears. More tears were out of the question. When anguish in the soul exceeds what can be endured, what is the use of crying? Just as it is not possible for anyone to fathom the finer sentiments words can never fully express, none can know the inner sorrows that tears, though meant to lessen them, barely touch.

Debabrata said nothing, believing that trying to soothe a mind that is hurt and in despair is the same as mocking it. But Ramesh said, 'Auntie! The new bride hasn't left this world. We think she's gone to stay with a relative. You might have heard from Deba that she has a distant relation. She probably decided to visit him. Don't worry, everything will become clear in a month's time.'

Readers know that Subhadra Devi became very angry with Debabrata when Basanti left. After telling her Basanti had written to a lover asking for help, he did not say anything about finding the other half of Basanti's letter, afraid of how she would react. When he discovered that the person in question was being addressed as 'brother', he had lacked the courage to tell her. Ramesh knew nothing of all this. When he alluded to a relative as he was speaking to her, Debabrata looked away apprehensively. If a ripple of joy quickly arose in Deba's mother's mind, it was because even though she was certain of Basanti's good character some shadow of doubt would nevertheless rear its head from time to time in her subconscious mind. She now felt an unusual sense of peace because that shadow was now dispelled and because she had not allowed herself to cast aspersions on Basanti.

Debabrata had a vacant look on his face, like a person accused. He did not have the courage to look his mother in the eye. After glancing at her son, Subhadra Devi addressed Ramesh. 'Ramu dear! For how long will you keep me alive by giving me false hope? I know my days are numbered. My wishes will have been realised if I have placed this foolish fellow back in the hands of the person I cherish. I'm not hopeful he'll ever become less capricious. And no one else in this world except Basa can get him to change his whimsical and cavalier ways. Who will look after him if I close my eyes today?' It was as though her love for her son was springing forth from some boundless source, almost choking her as it forced its way through her.

They were gently massaging Subhadra Devi's arms and feet. She addressed Deba. 'Your friend has come. Instead of taking care of him, you're punishing him.' Ramesh protested. 'What are you saying auntie? Isn't Deba's house my own, or do I not deserve to be your son as much as he does? I haven't seen you in a long time and have often thought of calling on you.'

At Deba's mother's insistence the two friends went out for a walk.

'Let's sit in the shade of this tree.'

Ramesh was feeling tired. They sat down.

Ramesh had not yet had a good look at Debabrata—his body was emaciated, his eyes pale, and his hair unkempt. In the quiet of where they were he could now see that. Although a strong-willed person he was cut to the quick. Ramesh spoke. 'Brother, after seeing the state you're in I haven't the slightest wish to criticise you, even though I came with the intention of saying some harsh words to you.'

Debabrata's eyes welled up. The utter shame he felt at Ramesh's heartfelt statement crushed him. He somehow got hold of himself. 'I expressed all my feelings in the letter I wrote to you. What more can I say? My cursed mind finds its only solace in thinking that in Basanti's absence I'm still able to take care of mother. But then, brother, it's beyond me to fill the void Basanti has left. If mother dies while this void still exists, then her unfulfilled wish will be a cause of lament for the rest of my life. That she has been able to survive despite the condition she's in means the most to me, as I'm reminded daily of the futility of my life.'

Ramesh understood his friend's remorse and anguish and spoke to comfort him. 'Forget that; it's no use thinking about that. Have you had any news? Have you looked for her in Puri and other places?'

'Do you think I haven't searched for Basanti all over Orissa? Brother, you're my only hope. Please give mother some strength. Looking for her has used up all my energy. The next course of action is up to you.'

'Why are you worrying so much? You've already more than paid for your misguided actions. I have reassured auntie. Please don't despair. If you do, and she suspects that, then her trust in me will vanish.'

They saw Dhania walking quickly towards them. Sensing something was wrong, Debabrata's face became pale. 'The old Saantani is desperately looking for you,' said Dhania. 'Saantani Nisa's mother sent me to fetch you.' The two friends ran quickly back home.

'She was fine when we were with her and wouldn't let us stay. How did things take a turn for the worse so soon? Ramesh used a stethoscope to examine Subhadra Devi. In answer to Debabrata's questioning he said, 'I find her heart is beating very rapidly.' Ramesh's words splashed on Debabrata's face like ink. He stood up. 'Let me call a doctor.'

After the doctor had applied cold compresses to the patient for a while, she seemed to be feeling better. Her condition would improve for two days, but then worsen for the next two, and people would say she was on her way to heaven. Debabrata and Ramesh applied themselves to her care with redoubled vigour. Constant physical work, worry, and anxiety began to tell upon Debabrata's mind as well as his body. There were signs he was close to a nervous breakdown. When the doctor told Debabrata he should not continue his vigils at his mother's bedside day and night, he began to feel the blackness of despair solidify in his mind. Ramesh would leave in a day or two. If Debabrata did not survive, who would take care of mother and from whom would she hear words of solace in her final hours? If only Basanti were here! But there was still no clue as to where she was. Nothing had come of frantic searching and writing letters. Ramesh was beginning to be more worried about the situation than Debabrata. When the postman arrived auntie would always ask, 'Ramu, did you receive any news? Won't I be able to catch one more glimpse of my Lakshmi? Are you people doing anything or only telling me stories?' This would leave Ramesh at a loss for words. Later, he would once again make up stories to give her hope. Two to three weeks went by like this. A letter from Dhania in Calcutta brought the news that there was still no trace of the young Saantani. This was too much to bear.

Subhadra Devi improved somewhat. As Ramesh was taking leave of her, she said in a feeble voice, after giving him her affectionate blessings, 'Ramu, so you are off. Be sure to write back quickly with news of Basa. I am waiting. Her touch might improve my health. Don't mind the expense. I will spend all I have to find my daughter-in-law. If I were fully recovered,

I would set out tomorrow with a pouch for alms in search of the Lakshmi of my home. Yes, God to the rescue. All right, son, go. It's getting late. But remember what I said, son, don't forget....' Ramesh made his exit, tears in his eyes.

When the long sighs of the two friends, expressing grief at their parting, had dissolved in the smoke from the train at Balasore railway station, Ramesh poked his head out through the window. 'Write that message,' he said, 'and send it today.' On his return Debabrata gave four large packets to the old account-keeper and asked him to put them in the post. Two days later the major daily newspapers in Calcutta, Bombay, Madras, and Lahore published a notice in larger than normal letters:

'Basa, please come back. Mother is on her deathbed. I myself am very close to death. Deba.'

Twenty-Eight*

That autumn morning had been clear and bright; this evening in spring was charmed and scarlet. The fresh and beaming smile of that morning in autumn had, however, faded from Basanti's face. It was as though the dull pain of her wounded heart had been scattered across the sky and the earth. She was revisiting pages from her eventful life and softly singing a mournful tune, as she saw her thwarted innermost desire mirrored in the painful blood-red twilight:

> Oh, my beloved,
> My beloved in this life and the lives to come,
> Spill onto the plate of grief
>   More of your tears.
> If spurned by the entire world,
> Oh my friend of the solitary path,
> I offer my anguished appeal to the crimson sky.
> Accept it my dear
> Oh my beloved, my love in this life and the lives to come.

Basanti was remembering that time, as she intoned the song. The rays of the dawning sun, streaming through the window,

* By Kalindi Charan Panigrahi.

brightened the room. Mother was on her sick bed. The bell of
Debabrata's bicycle rang out, and Deba bhai entered the house
like a fragrant breath of air. She was much younger then, blooming forth much like the wild sugarcane flowering in autumn
out of growing indescribable joy. She had no thought or care
for either the past or future. She only knew to go through life,
fleet-footed and delicate as a feather in the wind, laughing with
gay abandon.

Then there was another day—a blood-red evening like this
one, with the golden waters of the pond glistening amid the
stand of trees. Little ripples moved forward in a dance and
caressed the shore like the scene before her today. Her eyes were
lotuses in full bloom, afloat in the waters of beauty. Yes, that
very day at around this time someone had come up from behind
and covered her eyes. Her whole body had shrunk from a sense
of shame. She could not utter a word. She only sighed and tried
to uncover her eyes with her shaking hands by placing them on
Debabrata's. But slowly, very slowly. She had no wish to remove
those hands; rather, her mind longed to remain blindfolded all
her life and to lean against the young man standing behind her.
The happy memory of that time, overlaid with terrible pain,
was a source of deep sadness for her. She yearned for nothing
more than to rest her languid, pregnant body in the lap of her
beloved and forget herself.

Eight long months have passed and during this entire time
Basanti has found asylum in Binod Bihari's house. She has
spent these months thinking about different things, counting
each moment as it passed. Yes, Debabrata had abandoned her
because he no longer trusted her, but who was responsible for
that? Wasn't she herself partially to blame? Had she not understood Debabrata after so much time together? Could she doubt
his innocent heart, his simple and charming ways, and his
deeply loving nature? No, not at all. Why then had she given
such importance to the words he had uttered. Why had she

distanced herself so easily from her old sentimental 'Deba bhai'? Granted, Debabrata had wronged her seriously and arbitrarily, but could she not have forgiven her beloved, who was as dear to her as her own life? Why had she been so emotional as to walk away? Debabrata had spurned her values and disregarded her as a woman, but did she not share a part of the responsibility for that? If space for doubt had opened up in Debabrata's mind, Basanti, through her own fault, had not been able to remove it. Today she was able to understand her real self as a result of her distance from her beloved as well as from her world in the village. She was able to see clearly the difference between the Basanti whose sphere was in the home and the Basanti who existed outside the house. She had not excelled as much in her domestic setting as she had been able to outside. How otherwise could doubt have crossed Debabrata's mind, he who so doted on Basanti?

And then there was her elderly mother-in-law, a strong and exceptional woman! Much before a command had escaped her lips her servants and clerks would cower and shake in fear. At first she had been angry because her son had married a woman of uncertain background. Once she had come to know Basanti well, with her surprising ability to assess people, she had shown her a great deal of care and love. Many a time she had said, 'I was on the lookout for exactly such a daughter-in-law. A woman who hasn't the slightest strength of mind, one who wilts like a touch-me-not, one who's incapable of giving another person a piece of her mind, well, the very sight of such a woman sets my bones on fire. Does a woman have to give up everything just because she was born a woman? Without confidence or strength, such a woman would give a wide berth even to servants. Fie, fie, how can such a woman be a Saantani; she's only fit to be a maid. I would never agree to give such a woman a share in all I own.' Basanti could see very well that more than anyone else it was her old mother-in-law who had judged her properly and had learned to value her ideals. The same mother-in-law was now on her deathbed, and Basanti had left without being able to speak a word to her. What would her mother-in-law, so conscious of her prestige, be thinking of such behaviour on her part? All these thoughts assailed Basanti today, taking over her life.

She read Debabrata's message in the newspaper over and over: 'Please come back. Mother is on her deathbed. I myself am close to death.' How could she be so angry with Debabrata?

Today, Basanti no longer held anything against anybody. Tears began to stream from her eyes in helpless anger against some unknown God, whose secret command had made her life go awry like a boat lost in a storm.

It was at this point that someone covered her eyes from behind. A cold shiver passed through her body. Could it be 'Deba bhai'? Quickly she understood it was none other than her 'A'. Basantakumari felt her tears, and went around to face Basanti, asking in a quiet voice, 'Hello my dear "I", are you crying? Why? For heaven's sake, tell me if you're facing any problems here.' Basanti smiled softly. 'No, sister, what sort of difficulty could I be having? Would my life be happier anywhere else?' Immediately after saying this, Basanti realised that if Debabrata were with her, amid all the differences and disturbances, she would be happier than anywhere else in the world. She could not hold in her tears; they rolled down faster. It was not misery that was making her unhappy; the main reason for her sorrow was her husband's remorse, he who was as dear to her as life itself. Basanti was aghast, thinking about how her earlier courage, the indomitable courage she had shown as a champion of women's emancipation, had deserted her. How could she have become so soft and weak?

When Basantakumari, her eyes brimming, asked in the tearful voice of a child, 'Oh, dear, you're weeping. Please, for my sake, tell me what has hurt you'. Basanti drew her guileless face to her lap. Basantakumari knew the story of Basanti's life, but was unable to understand why she was crying inconsolably. Nor could she find words of solace. Basanti's heart was overwhelmed by the deep empathy shown by this loving girl.

Darkness had descended from the eastern sky, and the dusty shadow of evening had fallen across the pond. Through the spaces between the trees stars could be seen blooming in the sky in ones and twos. Basantakumari's tears had soaked Basanti's sari. Basanti raised her face and wiped the tears from her eyes as she tried to console her.

The two friends went inside the house and saw Binod Bihari bent over a book of medicine. At the sound of their footsteps he looked up at their faces. Sensing that something had happened, he asked, 'So what's wrong this time?'

Basanta's eyes welled up again. She went to her husband and said to him in a teary voice, 'Please find out what's wrong. Why was she crying so piteously, sitting by the side of the pond?' It was clear to Binod Babu that Basanti's tears were the reason for his wife's swollen eyes. He would have liked to engage in banter with his wife, but Basanti's sorrow made him unhappy too. He spoke softly. 'No, Basanti, don't you realise how much injustice you are doing to the sacred manifestation you are carrying within you?' Basanti quietly went over to Binod Babu and showed him the message in the newspaper. Binod understood everything once he had read it. 'Fine,' he said. 'We'll give Debabrata all the news. But it would be unwise for you to leave before the child has been delivered.' A stunned Basantakumari heard everything and determining to get the story from her husband later, took Basanti away to another part of the house.

x x x

Hardly had the lights come on in the shops, and the market area of Cuttack that evening than groups of school students could be seen heading briskly towards Choudhury Bazaar. There was going to be a meeting in the town hall. Some rowdy boys were among them and they were going with the intention of buying gudakhu in the bazaar; the meeting was strictly an excuse. They only had a vague idea about who would be chairing the meeting, who would be speaking, or what the subject would be. All they knew was that the chairman was an influential local person, that the speaker was a distinguished professor from abroad and that the subject was 'marriage' or something related to that. Every place has people who flow with the current. These boys were like that. Their main reason for attending meetings was to buy gudakhu, clothes, gamchhas, etc. In addition to these boys, most of the students were attending today's meeting. They had turned out in large numbers because the subject—'Marriage in the Modern Age'—was aimed at them.

The gist of what the speaker had to say was this: For the good of India and of humankind as a whole the time had come to defy narrow differences based on caste and to promote a new practice of marriage based on individual preferences. Every educated person should try to think of how this idea could take root among the people.

Since opinions on the subject might differ, the chairman, at the speaker's suggestion, requested questions and criticism from the floor.

It is up to the readers to guess what the members of the educated community of Utkala would have said. It is not possible to say who offered a just criticism. All that was heard was unspeakable, obscene, and not fit for anyone's ears. There was no lack of personal attacks, and even the poor chairman and the speaker did not escape the slurs.

The views of one particular person, a recent graduate, on this subject are worth noting. Unlike the others, this gentleman did not engage in abstract arguments but offered to cite a few cases from his own experience at college. Two of his friends, for example, were now reaping the damaging consequences of their irrational decision to marry for love. One married an educated woman of unknown background (this was a pure fabrication on the speaker's part) without his guardian's permission and drove her out of his house after a few days, on the grounds of misconduct. The other was poised to marry a Christian woman. Before society could give its views on the matter God had provided an indication of the judgement he would face. The Christian woman was now suffering from a serious disease. This was a sign from God of what happiness the couple would experience if they were to marry. The speaker continued. The educated community is the brains of a country; students are the country's hope for the future. Beware! Think long and hard to discover what your responsibility is on this earth. I dare any pundit or logician to refute these two examples from my own experience. Please, don't break into rounds of applause like some unruly crowd. The poet has rightly said:

The wise are at their wit's end at your ways
The mob, however, chants out its frenzied cheers.

Some mischievous college boys were taunting the learned gentleman, shouting 'sit down', 'stop speaking', but that did not stop him. A few others, moved by the speaker's exemplary courage, were encouraging him with smiles and shouting 'go on.' Some were sitting staring at the floor, their hands over their ears; others were adding to the uproar with their shouts of 'quiet,' 'quiet' .

Certain members of the audience started to quietly leave the hall. The first was a man who had been standing on the veranda earlier. Tall and broad chested, he had a long beard and unkempt hair, and was holding a suitcase, his face lit by a square of light filtering outside through the window. He had an expressive face and his complexion was fair. But his face had lost its lustre. His eyelids were black, as if they had been singed by the heat.

Suddenly, for some inexplicable reason, he began walking hur-
riedly down a dark road, taking himself out of the light. He
seemed eager to leave behind the shops, bazaar, and lanes. He
stayed away from heavily frequented, shop-lined roads, moving
towards outlying areas shrouded in darkness. It was as if he was
well known and wanted to keep his identity concealed.

Seeing the man step off the road and wander into darkness,
the constable on the beat shouted in Hindi, 'Who goes there?'
The man stood stock still, wordless, and exhausted. The constable shone his flashlight in the man's face, and then prostrated
himself before him in an instant. 'Please forgive me, sir. Where
are you off to at such a late hour and dressed so shabbily? Is
anyone in trouble?' The bearded man, unable to make out anything, asked mildly, 'Who are you?' The constable stood with
folded hands. 'I'm Mohammad, sir.' But it seemed as though
the man's memory had been washed clean and he was trying to
summon up remembrance of what had been lost. Looking up,
he said, 'Mohammad!'

'Yes, sir, the same Mohammad whose life was saved because
of your excellency. It seems your excellency has not taken long
to forget someone he helped! Have you forgotten the house
burning? The mob, after thrashing me for no fault of mine, was
about to throw me into the fire. I was screaming for dear life.
Don't you remember, sir, how you saved me, took me to the
hospital and had me treated, spending your own money? What
needy and suffering person in the bazaars and lanes of Cuttack
doesn't know you? My life was saved thanks to your excellency,
so of course I know you!'

The man seemed tense. Then he smiled drily. 'All right
Mohammad, I've some urgent business to attend to.' Mohammad,
however, was not one to give up. Disregarding orders, he stayed
with the man who had saved his life and insisted on escorting
him to his destination. Responding gravely—'No need for that
Mohammad'—the man resumed walking at his previous pace.

Mohammad thought to himself, 'This man's mission is to search out and take care of people others brush aside and have no concern for—someone dying with no shoulder to rest his head on, some old woman lying ill in bed with no one who thinks she's worth attending to, or someone who hasn't eaten for three days.' He took a drag on his cheroot and went back to his work.

The man entered Petin Sahi, walking briskly. He stood before a single-storey building and thought for a long time before laying his hand softly on the door. A woman's voice could be heard from inside. 'Who's there?'

'Open the door please.' A maid came to the door. She eyed the strange-looking man from head to toe and asked in an irritated voice, 'What do you want?'

The man's tone was serious. 'Is Ramesh Babu home?'

'Yes, but he doesn't have a moment to spare.'

'Send him word to come here for two minutes.'

'He's busy.'

'Send word I'm telling you.' The maid did not have to say anything more. A man appeared and without even looking at the visitor embraced him tightly. 'It's you Debabrata. God, what a sight you are! You're so tall and stand so straight, but today you seem completely broken. Do you think the struggle's over; it has just begun.' Saying this, the young man prepared to drag Debabrata inside the house, but the visitor stopped him. 'Wait brother. Let's first decide whether it's proper for me to meet with Suniti Devi.' The young man shook the visitor's hand and said, smiling, 'What do you mean? Suniti's been taken ill. Won't you see her at least once?'

'Yes, I came when I learned of her illness at the meeting. Otherwise, I had decided to...'

'... To leave town, you mad man. Come we'll talk about that afterwards.'

Without waiting for Debabrata to reply, Ramesh pulled him into the house. Entering Suniti's room, Debabrata could see in the faint light that she was lying on a bed in the corner. By the bedside was a table with her medicine. Suniti knew everything about what had happened to Debabrata. When her eyes fell on Debabrata as she turned on her side, she was surprised. 'Oh my God, Deba Babu, why do you look like that? What crime have you committed that you would have to do such penance? Yes, that capricious girl has left you in a sudden fit of anger, but her Boula can well imagine in what condition she must be now.'

Debabrata listened, his head bowed. He could neither speak nor lift his face to look at Suniti. He only asked Ramesh, 'How long has Suniti Devi been ill like this? What do the doctors say?' Ramesh glanced at Suniti affectionately. 'She's been suffering like this for the past two weeks but has recovered to a great extent. The doctors are no longer worried.' Ramesh then took up Debabrata's case. 'All right, Deba, tell me how mother is. How could you leave so soon? I never expected that!'

'Mother is greatly improved and wouldn't let me wait at home until she had recovered completely.'

'There's no one with you. Did you set off by yourself like a wandering Kabuli?'

'No brother. Mother had a servant and a cook come with me, but I sent them back when I was halfway through my journey. I have no idea where my fate will take me. Why would I have company and set out in style with drums and fireworks? Only Dhania has stayed with me.'

'Fine, but where will you set off to now since you don't know where you should be heading?'

A slight smile crossed Debabrata's face. 'How can I say where? I'll just wander aimlessly. But, for the time being at least, I'm headed for Calcutta.'

'Do write.'

'Well, if I get a chance.'

Ramesh then asked for details of the meeting he had not been able to attend because of Suniti's illness.

Debabrata had planned to set off there and then, but Ramesh and Suniti forced him to accept their hospitality for a day.

By the time Binod Bihari's letter giving a detailed account of Basanti reached Balasore, Debabrata had already left. He had more or less promised to Ramesh he would write, but he felt so utterly shamed in the eyes of society and of the world at large for having exiled Basanti that he could not decide if it would be proper to convey any news about himself either to Ramesh or to his own mother. He had sent a helpless Basanti off alone, and, like a person under a spell, had abandoned her thoughtlessly. Hadn't he, as well as the others, allowed a helpless woman to be exiled? Why would anyone be concerned about a man like him going astray and remaining beyond the pale? No, he would not tell anyone anything about himself until he had tracked down Basanti.

Twenty-Nine[*]

When Subhadra Devi learned the news of Basanti from Binod Bihari's letter, she summoned Nisamani. 'Nisa dear, my lost gem has been found. Now my health will improve.' Nisamani had also received a letter, but from Basanti herself. It dealt at length with the school Basanti had set up to educate girls. It was a long letter addressed to her protégé Nisamani, exhorting her to work to raise the standards of the school to ever loftier heights, to equip both young girls as well as older women with a variety of skills, and to bring them into the modern world, while at the same time making them conscious and proud of their Indian heritage. The letter ended by expressing respect for her mother-in-law and love to all her other friends. Hearing this from Nisamani, the old lady was overjoyed.

Even in Basanti's absence, Subhadra Devi's opinion of her had grown more favourable. When she heard everything she placed her hand on Nisamani and blessed her, hoping the noble work they had undertaken would be accomplished and encouraging her to devote most of her time to this task. Then Subhadra Devi asked, 'Nisa dear, can you tell me what my daughter-in-law will be blessed with?'

* By Kalindi Charan Panigrahi.

Nisa smiled gently. Wanting to probe the old lady's mind, she said, 'A son would, of course, be wonderful.'

'May your words bear fruit, Nisa dear. If it's a son, I'll be able to die in peace, knowing that the rites after my death will be taken care of. But do you think I would be unhappy if it's a daughter?'

'No, elder mother. A son or a daughter, it's your flesh and blood.'

'What you've said is correct. With a daughter like my daughter-in-law, not having a son would not matter to anyone. The doors of heaven would be wide open for their ancestors.'

Subhadra Devi was not aware Saniama had sneaked in and been standing near her for some time. These days she could not be so fresh with Saantani. Subhadra Devi had realised that Saniama, not being an equal, should not be spoken to as one. From that time Saniama not only lived in awe of Saantani; she also did not dare utter a word about Basanti in front of the neighbours. Seeing Saniama standing near her today, Subhadra Devi looked at her pointedly and said, 'Hey you, why are you standing there; go and clean the pots and pans.' Saniama backed away in fear.

Subhadra Devi returned to her conversation. 'Well, my dear Nisa, there hasn't been any news of Deba for a long time. Are these children taking it out on their old mother?'

'Don't worry about that elder mother. Deba bhai is not a child; he won't get lost.'

'No, I don't mean that. I'm just saying he should keep his old mother posted.'

'He must be wandering here and there and may not have the time or the chance to do that.'

'Yes, that's true. I have no misgivings about him, especially as he left after touching my feet. But then the thing is that without any knowledge about where my daughter-in-law is how long might the boy wander aimlessly? I would like to go in search of my daughter-in-law myself, but how would affairs be managed here? These greedy servants are lying in wait like vultures. The moment you turn your back, they pounce.' 'Right, how could you leave this place, elder mother? Send someone else to look for Deba bhai.'

'Yes, let's do that. You should write a letter to my daughter-in-law, giving her all the details relating to Deba, myself, and the school. By the way Nisa, haven't you written anything to her about yourself?'

Nisamani blushed a little. 'What would there be to say?'

Deba's mother smiled. 'About your marriage, my dear.'

Nisamani's cheeks reddened, and she hung her head. 'No, I haven't mentioned that.'

'Remember to write about it this time; it'll make my daughter-in-law very happy. What did the man say? That he would not marry a girl like you unless he was paid five thousand rupees in cash? Well, the girl's father might have money, but is the girl without qualities just because she's a girl? The fellow has a B.A. and an M.A., yet he still has so little intelligence. You may marry anyone you like for money, but will you ever get a girl with so much talent and virtue? You were wise to say no to him, Nisa. Would you be happy if you married such a man? How can one pass for a man if one only values money?'

A few days ago there had been a proposal in marriage for Nisamani from a highly qualified young man. As the young man had demanded five thousand rupees in cash, Nisamani had fallen at her father's feet saying she was not willing to marry him. She couldn't have as her husband some monster whose first thought was for money. Subhadra Devi was asking Nisamani to write about this to Basanti. She was no longer old-fashioned; Basanti had given her a new outlook on life.

At that point someone entered the house, shouting 'Ma Saantani, Ma Saantani'. Deba's mother recognised Dhania's voice. Dhania came in and slumped down at the mistress's feet in a heap. Smiling, the mistress asked, 'Hey burnt face. Have you come back after having your fill of fun or have you brought news of my daughter-in-law?'

Dhania answered pitiably and with folded hands. 'I have no news, Saantani. I could find no trace of her, even after ransacking the whole of Calcutta.'

'Yes, that is what you said in your letter. It's all right. It doesn't worry me. Look here, you misshapen creature, what you have not been able to do while wasting my money, I have been able to accomplish sitting at home.' Having said this, Subhadra Devi showed him Binod Bihari's letter.

Curious, Dhania asked, 'What's that Saantani?' Deba's mother replied in a voice full of delight, 'What do you think it is, it's a letter about my daughter-in-law.'

Dhania was delighted. 'Where is she?' he asked.

'Burdwan.'

'I'll go there today then. Saantani, where is babu Saanta?'

'Wait you misshapen creature; you're all set to go off without understanding anything. The babu left on his search before the letter arrived and has been gone for 10 days. First go and track him down. He doesn't have a servant or a cook. God knows what he's eating and drinking.'

Dhania was concerned. 'Saantani, why did you send babu out all alone when there are scores of servants around? That was certainly a rushed decision.'

Saantani's voice grew serious. 'Keep quiet, why are you worrying your head about this?' After a while she spoke, but with Nisamani in mind. 'Yes, dear Nisa, what's the point in sending Dhania to Calcutta today or tomorrow? How would he be able to find any trace of Deba in the big city? He'll only return as he did before. Like him, Deba too will head back in 10 or 15 days when he comes up with nothing. What do you think? My only worry is about how the boy will manage for food and drink?'

Nisamani could see a loving mother's heart being expressed in this concern. Smiling, she asked, 'Why worry so much about such things? Is he such a rustic that he'll starve in a city like Calcutta when he has money with him?'

It was decided not to send Dhania off in a rush, and the plan was put on hold for a few days. Instead, a letter, detailing everything, was posted to Basanti.

Thirty*

The train from Puri carrying mail pulled into Calcutta at about eight in the morning. After disembarking Debabrata set out on foot. He had no wish to get away quickly in a taxi or bus and surge past the huge crowd of men. On the contrary, he felt the need to become one among the thousands of people on foot. Grief had broken his heart, but this vast mass of men brought his will-power, lying dormant until then, into a state of wakefulness. He noticed that in this stream of humanity everyone was laughing and enjoying himself.

Everyone seemed to feel part of a larger community, and, like him, they were all headed towards their own goals, each different from the other. Yes, some in this crowd were troubled and torn by misfortune and suffering, as he was, but there was no end of laughter and high spirits. Each seemed to feel that his pain belonged not solely to himself but to the entire world. One of the many tidal waves in this sea of grief extending across the world had touched his core. Countless others were striking innumerable hearts. People suffer when they remain confined within themselves. But when they see themselves as tiny specks in the vast human congregation, they forget their own suffering

* By Kalindi Charan Panigrahi.

and become one with the entire universe, melting in pity at the huge shadow of suffering that has enveloped it. The blinders of selfishness instantly fell from Debabrata's eyes, and he felt himself part of the universal human community. His heart went out to each individual in this vast collective who had harboured grief deep within himself. He was no longer concentrating on his own suffering, but he did not forget his resolve to find and bring back Basanti, even if that meant risking his own life. He was human after all, not a creature without feelings or reactions.

Debabrata had decided not to write to anyone unless he had news of Basanti. This was not out of anger or unhappiness, but simply his resolve. Three months had gone by in the meantime. He had left Calcutta and travelled to cities such as Patna, Gaya, Allahabad, and Benares. Finally, he made his way back to Calcutta, feeling rebuffed. While on the road he would stare into every house and glance inside every passing vehicle hoping to catch sight of Basanti peering out from somewhere and then quickly withdrawing her pale face. When he was inside a bus, speeding along like an arrow, he would look out and expect to see Basanti standing alone in a lush green field or on the wooded hills, searching for her beloved in some moving bus. He thought that if he caught sight of the beautiful face he had stored in his heart's most delicate region he would leap from the moving bus. The next moment he smiled wryly to himself and thought 'am I going insane?'

Despite his resolve, the memories of Basanti would at times so overwhelm Debabrata that he would have to muster all his forces to stop himself from wailing like a child. Indeed, Basanti had so engulfed his day-to-day existence that he often assumed that if she was not present in a place, then nothing else was either. He bore the brunt of all this patiently and put his heart and soul into finding Basanti.

After travelling to many places and finally making his way back to Calcutta, Debabrata felt disappointed and could not decide what to do next. He was exhausted in both body and spirit. His large frame had shrunk and thinned, and he resembled a patient suffering from malaria. His long hair and beard, like that of a person newly released from jail, made him unrecognisable.

Sitting in a cramped room in Utkala Nivas, Debabrata was busy reading the letters Basanti had written to him before their marriage, as if trying to memorise them. Outside, the bell rang on the tram as it moved along its tracks. Taxis, buses, cars, and horses sped breathlessly every which way with a screech, a clatter, and a clop. Debabrata was aware of none of this. He read the letters over and over again, concentrating on them alone. On the cot in his room there was only a bed sheet—no pillow or quilt.

Hearing a noise in the room, Debabrata looked up. He saw a man sitting propped up against the wall, a bundle by his side. The man was sobbing, his head between his knees.

'Who's that?' Debabrata asked. The man did not raise his head or say anything; he only began to cry more miserably. Debabrata went over and lifted his head. My god, what's this? Servant boy Dhania! Debabrata was full of misgivings. Impatiently he asked, 'Dhania, how long have you been sitting here crying? Is mother well? Have you any news of the young Saantani?'

Dhania's teeth were chattering under the pressure of intense emotion. Tears streamed from his eyes like rain from the clouds. With great difficulty Debabrata was able to learn that everyone at home was keeping well and that there was good news about the young Saantani. He was able to understand that his bed, lack of shoes, and long hair and beard had shocked his servant. Dhania knew what sort of bed Debabrata was used to. Many times he had been scolded for not sending the bed linen to the washerman even if it was only slightly soiled. If the creases in his pajamas and shirt were not perfectly straight, they had to be pressed immediately. If his expensive shoes did not fit, they were given away to the employees and servants.

Debabrata patted Dhania on the back. 'Go wash your face in the sink.' Dhania did not move. At the sound of his master's tender and affectionate voice his tears increased. Dhania's distress grew even greater when he thought of what the Saantani would say if she saw his master in this state. The bed he slept in, his face, his shoeless feet! It did not take Dhania long to understand that Debabrata was in this state because he had neglected to eat and bathe regularly. He knew Debabrata was not attending to the daily demands of his body. The hope of regaining Basanti had taken firm hold of his mind. Only he could say how agitated by sorrow and joy his mind became when he learned all the details about Basanti from Dhania. The excitement caused by the thought of winning back Basanti soon made his body, already weakened by neglect, give way.

For Debabrata, Dhania acted as four servants in one: he called in the doctor, fetched medicine, prepared food to suit the patient's diet, and ran errands. Debabrata's feverish body and weak mind, restless with the desire to see Basanti, wanted to ignore the doctor's advice. At Dhania's repeated entreaties and because he was so weak he restrained himself with great effort and stayed on at Utkala Nivas.

After two days Debabrata was a little better. He no longer had a fever, although he felt twice as weak as before. But no further delay was possible—he had to set off for Burdwan to recover his darling Basanti. When he saw Dhania untying a bundle, Debabrata asked in a feeble voice, 'What's that?'

'Ma Saantani has sent some sweet gourd, pumpkin, badi, and pickle.'

Debabrata's eyes welled up. He had not been in communication with his loving mother since arriving in Calcutta. Though she would never think he was keeping silent because he was sulking, she must have felt anxious at not hearing from him. He immediately wrote her a letter, giving her all his news. And he did not forget to write to Ramesh.

Seeing how feeble his master was, Dhania asked him to rest another two days before setting off for Burdwan, but Debabrata would not listen. The arrangements for the trip were made. It was then that Debabrata realised he did not know where Basanti was staying. His mind had been so full of joy at the prospect of regaining her he had paid no attention to her address. But when he looked for the letter from Binod Bihari, he could not find it. Dhania saw his master was frantically searching for something. 'Babu, what are you looking for?' he asked.

Debabrata was worried. 'Where's the letter with the news about the young Saantani?'

'I gave it to you.' Saying this, Dhania started to rummage through the bag and shirt pockets. He could not find the letter.

'All right. Do you know the name of the person who wrote the letter?' Debabrata asked, despair in his voice.

'Babu, I only know this—he's a doctor.'

'Do you remember the lane or part of town where his house is?'

'No Babu.'

Debabrata was angry with Dhania for not having kept the letter in safe custody. The next moment, however, he felt ashamed of his reaction. He told Dhania to make the preparations for the journey to Burdwan. It would not be very difficult to trace Basanti's whereabouts once he got there.

In his feeble state, the journey was too much for Debabrata. Even before the train reached Burdwan he had a relapse of fever. Dhania was at his wit's end. What should he do? His master was unconscious. After getting down at the station he wondered where to look for the young Saantani, with his master in such a state. So he called a coach, had his master put inside, and ordered the coachman to drive to a hospital.

When Debabrata opened his eyes and looked around, he could not make out where he was. Dhania explained, 'Babu, this is a hospital. When master gets well, I'll go and enquire about the young Saantani.' Debabrata looked outside at the mention of Basanti. The sky was overcast; it was drizzling. It was as if someone had sucked out all the form and colour from the face of the earth and the sky. Debabrata's soul was awash in melancholy—Basanti! Ah, Basanti!

It was then that the doctor appeared. Whereas to Debabrata his looks as well as his manner seemed very gentle, Dhania felt the gentleman was acting strangely. He could not understand why the doctor was so surprised and worried when he saw Debabrata and heard his story. Nor why the doctor looked in on Debabrata every hour during the day, why he was giving Debabrata so much attention. The doctor spoke pure Bengali. After living in Balasore and travelling with Debabrata, Dhania had become used to speaking this language.

The doctor realised from Debabrata's symptoms that he was suffering from pneumonia and began treating him accordingly. After three days he was on the road to recovery. During that time Dhania applied himself to taking care of his master and making him comfortable, without thinking of his own food and sleep. Today—after three days—he had been able to sleep soundly. Then, while gently massaging his master's feet, Dhania heard two people speaking outside. Snatches of Oriya hit his ears. Hearing someone speaking his mother tongue in this remote place after so many days, he was curious and quietly left the patient's room, peering out the door to see who it was. He was taken aback to see the doctor speaking quietly with someone. Dhania rushed out and fell at the doctor's feet, his voice filled with emotion. 'Babu, our young Saantani is in your house, I'm sure of that.' Whatever he had suspected from the doctor's manner was confirmed when he heard the doctor speak Oriya. The doctor asked him to be quiet and explained everything. Yes, the young Saantani was in his house and was fine, but in Debabrata's state it was not safe to give him any news that might excite him. This was why he had arranged for Debabrata to stay in the hospital and not at his home. Dhania too should observe this rule and not tell his master anything without first consulting him. Dhania respectfully gave his consent, but his chest was aflutter; how he wished he could tell his master the good news!

Not one to be easily put off, Dhania collected every bit of news he could about the young Saantani from the doctor. When he heard that the baby Saanta had been born two months earlier, he was elated. He pleaded to be allowed to see the little Saanta once, but Binod Bihari explained that Debabrata's state ruled out his being left alone, even for a moment. He assured Dhania the young Saantani and the little Saanta would come to the hospital.

Basanti's motherly form had grown delicate and serene like the dew-washed landscape in autumn. She only had eyes for her baby boy. The baby, after tumbling from her womb two months ago, nestled in her tender lap. Her eyes had filled with tears many times as she gazed at this two-month-old baby, and just as she had erased her sorrows in the past, she wiped away those tears with the end of her sari. It was as though pure laughter and joy had been abolished from the world since the day she had parted from Debabrata. Despite repeated requests from Basantakumari she had not given her son a name.

One day she was sunning the child as she rubbed oil on its skin. Just then Basantakumari rushed in. 'Have you heard my dear "I"? Two people from Orissa have come to the hospital.'

Basanti took her eyes off the child. 'Who could they be?'

Basantakumari smiled gently. 'God only knows. A bearded gentleman with a servant.' Not wishing to enquire further, Basanti remarked, 'Must be someone then,' and went back to what she was doing. Basantakumari ran and hugged Basanti. 'It's him dear. He has come here to take you away from us.'

It was as if lightning had hit Basanti. Thunderstruck, she asked, 'Who is this "he"?' Smiling, Basantakumari replied, 'Who else do you think? Him!'

This seemed impossible to Basanti. The words 'bearded gentleman' and 'hospital' made her anxious. 'Come on now, should you make light of such serious matters?'

Basanta replied with childlike simplicity this time. 'For God's sake "I", would I joke with you about a matter like this? Servant boy Rama heard everything from your brother and told me. He has been here for three days; your brother has kept it hidden from us. He did not trust me with the news. Supposedly I can't keep a secret and would have leaked the matter to you immediately. Yes, he was taken ill; now he's better.'

Basanti felt as if the ground had slipped beneath her feet. Debabrata had been lying ill in the hospital for three days with God knows who taking care of him! She was so unlucky! Even though he was so close she could not see him.

Noticing Basanti's anxiety, Basantakumari said, 'Deba Babu has rallied a good deal and is resting. Will you go and see him "I"?' Forgetting her child, Basanti stood up in a rush and answered like a little girl, 'Yes, let's go.' This bewildered Basanta. 'What are you saying? You'll go, leaving your child exposed to the sun like this?' Basanti was beyond hearing or seeing anything. Like a young girl she lowered her face and repeated, 'Yes, let's go.'

Basantakumari burst into laughter. 'What a thing to say! You'd go and leave a two-month old baby in the sun? Has someone hypnotised you "I"? And do you want to go out without being properly dressed?'

Basanti went out dressed the way she was. She left the baby in the care of Paschima, the nanny, asking her to give him a bath. Basantakumari also had to leave without changing her clothes. Debabrata was still asleep. Dhania sat by his side, massaging his feet. When Binod Babu saw his own coach heading towards the hospital he went to intercept it. Then he checked if Debabrata was asleep, as he knew Basanti's presence would not be safe for the patient unless he was sleeping.

When Binod Bihari came out of the patient's room and signalled for them to approach, Basanta stepped out of the carriage first, followed by Basanti. The two friends quietly entered the room. Basanti was the first to see this large man as he slept peacefully. Dhania was ready to fling himself at the young Saantani's feet, but the doctor's 'no' made him sit quietly. When her gaze shifted from Debabrata's pale worn-out face to Dhania sitting with his eyes full of tears and a face heavy with sorrow, she could no longer remain calm. Wiping her eyes with the folds of her sari, she went straight back to the coach and sat there. When Basantakumari returned, she saw Basanti's sari soaked in tears.

As Debabrata's condition improved, he began to miss Basanti more and more. If he sought an answer from Dhania, Dhania would say, 'The doctor knows.' The doctor, in turn, would say, 'Yes, I've heard of an Oriya doctor who lives not far from here, but I'm not close to him.' Debabrata wrote many letters to this Oriya doctor and requested his doctor to have them delivered, but he never received a reply.

One day Debabrata's doctor informed him that the gentleman he had been trying to reach had returned from leave and had invited him to his house. If Debabrata would accept the invitation, they would be able to meet and talk. Debabrata seized the opportunity, more than pleased to accept. By that time his health had improved; there was no reason to worry.

The doctor's coach arrived as scheduled and picked up Debabrata. The Oriya doctor's home was nicely furnished, modern in taste. Debabrata was surprised, however, not to find anyone else there. He could not understand why the doctor ushered him past the drawing room straight into the bedroom with a lavish display of hospitality. They carried on a conversation in

Bengali, sitting in the bedroom. At times the sound of a woman laughing in another part of the house interrupted them. Out of politeness Debabrata refrained from asking any questions, but was baffled by what was happening.

Debabrata's health had mended. The doctor mentioned he would be discharged from the hospital the following day and asked, 'Sir, could you please tell me what work you have with the Oriya doctor?' Debabrata answered calmly. 'I have a private matter to discuss with him.'

The doctor smiled gently. 'Is he a relative of yours?'

'No.'

'Then he must be a friend you've known for a long time.'

'No.'

'Then I think you are visiting in connection with some business.'

Debabrata replied calmly. 'Please excuse me sir, I'm not ready to discuss anything regarding this.'

Changing the subject, the doctor asked, 'All right sir, please tell me what has happened to the project of reunification of Orissa? With whom will Orissa merge?'

'The Government of India has not yet reached its decision.'

The doctor said, somewhat sarcastically, 'It seems this will lead to major trouble, like what followed the Partition of Bengal.'

'No, it's unlikely to be like the Bengal Partition. The trouble in Bengal began because the Government divided Bengal right when the national movement was at its height. There's no plan to divide Orissa; on the contrary, the problem for now is the reunification of a long-dismembered Orissa.'

The doctor said, smiling wryly, 'Well sir, don't you think it would be good for Orissa to join with Bengal? Bengal is a developed community, and Oriyas consider Bengalis worthy of imitation.'

Debabrata could not understand why this Bengali gentleman was being so provincial. Becoming excited, Debabrata was about to add something more when Dhania came into the room panting and gasping, and handed him two telegrams. He opened them. One announced that Ramesh and Suniti's wedding would be held in a week's time and that Debabrata should grace the occasion with his wife. The other said that after learning about his illness, his mother would be reaching Burdwan tomorrow morning.

Debabrata stared at Dhania. 'Who wrote to mother about my illness?' he asked.

'I know nothing about that, Babu.'

A concerned Debabrata stood up to take leave of the doctor. It was then that he saw the form of a woman he didn't recognise standing in the doorway, holding a baby. Only he could say whether, when he saw his own child in the arms of this woman, he experienced the same feelings as Ramachandra did on seeing Laba and Kusha for the first time or as Dushyanta did when he beheld Bharata. The child, however, began to cry when he saw this tall, bearded, strange-looking person. The woman called someone, laughing. 'I cannot hold your child any longer "I". Come and take him.'

Hearing the woman speaking his own language, Debabrata turned in surprise to look at the doctor, but both the doctor and Dhania had left by then. When Debabrata, feeling bewildered, looked back, he saw another woman, her face soaked in tears, being handed back the baby. Who was she? He stared at her in disbelief. The baby, now safely in his mother's arms, gazed at the strange-looking person without fear.

Debabrata's glance settled on Basanti. He did not look at his baby boy, but only moved forward to take him into his arms. Seeing the man inching towards him, the baby hid his face in his mother's bosom. If today he were able to remember what happened, this is how he would put it: when he raised his head from his mother's bosom, he saw the bearded man holding his mother in an embrace, while his mother held him in one arm and encircled the man's back with the other. His mother, her face pressed against the man's shoulder, was sobbing, 'Deba bhai!' And the man, his bearded face thrust into his mother's shoulder, was saying 'Basa', with all the emotion he could muster.

About the Authors and Translators

Authors

Baishnab Charan Das (1899–1958): Closely connected with the **Sabuja Group**, although not a core member of the group, Das is best known for the first psychological novel in Odia, called *Mane Mane*, available in an English translation by Snehaprava Das as *The World Within* (2008). He was the Chief of Police of the ex-feudatory state of Mayurbhanj and became the Inspector General of Odisha after Odisha became an independent state. Das's complete works have been published in a volume by the Odisha Sahitya Akademi.

Prativa Devi (1898–1949): The daughter of Biswanath Kar, renowned litterateur and editor of *Utkala Sahitya*, Prativa was inclined to an intellectual and literary career. She embellished the pages of *Utkala Sahitya* with her translated stories. She was one of the earliest Odia women to have matriculated. She contributed one chapter to the novel *Basanti*.

Sarala Devi (1904–1986): Mostly self-taught, Sarala Devi rose to be a feisty writer and crusader for women's freedom. She wrote a prodigious amount of poetry, essays, and criticism. Among her essays is the iconic 'Narira Dabi' (The Rights of Women), which is considered a manifesto of feminism in Odisha. She was a leading woman freedom fighter. She has the distinction of being the first woman legislator of the Odisha Assembly. She contributed the largest number of chapters (nine) to *Basanti*. A comprehensive collection of her Odia writings in English translation, titled *The Best of Sarala Devi*, was published by Oxford University Press in 2016.

Suprava Devi (1900–1982): As the daughter of Biswanath Kar, Suprava was initiated into a literary career early in her life. As a regular contributor of short stories and essays (under the celebrated column 'Nari Prasanga'[Women's issues]) to *Utkala Sahitya*, she played a major role in introducing the Odia readership to important literary and cultural trends as well as renowned women writers like Ellen Carolina Sofia Key and Sigrid Undset. She contributed two chapters to the novel *Basanti*.

Muralidhar Mahanti (1902–1978): Closely connected with the **Sabuja Group** while studying for his Masters in English at Ravenshaw College, Mahanti felt an attraction for a literary career, developed an interest in Northern Indian classical music. With a Bar-at-Law from the Inner Temple, London, a rarity in those times, Mahanti became a legal luminary. He was the first practicing barrister in the state, not only in Odisha but in the country as a whole. He acquired a reputation as a columnist, writing polemical pieces on topical issues in prestigious Odia dailies such as *Samaj* and *Matrubhumi*.

Harihar Mahapatra (1904–1994): One of the core members of the **Sabuja Group**, Mahapatra went from serving on the Bar of the Odisha High Court to serving on the Bench of the Patna High Court. He was the editor of *Juga Bina*, the mouthpiece of the **Sabuja Sahitya Samiti**. He also acted as the chief editor of *Jhankar*, a celebrated monthly literary magazine in Odia. Mahapatra's poems and essays have been collected in a volume titled *Bina Seshare Arambha*. His autobiography in Odia, *Jibana O Jibika*, has been published in an English translation by Ashok Mohanty under the title *My Life and Work* (2011).

Sarat Chandra Mukherjee (1902–1987): One of the five core members of the **Sabuja Group**, Mukherjee went on to write poetry and books on the art and architecture of Odisha. He functioned as the secretary of the **Sabuja Sahitya Samiti** as the long as the literary society was in existence and took the initiative of publishing *Basanti* as a book after it had been serialised in *Utkala Sahitya*. *Konarka, The Great Temple* of *Odisha* is among his well-known books. His poems have been collected in a volume titled *Panchapuspa*. He too was a member of the distinguished Indian Civil Service.

Kalindi Charan Panigrahi (1901–1991): Panigrahi's literary career blossomed in Ravenshaw College, where he, along with four other young and enthusiastic friends, formed the **Sabuja Group** with the intention of creating a new literature for Odisha. The Group was supremely productive collectively, which was of course a result of the individual creativity of each member. Panigrahi went on to become a prominent writer in Odia, contributing to the novel, poetry, short stories, drama, and essays. He is famous for his novel *Matira Manisha*, which was first translated into English by Lila Ray as *A House Undivided* and made into an acclaimed Odia movie by the renowned film maker Mrinal Sen. The novel has recently appeared in a new English translation by Bikram Das as *Born of the Soil* (2016).

Annada Shankar Ray (1904–2002): One of the five core members of the **Sabuja Group**, Ray started by writing in

Odia during his student days at Ravenshaw College and later on switched over to writing in Bengali, becoming a prominent writer in that language. The idea of a collective novel in Odia, a first for Odia literature, was conceived by him and Kalindi Charan Panigrahi during a summer stay at Puri. Though Ray's poetic output in Odia is very small, consisting of only 15 poems, he is considered a prodigious talent in poetry. He contributed significantly to Odia prose and criticism during his five years of literary activism in Odia. His open letters, essays, and poems have been collected in a volume called *Sabuja Akhyara* (Sabuja Alphabet). He was a member of the distinguished Indian Civil Service.

Translators

Himansu S. Mohapatra is widely published in the fields of criticism and comparative studies of Western and Indian, mostly Odia, fiction of the nineteenth and twentieth century. He has simultaneously pursued a deuxième carrière, writing reviews, belles-lettres, and light literary journalism. From 2008 onwards he has written on translation and has translated in collaboration with Paul St-Pierre. *The Other Side of Reason* (2008), his first collaborative work, is a translation of selected contemporary Odia short stories into English. *Basanti* is his second collaborative translation project. He taught at the P.G. Department of English, Utkal University, Bhubaneswar, Odisha, India, from 1994 to 2018.

Paul St-Pierre is former professor, Department of Linguistics and Translation, Université de Montréal, Canada. He taught in translation programs in Canada for more than twenty-five years and served as president of both the Canadian Association for Translation Studies and the Canadian Association of Schools of Translation. He has collaborated on many translations of literary texts from Odia into English. Among these are: *Ants, Ghosts and Whispering Trees* (an anthology of Odia short stories, with K.K. and Leelawati Mohapatra, 2003); *Six Acres and a Third* (the first social realist novel in an Indian language, by Phakirmohan Senapati, translated with R.S. Mishra, S.P. Mohanty, and J.K. Nayak, 2005); *Medieval Odia Poetry* (with Ganeshwar Mishra, 2010); and *Atmacharita* (the first autobiography in Odia, also by Phakirmohan Senapati, 2016; translated with D.R. Pattanaik and B.K. Tripathy).